VISIONARY IN RESIDENCE

VISIONARY IN RESIDENCE

STORIES

BRUCE STERLING

THUNDER'S MOUTH PRESS

NEW YORK

Visionary in Residence

Thunder's Mouth Press
An Imprint of Avalon Publishing Group, Inc.
245 West 17th Street • 11th Floor
New York, NY 10011

AVALON
publishing group incorporated

All stories © Bruce Sterling unless otherwise noted.
"In Paradise" first appeared in *The Magazine of Fantasy and Science Fiction*, Sep-
tember 2002. "Luciferase" first appeared in *SciFiction*, December 2004. "Homo
Sapiens Declared Extinct" first appeared in *Nature*, November 11, 1999. "Ivory Tower"
first appeared in *Nature*, April 7, 2005. "Message Found In a Bottle" appears here for
the first time. "The Growthing" first appeared in *Metropolis*, January 2004. "User-
Centric" first appeared in Designfax, December 1999. "Code" first appeared in *Men
Seeking Women: Love and Sex On-line* edited by Jonathan Karp, Atrandom.com, 2001.
"The Scab's Progress" (with Paul Di Filippo) first appeared in *SciFiction*, January 2001;
© Bruce Sterling and Paul Di Filippo. "Junk DNA" (with Rudy Rucker) first appeared in
Asimov's, January 2003; © Bruce Sterling and Rudy Rucker. "The Necropolis of Thebes"
first appeared in *Panorama*, November 2003. "The Blemmye's Stratagem" first
appeared in *The Magazine of Fantasy & Science Fiction*, January 2005. "The Denial"
first appeared in *The Magazine of Fantasy & Science Fiction*, September 2005.

Library of Congress Cataloging-in-Publication Data is available.

ISBN: 1-56025-841-1
978-1-56025-841-4

Book design by Maria E. Torres
Printed in the United States of America
Distributed by Publishers Group West

CONTENTS

I. Science Fiction
In Paradise ∗ 1

II. Fiction about Science
Luciferase ∗ 19

III. Fiction for Scientists
Homo Sapiens Declared Extinct ∗ 41

Ivory Tower ∗ 45

Message Found in a Bottle ∗ 49

IV. Architecture Fiction
The Growthing ∗ 55

V. Design Fiction
User-Centric ∗ 65

VI. Mainstream Fiction
Code ∗ 87

VII. Cyberpunk to Ribofunk

The Scab's Progress (with Paul Di Filippo) * 109

Junk DNA (with Rudy Rucker) * 165

VIII. The Past Is a Future That Already Happened

The Necropolis of Thebest * 217

The Blemmye's Stratagem * 225

The Denial * 271

* I *

Science Fiction

(I'm a science fiction writer. This is a golden opportunity to get up to most any mischief imaginable. With this fourth collection of my stories, I'm going to prove this to you. It'll take thirteen stories and about 70,000 words. We'll start nice and simple, with a story that couldn't be more traditional in its SF thematics. A real-time voice-translation device is one of the hoariest gizmos in the eighty-year-old arsenal of popular science fiction. It's nevertheless an idea brimming over with fresh possibilities. Here: just look at the mileage one can wring out of a conceit like that.)

In Paradise

The machines broke down so much that it was comical, but the security people never laughed about that.

Felix could endure the delay, for plumbers billed by the hour. He opened his tool kit, extracted a plastic flask, and had a solid nip of Scotch.

The Muslim girl was chattering into her phone. Her dad and another bearded weirdo had passed through the big metal frame just as the scanner broke down. So these two somber, suited old men were getting the full third degree with the hand wands, while daughter was stuck. Daughter wore a long baggy coat and a thick black head scarf and a surprisingly sexy pair of sandals. Between her and her minders stretched the no-man's land of official insecurity. She waved across the gap.

The security geeks found something metallic in the black wool jacket of the Wicked Uncle. Of course it was harmless, but they had to run their full ritual, lest they die of boredom at their posts. As the Scotch settled in, Felix felt time stretch like taffy. Little Miss Mujahideen discovered that her phone was dying. She banged at it with the flat of her hand.

The line of hopeful shoppers, grimly waiting to stimulate the economy, shifted in their disgruntlement. It was a bad, bleak scene. It crushed Felix's heart within him. He longed to leap to his feet and harangue the lot of them. *Wake up*, he wanted to scream at them. *Cheer up, act more human.* He felt the urge keenly, but it scared people when he cut loose like that. They really hated it. And so did he. He knew he couldn't look them in the eye. It would only make a lot of trouble.

The Mideastern men shouted at the girl. She waved her dead phone at them, as if another breakdown was going to help their mood. Then Felix noticed that she shared his own make of cellphone. She had a rather ahead-of-the-curve Finnish model that he'd spent a lot of money on. So Felix rose and sidled over.

"Help you out with that phone, ma'am?"

She gave him the paralyzed look of a coed stuck with a dripping tap. "No English?" he concluded. *"¿Habla español, señorita?"* No such luck.

He offered her his own phone. No, she didn't care to use it. Surprised and even a little hurt by this rejection, Felix took his first good look at her and realized with a lurch that she was pretty. What eyes! They were whirlpools. The line of her lips was like the tapered edge of a rose leaf.

"It's your battery," he told her. Though she had not a word of English, she obviously got it about phone batteries. After some gestured persuasion, she was willing to trade her dead battery for his. There was a fine and delicate little moment when his fingertips extracted her power supply, and he inserted his own unit into that golden-lined copper cavity. Her display leapt to life with an eager flash of numerals. Felix pressed a button or two, smiled winningly, and handed her phone back.

She dialed in a hurry, and bearded Evil Dad lifted his phone to answer, and life became much easier on the nerves. Then, with a groaning buzz, the scanner came back on. Dad and Uncle waved a command at her, like lifers turned to trusty prison guards, and she scampered through the metal gate and never looked back.

She had taken his battery. Well, no problem. He would treasure the one she had given him.

Felix gallantly let the little crowd through before he himself cleared security. The geeks always went nuts about his plumbing tools, but then again they had to. He found the assignment: a chichi place that sold fake antiques and potpourri. The manager's office had a clogged drain. As he worked, Felix recharged the phone. Then he socked them for a sum that made them wince.

On his leisurely way out—whoa, there was Miss Cellphone, that looker, that little goddess, browsing in a jewelry store over Korean gold chains and tiaras. Dad and Uncle were there, with a couple of off-duty cops.

Felix retired to a bench beside the fountain, in the potted plastic plants. He had another bracing shot of Scotch, then put his feet up on his toolbox and punched her number.

He saw her straighten at the ring. She opened her purse and placed the phone to the kerchiefed side of her head. She didn't know where he was, or who he was. That was why the words came pouring out of him.

"My God you're pretty," he said. "You are wasting your time with that jewelry. Because your eyes are like two black diamonds."

She jumped a little, poked at the phone's buttons with disbelief, and put it back to her head.

Felix choked back the urge to laugh and leaned forward, his elbows on his knees. "A string of pearls around your neck would look like peanuts," he told the phone. "I am totally smitten with you. What are you like under that big baggy coat? Do I dare to wonder? I would give a million dollars just to see your knees!"

"Why are you telling me that?" said the phone.

"Because I'm looking at you right now. And after one look at you, believe me, I was a lost soul." Felix felt a chill. "Hey, wait a minute. You don't speak English, do you?"

"No, I don't speak English—but my telephone does."

"It *does?*"

"It's a very new telephone. It's from Finland," the telephone said. "I need it because I'm stuck in a foreign country. Do you really have a million dollars for my knees?"

"That was a figure of speech," said Felix, though his bank account was, in point of fact, looking considerably healthier since his girlfriend Lola had dumped him. "Never mind the million dollars," he said. "I'm dying of love out here. I'd sell my blood just to buy you petunias."

"You must be a famous poet," said the phone dreamily, "for you speak such wonderful Farsi."

Felix had no idea what Farsi was—but he was way beyond such fretting now. The rusty gates of his soul were shuddering on their hinges. "I'm drunk," he realized. "I am drunk on your smile."

"In my family, the women never smile."

Felix had no idea what to say to that, so there was a hissing silence.

"Are you a spy? How did you get my phone number?"

"I'm not a spy. I got your phone number from your phone."

"Then I know you. You must be that tall foreign man who gave me your battery. Where are you?"

"Look outside the store. See me on the bench?" She turned where she stood, and he waved his fingertips. "That's right, it's me," he declared to her. "I can't believe I'm really going through with this. You just stand there, okay? I'm going to run in there and buy you a wedding ring."

"Don't do that." She glanced cautiously at Dad and Uncle, then stepped closer to the bulletproof glass. "Yes, I do see you. I remember you."

She was looking straight at him. Their eyes met. They were connecting. A hot torrent ran up his spine. "You are looking straight at me."

"You're very handsome."

It wasn't hard to elope. Young women had been eloping since the dawn of time. Elopement with eager phone support was a snap. He followed her to the hotel, a posh place that swarmed with limos and videocams. He brought her a bag with a big hat, sunglasses, and a cheap Mexican wedding dress. He sneaked into the women's restroom—they never put videocams there, due to the complaints—and he left the bag in a stall. She went in, came out in new clothes with her hair loose, and walked straight out of the hotel and into his car.

They couldn't speak together without their phones, but that turned out to be surprisingly advantageous, as further discussion was not on their minds. Unlike Lola, who was alway complaining that he should open up and relate—"you're a plumber," she would tell him, "how deep and mysterious is a plumber supposed to be?"—the new woman in his life had needs that were very straightforward. She liked to walk in parks without a police escort. She liked to thoughtfully peruse the goods in Mideastern ethnic groceries. And she liked to make love to him.

She was nineteen years old, and the willing sacrifice of her chastity had really burned the bridges for his little refugee. Once she got fully briefed about what went inside where, she was in a mood to tame the demon. She had big, jagged, sobbing, alarming, romantic, brink-of-the-grave things going on, with long, swoony kisses, and heel-drumming, and clutching and clawing.

When they were too weak, and too raw, and too tingling to make love any more, then she would cook, very badly. She was on her phone constantly, talking to her people. These confidantes of hers were obviously women, because she asked them for Persian cooking tips. She would sink with triumphant delight into a cheery chatter as the basmati rice burned.

He longed to take her out to eat; to show her to everyone, to the whole world; really, besides the sex, no act could have made him happier—but she was undocumented, and sooner or later some security geek was sure to check on that. People did things like that to people nowadays. To contemplate such things threw a thorny darkness over their whole affair, so, mostly, he didn't think. He took time off work, and he spent every moment that he could in her radiant presence, and she did what a pretty girl could do to lift a man's darkened spirits, which was plenty. More than he had ever had from anyone.

After ten days of golden, unsullied bliss, ten days of bread and jug wine, ten days when the nightingales sang in chorus and the reddest of roses bloomed outside the boudoir, there came a knock on his door, and it was three cops.

"Hello, Mr. Hernandez," said the smallest of the trio. "I would be Agent Portillo from Homeland Security, and these would be two of my distinguished associates. Might we come in?"

"Would there be a problem?" said Felix.

"Yes there would!" said Portillo. "There might be rather less of a problem if my associates here could search your apartment." Portillo offered up a handheld screen. "A young woman named Batool Kadivar? Would we be recognizing Miss Batool Kadivar?"

"I can't even pronounce that," Felix said. "But I guess you'd better come in," for Agent Portillo's associates were already well on their way. Men of their ilk were not prepared to take no for an answer. They shoved past him and headed at once for the bedroom.

"Who are those guys? They're not American."

"They're Iranian allies. The Iranians were totally nuts for

a while, and then they were sort of okay, and then they became our new friends, and then the enemies of our friends became our friends . . . Do you ever watch TV news, Mr. Hernandez? Secular uprisings, people seizing embassies? Ground war in the holy city of Qom, that sort of thing?"

"It's hard to miss," Felix admitted.

"There are a billion Muslims. If they want to turn the whole planet into Israel, we don't get a choice about that. You know something? I used to be an accountant!" Portillo sighed theatrically. " 'Homeland Security.' Why'd they have to stick me with that chicken outfit? Hombre, we're twenty years old and we don't even have our own budget yet. Did you see those gorillas I've got on my hands? Do you think these guys ever listen to sense? Geneva Convention? US Constitution? Come on."

"They're not gonna find any terrorists in here."

Portillo sighed again. "Look, Mr. Hernandez. You're a young man with a clean record, so I want to do you a favor." He adjusted his handheld and it showed a new screen. "These are cellphone records. Thirty, forty calls a day, to and from your number. Then look at this screen. This is the good part. Check out *her* call records. That would be her aunt in Yerevan, and her little sister in Teheran, and five or six of her teenage girlfriends, still living back in purdah . . . Who do you think is gonna *pay* that phone bill? Did that ever cross your mind?"

Felix said nothing.

"I can understand this, Mr. Hernandez. You lucked out. You're a young, red-blooded guy, and that is a very pretty girl. But she's a minor, and an illegal alien. Her father's family has got political connections like nobody's business, and I would mean nobody, and I would also mean business."

"Not my business," Felix said.

"You're being a sap, Mr. Hernandez. You may not be interested in war, but war is plenty interested in you."

There were loud crashing, sacking, and looting noises coming from his bedroom.

"You are sunk, *hermano*. There is video at the Lebanese grocery store. There is video hidden in the traffic lights. You're a free American citizen, sir. You are free to go anywhere you want, and we're free to watch all the backup tapes. That would be the big story I'm relating here. Would we be catching on yet?"

"That's some kind of story," Felix said.

"You don't know the half of it. You don't know the tenth."

The two goons reappeared. There was a brief exchange of notes. They had to use their computers.

"My friends here are disappointed," said Agent Portillo. "Because there is no girl in your residence, even though there is an extensive selection of makeup and perfume. They want me to arrest you for abduction, and obstruction of justice, and probably ten or twelve other things. But I would be asking myself: why? Why should this young taxpayer with a steady job want to have his life ruined? What I'm thinking is: there must be *another* story. A *better* story. The flighty girl ran off, and she spent the last two weeks in a convent. It was just an impulse thing for her. She got frightened and upset by America, and then she came back to her people. Everything diplomatic."

"That's diplomacy?"

"Diplomacy is the art of avoiding extensive unpleasantness

for all the parties concerned. The United Coalition, as it were."

"They'll chop her hands off and beat her like a dog!"

"Well, that would depend, Mr. Hernandez. That would depend entirely on whether the girl herself tells that story. Somebody would have to get her up to speed on all that. A trusted friend. You see?"

After the departure of the three security men, Felix thought through his situation. He realized there was nothing whatsoever in it for him but shame, humiliation, impotence, and a crushing and lasting unhappiness. He then fetched up the reposada tequila from beneath his sink.

Some time later he felt the dull stinging of a series of slaps to his head. When she saw that she had his attention, she poured the tequila onto the floor, accenting this gesture with an eye-opening Persian harangue.

Felix staggered into the bathroom, threw up, and returned to find a fresh cup of coffee. She had raised the volume and was still going strong. He'd never had her pick a lover's quarrel with him, though he'd always known it was in her somewhere. It was magnificent. It was washing over him in a musical torrent of absolute nonsense. It was operatic, and he found it quite beautiful. Like sitting through a rainstorm without getting wet: trees straining, leaves flying, dark, windy, torrential. Majestic.

Her idea of coffee was basically wet grounds, so it brought him around in short order. "You're right, I'm wrong, and I'm sorry," he admitted tangentially, knowing she didn't understand a word, "so come on and help me," and he opened the sink cabinet, where he had hidden all his bottles when he'd noticed the earlier disapproving glances. He then decanted them down the drain: vodka, Southern Comfort, the gin, the party jug of tequila, even the last two inches of his favorite single malt. Muslims didn't drink, and really, how wrong could any billion people be?

He gulped a couple of aspirin and picked up the phone. "The police were here. They know about us. I got upset. I drank too much."

"Did they beat you?"

"Uh, no. They're not big fans of beating over here: they've got better methods. They'll be back. We are in big trouble."

She folded her arms. "Then we'll run away."

"You know, we have a proverb for that in America: 'You can run, but you can't hide.' "

"Darling, I love your poetry, but when the police come to the house, it's serious."

"Yes. It's very serious. It's serious as cancer. You've got no ID. You have no passport. You can't get on any plane to get away. Even the trains and lousy bus stations have facial recognition. My car is useless, too. They'd read my license plate a hundred times before we hit city limits. I can't rent another car without leaving credit records. The cops have got my number."

"We'll steal a fast car and go very fast."

"You can't outrun them! That is not possible! They've all got phones like we do, so they're always ahead of us, waiting."

"I'm a rebel! I'll never surrender!" She lifted her chin. "Let's get married."

"I'd love to, but we can't. We have no license. We have no blood test."

"Then we'll marry in some place where they have all the blood they want. Beirut, that would be good." She placed her free hand against her chest. "We were married in my heart the first time we ever made love."

This artless confession blew through him like a summer breeze. "They do have rings for cash at a pawnbroker's . . . But I'm a Catholic. There must be *somebody* who does this sort of thing. Maybe some heretic mullah. Maybe a Santeria guy?"

"If we're husband and wife, what can they do to us? We haven't done anything wrong. I'll get a green card. I'll beg them, I'll beg for mercy. I'll beg political asylum."

Agent Portillo conspicuously cleared his throat. "Mr. Hernandez, please! This would not be the conversation you two need to be having."

"I forgot to mention the worst part," Felix said. "They know about our phones."

"Miss Kadivar, can you also understand me?"

"Who are you? I hate you. Get off this line and let me talk to him."

"*Salaam alaikum* to you, too," Portillo concluded. "It's a sad commentary on federal procurement when a mullah's daughter has a fancy translator and I can't even talk live with my own fellow agents. By the way, those two gentlemen from the new regime in Teheran are staking out your apartment. How they failed to recognize your girlfriend on her way in, that I'll never know. But if you two listen to me, I think I can walk you out of this very dangerous situation."

"I don't want to leave my beloved," she said.

"Over my dead body," Felix declared. "Come and get me. Bring a gun."

"Okay, Miss Kadivar, you would seem to be the more rational of the two parties, so let me talk sense to you. You have no future with this man. What kind of wicked man seduces a decent girl with phone pranks? He's an *aayash*, he's a playboy. America has a fifty percent divorce rate. He would never ask your father honorably for your hand. What would your mother say?"

"Who is this awful man?" she said, shaken. "He knows everything!"

"He's a snake!" Felix said. "He's the devil!"

"You still don't get it, compadre. I'm not the Great Satan. Really, I'm not. I'm the *good guy*. I'm your guardian angel, dude. I'm trying really hard to give you back a normal life."

"Okay, cop, you had your say, now listen to me. I love her body and soul, and even if you kill me dead for that, the flames from my heart will set my coffin on fire."

She burst into tears. "Oh God, my God, that's the most beautiful thing anyone has ever said to me!"

"You kids are sick, okay?" Portillo snapped. "This would be *mental illness* that I'm eavesdropping on here! You two don't even *speak each other's language*. You had every fair warning. Just remember, when it happens, you *made me* do it. Now try this one on for size, Romeo and Juliet." The phones went dead.

Felix put his dead phone on the tabletop. "Okay. Situation report. We've got no phones, no passports, no ID, and two different intelligence agencies are after us. We can't fly, we can't drive, we can't take a train or a bus. My credit cards are useless now, my bank cards will just track me down, and I guess I've lost my job now. I can't even walk out my own front door . . . And wow, you don't understand a single word I'm saying. I can tell from that look in your eye. You are completely thrilled."

She put her finger to her lips. Then she took him by the hand.

Apparently, she had a new plan. It involved walking. She wanted to walk to Los Angeles. She knew the words "Los Angeles," and maybe there was someone there that she knew. This trek would involve crossing half the American continent on foot, but Felix was at peace with that ambition. He really thought he could do it. A lot of people had done it just for the sake of gold nuggets, back in 1849. Women had walked to California just to meet a guy with gold nuggets.

The beautiful part of this scheme was that, after creeping out the window, they really had vanished. The feds might be all over the airports, over everything that mattered, but they didn't care about what didn't matter. Nobody was looking out for dangerous interstate pedestrians.

To pass the time as they walked, she taught him elementary Farsi. The day's first lesson was body parts, because that was all they had handy for pointing. That suited Felix just fine. If anything, this expanded their passionate communion. He was perfectly willing to starve for that, fight for that, and die for that. Every form of intercourse between man and woman was fraught with illusion, and the bigger, the better. Every hour that passed was an hour they had not been parted.

They had to sleep rough. Their clothes became filthy. Then, on the tenth day, they got arrested.

• • •

She was, of course, an illegal alien, and he had the good sense to talk only Spanish, so of course, he became one as well. The Immigration cops piled them into the bus for the border, but they got two seats together and were able to kiss and hold hands. The other deported wretches even smiled at them.

He realized now that he was sacrificing everything for her: his identity, his citizenship, flag, church, habits, money . . . Everything, and good riddance. He bit thoughtfully into his wax-papered cheese sandwich. That was the federal bounty delivered to every refugee on the bus, along with an apple, a small carton of homogenized milk, and some carrot chips.

When the protein hit his famished stomach Felix realized that he had gone delirious with joy. He was *growing* by this experience. It had broken every stifling limit within him. His dusty, savage, squalid world was widening drastically.

Giving alms, for instance—before his abject poverty, he'd never understood that alms were holy. Alms were indeed very holy. From now on—as soon as he found a place to sleep, some place that was so torn, so wrecked, so bleeding, that it never asked uncomfortable questions about a plumber—as soon as he became a plumber again, then he'd be giving some alms.

She ate her food, licked her fingers, then fell asleep against him, in the moving bus. He brushed the free hair from her dirty face. She was twenty days older now. "This is a pearl," he said aloud. "This is a pearl by far too rare to be contained within the shell of time and space."

Why had those lines come to him, in such a rush? Had he read them somewhere? Or were those lines his own?

★ II ★

Fiction about Science

(This next story is about talking bugs. Huh? But look—it was directly inspired by a scientific paper by noted American entomologist Thomas Eisner, on the biochemistry and ecology of fireflies. Since I happened to be in Eastern Europe when the inspiration for this story struck me, I jimmied up a work of insectile fantastyka in the tradition of European writers Karel Capek (*The Insect Play*) and Viktor Pelevin (*The Life of Insects*). I rather prefer these two works to the superstar Eastern European talking-bug yarn of all time, Franz Kafka's "The Metamorphosis." Of course, I didn't have to write a story whose protagonists are romantic talking bugs. . . . But why not? This is a global era, folks.)

Luciferase

His flesh lit up with erotic need.

The urge within him was beyond comprehension. It was cosmic, its own pure justification.

Light shocked out of him in a tumbling chemical rush.

Someone smashed into him with a violent scrabble of claws. He lost his grip on the grass stem, and fell spinning into the dirt.

He lay there stunned, legs folded tightly across his belly.

His assailant plummeted after him from the twilight sky. It was Peck, a spider. Peck hit the rotting leaf litter and rebounded on powerful legs. He spun his spiny carcass, his domed eyes searching for prey like a set of black periscopes.

"Peck, it's me. It's Vinnie." Wisely, Vinnie stifled his

tremendous urge to flash. Peck would attack anything that lit his eight black eyes.

"I need to eat you right now," Peck said reasonably.

"Peck, you can't eat me, okay? Fireflies are poisonous."

Peck had molted since the last time their paths had crossed. His bristling, aggressive body had almost doubled in volume. Peck might be as dumb as a clod of earth, but you could never fault a jumping-spider for audacity.

The nights were growing longer, and Vinnie wasn't getting any younger. He bent his flat head and striped thorax, tumbled sideways with an effort, then clambered to his long hooked feet. He'd reached full size for a firefly, and the grueling effort of his nightly displays had cost him a lot of weight. He felt light-headed, giddy, and possessed by a frustrated lust.

Peck's fierce attack had just damaged his left midleg. The complex joint between Vinnie's coxa and femur had gone all leaky.

Peck looked a bit embarrassed. By his nature, Peck was susceptible to good sense; it was just that his all-consuming urge to leap, bite, and devour was more than he could handle. "Vinnie, was that you I jumped just now?"

"Yes, of course it was, and you've busted my leg. Get this straight, Peck: I'm a lightning bug. If you ever eat me, you're going to vomit and die."

"But I thought you were just a nice tasty beetle."

"We've had this discussion before, Peck. I *am* a beetle. All lightning bugs are beetles. Beetles of the family Lampyridae."

Peck drummed the littered earth with his murderous spiny forelegs. "You're awfully soft-bodied for a beetle."

"I don't need any armor, because I've got toxins," Vinnie

snapped. "I'm also built light 'cause I fly! You want to eat something soft? Kill a snail!"

"I don't like snails," Peck muttered. "Snails got no legs and they eat with their tongues. Plus they got big hard shells!"

Vinnie sighed gustily through his spiracles. Why were spiders so stubborn and picky? Snails were delicious. Vinnie himself had eaten snails, back when he was a grub.

When he had been a kid, all he had wanted to do was burrow, eat, and grow. No adult airborne displays. No burdensome public reputation as an artist. Yet he'd been so happy and excited, innocently writhing in the loamy dark. Kids were like that.

Vinnie leaned against a tall dandelion stem and unhinged his striped wing covers. His left midleg was screwed up, but he was itching to get aloft and shine. "Peck, I forgive you. You're a dumb, meat-eating spider, but at least you don't use webs. Those are just plain irresponsible, webs."

"I could chew your broken leg off," Peck mused. "Your legs aren't poisonous."

Vinnie wriggled his damaged joint cautiously. "How'd things work out with that lady friend I recommended?"

"Oh! She was so pretty!"

"How come you're still alive, then?"

"I tried my best to get close to her," Peck said gloomily. "I really hoofed it up for that chick, I did my big courtship peace-dance . . . But she gave me the brush-off. Wrong species."

"She didn't eat you," said Vinnie. He was genuinely curious. The spider tore at the earth in embarrassment. Peck was reluctant to engage in such personal confidences, but, being a lone predator, he rarely had the chance to talk things out with a sympathetic listener. "I was so ticked off by that. Really, I felt like attacking her and eating her myself. But . . . well . . . that's just the way chicks are. . . . All dames are trouble, basically. . . ." Peck's distress was growing. "When, Vinnie? When will I find a decent girl willing to eat me?"

Vinnie preened both his antennae. "It's a terrible thing, loneliness."

"It's all I can think about. I need to find the woman who's meant for me. I want to become one with her. I want to lay my body down . . . afterward, you know. . . . Feeling so nice and tired then, done with all this struggle of life. . . . Complete, like, fulfilledness. . . . Fulfillitude. . . ."

" 'Serenity,' that's the word you're looking for, Peck."

"And I want her to eat me. I do. Maybe she'll eat me real nice and slow, while I'm all full of venom, paralyzed, and still alive!"

"Romance." Vinnie sighed. "No, Peck, you won't see me scoffing about it. Not after what I've been through."

Warmed by his own dreams, the spider danced on the tips of his spiny feet. "Some nice girl should be drinking my vital fluids. Think of the size of that egg sac, and the pack of kids she'd have!"

"You're a one-woman guy."

"I want true happiness. It's my right!"

Vinnie sniffed through his vent holes. "Romance is one thing, kid. Happiness, that's another."

"I just don't get it. Am I so bad? I'm trying to do the decent thing!"

"Let the ol' firefly give you a tip here, kid. You're being a chump. You could court three spider ladies, fertilize the eggs of the first two, then sacrifice your body into the gut of number three. That way, you'd convey the metabolic benefits from being devoured, plus you'd get a lot more genetic variety in your progeny. You follow me? Let the first two pay the price for their own child support!"

Peck thought this proposal over. "Hey, that's cold-blooded!"

"So?"

"You'd really treat women like that? What is it with you?"

"Well, it's not like I'm given a choice." Vinnie had never met a woman who showed any interest in devouring him. On the contrary, once the night's glowing courtship was consummated, Vinnie's ladies simply scrammed down from their leafy boudoirs to lay some fresh eggs in the dirt.

Once his supple aviator's body had given women what they craved, they never wanted to talk to him again. All that bioluminescent signaling and sophisticated communication, then a moment or two of physical bliss, then that sudden cold and that lasting emotional silence. The irony of this had not escaped Vinnie. It gnawed at the core of him.

"Can I ask you something personal?" said the spider. "How many girls have you been with?"

"Oh, about as many as I have legs," said Vinnie airily. "And I was right to do it. They were gorgeous! Every moment was so deeply felt! Who wouldn't go for such classy dames!"

"Was it that good for you?"

"It was tremendous! Except for Sylvia. . . . That tramp!" Vinnie couldn't restrain his bitterness. He missed Sylvia worst of all. Sylvia was the one who just wasn't taken in by the story: the gallantries, the calculated showmanship. . . . Sylvia frankly understood what a man really needed in life. And boy, could she ever give it. Yet she'd walked off to lay her eggs just like the rest of them.

"You sure are lucky, Vinnie. I've never even *met* a woman of my own species. Us top predators are rare!"

Spiders seemed pretty common to Vinnie. If there was a local "top" predator, it was the grass snake. The grass snake had teeth, a tongue, bones, scales, ate anything, never stopped growing, and apparently lived forever. Vinnie had been tempted to communicate with the grass snake, maybe ask for its name, but he didn't quite know how to open the conversation. "Did you try signaling for some women, Peck? Flashing? Make a loud mating call of any kind?"

"I can't pull stunts like that!" Peck protested. "Because my flesh isn't poisonous! Some bird would pick me off in a hot second." Peck ran one foreleg through his venomed fangs. "All this sex talk sure makes me hungry."

"Don't you dare bite me," Vinnie said.

"But I'm ravenous! If I don't eat, I'm gonna die!"

"How about a tasty mosquito?" said Vinnie. "A female mosquito with a belly full of fresh blood! That's mammal blood! Right off the top of the food chain."

Peck perked up. "Now that's what I'm talking about!"

Vinnie loathed mosquitoes. Their brainless whining spoiled the limpid beauty of his evening flights. When mosquitos were full of blood, they were a serious collision hazard. "Over there at streamside where the water smells bad, those parasites are out of their heads on pheromones. There's a cloud of 'em there tonight, a big orgy. I'll take you there right away. You follow my taillight, and you'll make out like a bandit."

It was an enticing prospect and a genuinely friendly offer, but romantic rejection had made Peck jaded. "You know that I can't fly."

"You can hop! You can jump! I'll fly low for you," Vinnie promised. "I'll glow bright, just for your weak spider eyes."

"Look, my eyes are just fine," Peck lied. "I'm great at tracking motion! It's just, well, I can't focus too good. So once you're up there flashing, well, those big blurry lights could be anybody."

"Peck, give me a break. You'll know it's me, because my skills are second to none. Now pay some attention, and learn about the state of the art in aerobatic luminescence."

The tough climb up the tall stalk got Vinnie warmed up. He poised himself under the canopy of the dandelion bloom, flapped open his casings, extruded filmy black wings, and took flight.

Night was deepening, that vast abyss. Light shocked out of his slatted belly, and the world exploded with meaning. Nothing meant more than his glowing arc across the nullity of darkness. His very being was focused: to connect.

He and his fellow artists were chips of sunlight, smuggled from day into gloom. Illumination streamed from his being. When a woman responded from her private world in the vital undergrowth, he did not so much see her message as become it: that female response pressed directly on his soul.

He felt too bright to eat, these days. He knew that it was important to chew, to swallow, but he couldn't seem to focus any interest in anything but mating. It was as much as he could do to suck a little nectar in the after-hours, during the blue glow of dawn. Even tasty loaves of pollen seemed boring now, beneath him somehow. There was a clarity, a purity, in this radiant giving of his essence.

It could not last, he knew that. Yet each new gout of light, as it burst from his flesh, each bout of soul-bruising carnality, pushed him closer to wisdom.

Once airborne, he forgot Peck at once. It made no sense to waste his art on some dirt-bound spider. The evening air was a pageant of glittering rivals. The ground below was bejeweled with willing women.

The tender night was splendor itself. The air had just the right level of dampness to avoid dessication and a light, assisting breeze that was perfect for stunting. His powerful wing muscles blew heat through his long body. He lit up like a falling star.

He was reaching a personal best, this evening: he felt calm, mellow, yet tingling with anticipation. He looped, he swirled: masterful accents against the velvet darkness. No frenzy anymore, never too much zeal: his glittering arcs were a languid commentary on the universe, an invitation to enhance one's state of being.

The other flyboys in the evening air with him tonight. . . . Yes, these were his rivals, the genetic competition, but Vinnie couldn't help but admire their skill. Some ugly bitterness had died within him tonight. Even the worst among them . . . the guys pulling cheap stunts, the vulgar ones who just trawled the briar patch, same old same old. . . . At least they had heart. They had desire, need. Life meant something, even to them.

Then he saw her.

She had a woman's glow. Women didn't glow in the way men did. They didn't glow for the sake of fame; they glowed in response to others. He'd come to know them as practical, single-minded. There was a perfunctory quality to the glowing signals they sent from their posts on leaves, stems, blossoms. As if they had watched his antics long enough, and now they were saying: Very well. If that's what it takes to make you happy, here I am.

But this dazzling, feminine glow . . . It was very bright, and there was some piquant quality about it. . . . A teasing lag, a kind of ironic awareness. . . . He circled and sent a response. A query.

Her answer came, a bit too quickly. Bold, assertive. As if he were being a little foolish not to already know who she was, what she was, what their game was. An implicit challenge there. No coyness needed, no quarter taken or given.

He sent a long reply, a rising note, sustained.

Her answer was the very soul of allure. It was rich, self-conscious, and burningly voluptuous. It astounded him. He could no more have resisted that siren flash than a moth could resist a flame. His airborne body reoriented itself almost against his will.

She was on the broad leaf of a nettle. Vinnie wasn't crazy about nettle plants; the gummy, stinging barbs weren't likely to hurt a creature of his size, but they were inconvenient. The leaf was sticky, and his left midleg was wonky, so it wasn't the elegant, poised landing a man come courting would have hoped for.

Then she pounced on him. She came running from the base of the nettle leaf, and for all her great bulk—she seemed three times his size—she was lethally fast.

She knocked him backward with her headlong assault, and in a confused, writhing mass, they fought. They battled in a jumbled mess of multilegged wrestling, and somehow, the two of them ended up jammed down and half-trapped among the nettle barbs. She couldn't get the lethal grip she wanted, the crushing bite that would have finished him off; she had his bad leg in her huge jaws, but her wing case had gone askew in the struggle, and the tender veil of her wing was crumpled, gluey, and stuck into place. They were stalemated.

"Okay," he gasped. "Now you're going to tell me what this is about! Who are you? What are you?"

"I'm a Photuris," she muttered around the shaft of his leg. "So I'm eating you."

"What is that supposed to mean?"

"Well, you're a Photinus. Or you taste like one. And I'm a Photuris, so I prey on you."

"Would you stop chewing, please? Can't we discuss this matter like adults?"

" 'Adults'?" She pulled her fanged mandibles from the badly dented chitin of his leg. Her mouth looked somewhat like his own, but much larger, and highly suited to ripping men apart. "Do I look like a pupa to you, shorty?"

Vinnie heaved himself vigorously, struggling to find his feet in the gummy footing of the nettle leaf. She wasn't really three times his size—more like double it—and now that her sudden ambush had failed, she had a fight on her hands with him. Vinnie knew that she could kill him, and it was clear she intended to eat him. But he'd been in some fights of his own in younger days, and he knew how to handle himself. She could lose an antenna, maybe a leg.

"Look, back off, lady—or whatever you are."

"I just told you what I am: I'm a female Photuris. We lure and eat Photinus males. That's our niche, it's what we live for. I was luring you—practically perfectly—so I should be eating you right now. Stand still, and I'll make this quick."

"You're 'luring' me?" Vinnie scoffed. "Your head is three times too big! Your mouth is a mass of fangs! And your ass is enormous. You know what? You're not alluring. You're a giant, ugly cannibal."

"That's not fair. I'm not a cannibal. You're my prey species."

"But we're both beetles of the family Lampyridae. Plus, you used my own Photinus style of flashing!"

"Not exactly," she said. "I improved it. Given my profession, I'm better at flashing than any Photinus—male or female."

"Okay," said Vinnie, "I admit it, your display was fantastic. I never saw the like. It's a pity that, face to face, you're so hideous."

"Look, fella, I happen to be extremely attractive to Photuris men. Your limited standards of female beauty, those I don't care about. I don't need to please you. All I have to do is rip your head off, then eat you."

Vinnie considered this. He could recognize that his cannibal remark had been a little ungallant. Several million years ago, Photuris and Photinus had probably been the same species of beetle, but beetles had a genius for radiating into every conceivable evolutionary niche. That was why there were more beetles in the world than any other kind of creature.

It shouldn't have entirely surprised him to learn there was a class of firefly that ate fireflies.

"Okay, I guess I can accept that, but tell me something. Where are these Photuris men that you are supposed to attract?"

"What do you mean?"

"I wasn't hatched yesterday. I know every guy around here, by his style and his signal. If there were any Photuris men around, I'd know that. So where are they?"

"Top predators are rare," she admitted.

"You never met a male at all? Getting pretty late in the season."

"I met a lot of men of your species. Your type is very common. I ate about as many of you as I have legs."

"What were their names?" Vinnie paused. "Never mind that. You just kind of jumped on them out of the darkness, eh? Never bothered to, uh, get to know them as people."

"I knew what they wanted," she said. "What's to talk about?"

"Everything," he said. "There's everything to talk about. Love is a carnival! It's an adventure! There should be tenderness in all this, there should be soulfulness! The unexamined light is not worth flashing! A man and woman in sexual union are the very hinge of futurity! They are the opened door to the renewal of life. Flesh in a fertile unity, that is the gate through which all else must pass. . . ."

"You're kind of a cute guy, for a Photinus."

"I keep in shape."

"You came here to mate, not to talk philosophy. Sex is what you wanted, isn't it? Go on, admit that."

"Well, yeah. Of course I wanted it."

"Well, you're not so bad-looking. Suppose that I let you just do it. When you're nice and tired afterward, will you let me devour you without putting up a big fuss about it?"

Vinnie looked her over. She was colossally huge, crazily powerful, treacherous, grisly, and fanged, but she was kind of growing on him. A flash burst out of him, involuntarily lighting the leaf surface.

"We have chemistry," he admitted. "Frankly, I'm tempted."

"Well, what's stopping you?"

He drew a breath. "I've got a counterproposal. Why don't you let me go? Then, as a reward, I'll send you three or four other Photinus males, to make up for the loss of me."

"Would you really do that? Why?"

"I've got my reasons. It just so happens that certain flyers are aesthetically offensive. Those guys are unfit, and they shouldn't be reproducing. Seriously."

"I'm supposed to eat rivals whose work isn't up to your artistic standards?"

"Have you seen those clowns by the bramble pile? Every night they fly those tight little circles. . . ."

She laughed. "You mean them? They're the shallow end of the gene pool! They're beneath me."

"You're not being reasonable here. Do you want someone to appreciate your charm, or do you want food?"

She pulled in irritation at her soiled wing. It peeled free from the nettle's furry surface. "What's your name, anyway?"

"Vinnie."

"I'm Dolores."

"Hi."

"I've heard stories about situations like this," she said slowly. "Once I heard about a sister who actually fell for a Photinus guy."

"No kidding."

"He was so sweet that she just chewed his two midlegs

off. Because she wanted him to fly off and reproduce, and put more men like himself into the breeding population."

"That's a great evolutionary gambit, but I don't want my legs eaten off," Vinnie said. He lost his composure and began to flash uncontrollably.

"You should watch it, carrying on that way," she said. Reflexively, she flashed in response. Her flashes were hugely powerful, torrents of carnivorous vitality. "A little guy like you, you could blow some valve in your abdomen."

"Does that matter, Dolores? Summer's going to end! I'll die of natural causes! Let me go. I'll creep on back to you at the end of my lifespan. You can eat me then! What difference does it make to either one of us?"

"I might die before you came back," she said. "I might starve to death."

"So what? So what if we both burn out tonight in one last great performance? You don't scare me."

She backed away. "You have guts and talent," she admitted. "You can glow."

"I thought I was hot stuff till I met you," he said. Light poured from him. Now they were duetting. She had a wild, feral, overwhelming gift for expression. It was like standing next to the sun.

The nettle leaf trembled gently. Another lightning bug had arrived.

He was long and spindly and thin. He was too tall, and his proportions were off.

"What have we got here?" he drawled.

"I'm Vinnie. This is Dolores. Now get lost."

The stranger looked at Dolores quizzically. "Why is this piece of meat talking?"

"You're a Photuris male," said Dolores in awe. "At last! Where have you been all my life?"

"I'm a rarity, babe, the only one in these parts. You and the suppertime here sure are making a big bright ruckus. I never flew by this little nettle patch before, but you're hard to miss tonight. When do we eat?"

"Did you flash on your way here?" said Vinnie. "It would have been more polite to flash."

"Why would I bother? I know where she is." He turned to Dolores. "Would you kill him now, please? I'm hungry."

"Wait a minute," said Vinnie. "What flashing system do you use?"

"I beg your pardon?"

"It's a professional interest. She's a mimic, right? She mimics how a Photinus flashes. Are you a mimic, too?"

"I can mimic fourteen different genres of flashing," said the stranger.

"Okay, fine, yeah, I get that, very impressive. You're great at pastiche. But I'm asking you: how do *you yourself* flash, as a Photuris? What do you bring to the table, creatively speaking?"

"Well," said the stranger, "with an incident like this one, I don't need to flash at all. I can just watch her mimicking you. Then we eat you, and we reproduce, and everything's hunky-dory."

Vinnie turned to Dolores. "You know what? This creep can't flash for himself. He's got nothing authentic to say!"

"Is that true?" said Dolores.

With a groan of disbelief, the stranger lit up. "Okay, fine, be that way! You want a guy to flash at you, no problem. I can ripple through all kinds of patterns. You name it, I can do it. Whatever the market demands."

"That's not his point," said Dolores. "His point was, you can't communicate with me as a man of my own species should communicate with a woman."

"But we're carnivores! We exploit the flashing system in order to eat people who flash."

"Does this mean you're incapable of a sincere expression in your own idiom?"

"You need to knock those weird ideas out of your head," said the stranger. "Okay, fine, so I don't have a unique Photuris signal! Who cares? I don't need one, and I don't want one. I'll tell you what I *do* want and need—and you'd better give it to me. I want to eat his head and thorax. You can eat the rest of him, but leave those parts for me."

"Why?"

"Especially those big glands in his neck."

"Why is that?" she insisted.

"Because that's where he manufactures lucibufagin, the firefly poison. Once we eat those poison glands, we absorb the poison. Then we become poisonous, too."

"We're not poisonous by nature?" said Dolores.

"No. Not until we we eat Photinus beetles. See, we have no need to create our own poison. We just suck poison out of their flesh, and then it belongs to us."

"Okay, that does it!" Vinnie announced. "I was sympathetic to the situation up to this point, but that's just a plain rip-off! You've got no lightning pattern and you've got no poison either? You're not a predator at all! You're a parasite!"

"Watch what you say," said the stranger. He shielded his eyes from Vinnie's angry flashing.

"You want a piece of me? Come on, give me your best shot!"

"Kill him," the stranger urged.

"She doesn't *need* any more poison," Vinnie pointed out, "because she already killed and ate six men. You're the one who's begging her to do your dirty work."

"Why am I listening to this?"

"What kind of man do you call yourself? You're a complete poseur! You're a drone."

The male Photuris took a cautious step back to the edge of the nettle leaf. "I'm far too valuable to risk my unique genes fighting prey animals."

"You don't like this?" said Vinnie. "You're shaking all over! Come back here and tussle, you lackluster, poison-free wimp!"

"You know what he's up to, don't you?" called the stranger to Dolores. "If I get injured, there could be any number of women in this area who go unfertilized. Including you!"

A black shape hurtled from nowhere with a sudden jarring collision. It was Peck. In an instant Peck's jaws had crunched fatally through the stranger's back.

"Fly away!" Dolores screamed. In her panic, she failed to unfurl her delicate wings. Her heavy body collided with a dozen nettle leaves on her way down to earth.

"Wow, he tastes fantastic!" Peck muttered through a mouthful of pierced integument. "I always knew that a lightning bug would taste great!" Peck hauled the stranger's paralyzed carcass toward the smooth base of the nettle leaf. "Ow! Why'd you have to pick a nettle plant, Vinnie?"

Vinnie left. With a few discreet flashes, he located Dolores. She was terrified, and cowering under a wilting toadstool.

"What was that?" Dolores gasped.

"Jumping spider," said Vinnie. "Came out of nowhere and nailed him."

"What a horrible monster!"

"I've been around," said Vinnie. "They're all the same." He examined himself. His left midleg had frozen into position. One of Dolores's antennae was wrecked and cockeyed. Both of them were covered with gum and flecks of dirt. "Look how screwed up we are! Why'd you pick a nettle for a perch?"

Dolores loosened her enormous jaws. "That makes it harder for prey to get away."

"Well, we got away anyway."

"Yes, but now I'm starving!"

One of the Photuris's legs came tumbling down. It stuck to the side of a fallen leaf. It was followed by the entirety of his severed, glowing gut. Vinnie limped forward and sniffed. "Spiders sure are picky eaters. This leg here is practically whole."

"You can't eat that," she said.

"Are you kidding? Sure I can eat it."

"Well, save some for me!"

Vinnie reached out and sampled a bit of the broken, glowing abdomen. "You know what this is? This is practically pure luciferin! And that tangy spice is its catalyst, luciferase!" He stuck his entire head into his rival's exploded gut. It was as if the core of the sun had been made out of jam: yellow, rich, and thick.

Vinnie pulled himself free, and for, the first time in his life, he glowed from both ends. When he swallowed, he glowed so hard that light shone through his thorax.

"You shouldn't eat that stuff."

"What, like I can't metabolize my own biochemistry? You go ahead and eat his leg! Go on, chow down, you've got the fangs for it!" Vinnie opened his wing-cases. His back glowed straight through the veining of his wings. He glittered all over. It felt completely sublime.

"I couldn't possibly eat my own species," Dolores said primly.

"Oh come on, I won't tell! I bet I'm the first Photinus to devour a Photuris in about a million years." Vinnie burrowed right in and began to glut himself. "I haven't had a serious meal in ages! This is giving me my appetite back!"

"I've lost my best perch. I'm going to starve," said Dolores, bursting into sobs. "I'll never reproduce. I'm an evolutionary failure!"

"Quit fussing," shrugged Vinnie, wiping bright goo from his jaws. "I did my own bit for posterity. So what? It's not like we ever live to see posterity." He groomed his damaged leg, licking his own seeping juices. Maybe he would heal, if he swallowed enough protein. Fireflies were quick to heal.

"I'm totally disillusioned, Vinnie. Because I now know that there can be no true sincerity between a woman and a man. We can never have a genuine meeting of minds. Language fails us."

Suddenly Vinnie disgorged. "Oh dear. Oh, that was just too rich to keep down."

Dolores examined the brightly glowing pile of masticated paste. "That's interesting. . . . Now that you ate this and barfed it up, it smells just like a Photinus smells."

"Sure. We're all the same chemistry under the skin."

"It even tastes like you taste. It tastes pretty good, actually."

"I told you it was terrific." Vinnie burst into triumphant

laughter. "Look at me now! Look! I'm glowing fore and aft, port and starboard, inside and out! I have achieved the height of artistry! This is the happiest night of my life!"

Dolores dabbled her cruelly hooked feet in the glowing paste. In a mix of despair and frivolity, she anointed herself with gold. It made her gorgeous, splendid, luminous. She was terrible and beautiful, like a flaming angel.

Clarity flooded his mind. "I love you! Let's fly till dawn!"

★ III ★

Fiction for Scientists

(I've been reading the British science weekly *Nature* for many years. On occasion they ask me for fiction. Writing for *Nature* is a highly purified form of science fiction, in that it's fiction written specifically for a readership of scientists. It's exhilirating to write for an audience so thoroughly educated, and so entirely unperturbed by multisyllabic, sesquipedalian, ultra-technical forms of expression. At eight hundred words a pop, I wish I could write one of these pieces every week.)

Homo Sapiens Declared Extinct

AD 2380

After a painstaking ten-year search, from the Tibetan highlands to the Brazilian rainforests, it's official—there are no more human beings.

"I suppose I have to consider this a personal setback," said anthropologist Dr. Marcia Raymo, of the Institute for Retrograde Study in Berlin. "Of course we still have human tissue in the lab, and we could clone as many specimens of Homo sapiens as we like. But that species was always known primarily for its unique cultural activity."

"I can't understand what the fuss is about," declared Rita "Cuddles" Srinivasan, actress, sex symbol, and computer peripheral. "Artificial Intelligences love to embody themselves in human forms like mine, to wallow in sex and eating. I'm good for oodles of human stuff, scratching, sleeping, sneezing, you can name it. As long as AIs honor their origins, you'll see plenty of disembodied intelligences slumming around in human forms. That's where all the fun is, I promise—trust me."

The actress's current AI sponsor further remarked via wireless telepathy that Miss Srinivasan's occasional extra arms or heads should be seen as a sign of "creative brio" and not as a violation of "some obsolete, supposedly standard human form."

A worldwide survey of skull contents in April 2379 revealed no living citizen with less than 35 percent cultured gelbrain. "That pretty well kicks it in the head for me," declared statistician Piers Euler, the front identity for a collaborative group-mind of mathematicians at the Bourbaki Academy in Paris. "I don't see how you can declare any entity 'human' when their brain is a gelatin lattice, and every cell of their body contains extensive extra strands of industrial-strength DNA. Not only is humanity extinct, but, strictly speaking, pretty much everyone alive today should be classified as a unique, post-natural, one-of-a-kind species."

"I was born human," admitted 380-year-old classical musician Soon Yi, speaking from his support vat in Shanghai. "I grew up as a human being. It seemed quite natural at the time. For hundreds of years on the state-supported concert circuit, I promoted myself as a 'humanist,' supporting and promoting human high culture. But at this point, I should be honest: that was always my stage pretence. Let's face it: gelbrain is vastly better stuff than those grey, greasy, catch-as-catch-can human neurons. You can't become a serious professional artiste while using nothing but all-natural animal tissue in your head. It's just absurd!"

Gently fanning his wizened tissues with warm currents of support fluid, the grand old man of music continued: "Wolfgang Mozart was a very dull creature by our modern standards, but thanks to gelbrain I can still find ways to pump life into his primitive compositions. I also persist in finding Bach worthwhile, even in today's ultracivilized milieu, where individual consciousness and creative subjectivity tend to be rather rare, or absent entirely."

Posthumanity's most scientifically advanced group, the pioneer Blood Bathers in their vast crystalline castles in the Oort Cloud, could not be reached for comment.

"Why trouble the highly prestigious Blood Bathers with some trifling development here on distant Earth?" demanded President Arno Hopmeier of the World Antisubjectivist Council. "The Blood Bathers are busily researching novel realms of complex organization far beyond mere 'intelligence.' We should feel extremely honored that they still bother to share their lab results with creatures like us. It would only annoy Their Skinless Eminences if we ask them to fret over some defunct race of featherless bipeds."

A Circumsolar Day of Mourning has been declared to commemorate the official extinction of humanity, but it is widely believed that bursts of wild public enthusiasm will mar the funereal proceedings.

"When you sum them up," mused Orbital Entity Ankh/Ghih/9819, "it's hard to perceive any tragedy in this long-awaited event. Beasts, birds, butterflies, even the very rocks and rivers must be rejoicing to see humans finally gone. We should try to be adult about this: we should take a deep breath, turn our face to the light of the future, and get on with the business of living.

"Since I've been asked to offer an epitaph," the widely distributed poetware continued, "I believe that we should rearrange the Great Wall of China to spell out (in Chinese of course, since most of them were always Chinese)— 'THEY WERE VERY, VERY CURIOUS, BUT NOT AT ALL FAR-SIGHTED.'

"This historical moment is a serious occasion that requires a sense of public dignity. My dog, for instance, says he'll truly miss humanity. But then again, my dog says a lot of things."

Ivory Tower

O ur problem was simple. We needed an Academy, but professional careers in conventional science were out of the question for us. We were ten thousand physicists entirely self-educated by Internet.

Frankly, physics is a lot easier to learn than physicists used to let on. The ultimate size of the smallest particles—the origin and fate of the universe—come on, who could fail to take a burning interest in those subjects? If we were genuinely civilized, that's all we would talk about. In the new world of open access, ultrawide broadband, and gigantic storage banks, physics is just sort of sitting there. It's like a vast intellectual Tinkertoy!

We cranky Net-geeks had to find a way to devote every

waking moment to our overpowering lust for physics. Of course we demanded state support for our research efforts (just like real scientists do), but alas, the bureaucrats wouldn't give us the time of day.

So to find time for our kind of science, we had to dump a few shibboleths. For instance, we never bother to "publish"—we just post our findings on weblogs, and if that gets a lot of links, hey, we're the Most Frequently Cited. Tenure? Who needs that? Never heard of it! Doctorates, degrees, defending a thesis? Don't know, don't need 'em, can't even be bothered!

Organizing ourselves was a snap. If you are a math genius whose primary language is Malayalam and whose main enthusiasm is wave-particle duality, you stand out on the Net like a buzzing hornet in a spiderweb. You're one in a million, pal—but in a world of ten billion people, there's ten thousand of us. We immediately started swapping everything we knew on collaborative weblogs.

Since most of us were Indian and/or Chinese (most of everybody is Indian and/or Chinese), we established our Autodidacts' Academy on the sun-baked sandstone flats of the desert of Rajasthan, not too far from the deserted Mughal utopia of Fatehpur Sikri. We were dreamy, workaholic utopians trying to wrest a living out of barren wilderness—something like Mormons, basically. However, since it was the 2050s, we also had unlimited processing power, bandwidth, search engines, social software, and open-source everything. How could we fail?

Basically, we recast human existence as a bio-engineering problem. How do you move enough nutrient through human brain tissue to allow a city full of people to blissfully contemplate supersymmetric M-branes? The solutions were already scattered through the online technical literature; we just Googled it all up and set it right to work. Our energy is solar; water is distilled and recycled; and the ivory-gleaming domes and spires of our physics ashram are computer-fabricated grit, glue, and sawdust. All our lab equipment is made of garbage.

Our visitors are astounded to see (for instance) repurposed robotic vacuum cleaners equipped with tiller blades and digging out our 150-kilometer accelerator tunnel. But why not? In the 2050s, even the junk is ultra-advanced, and nobody knows how to repair it. Any sufficiently advanced garbage is indistinguishable from magic.

Our daily diet, which is free of charge, is fully defined "Purina Physicist Chow." It's basically sewage, with its bioenergetic potential restored by genetically altered yeasts. Some diners fail to appreciate the elegant mathematical simplicity of this solution to the age-old problem of a free lunch. But if they don't get it, then they don't belong here with us, anyway.

There's no money and no banking here. Instead, every object is tracked by RFID tags and subjected to a bio-energetic, cost-benefit, eBay-style arbitrage by repurposed stock-market buy-sell software agents. In practice, this means that when you need something new, you just pile up the things you don't want by your doorway until somebody shows up and gives you the thing you do want. Economists who visit here just flee screaming—but was economics ever really a "science"? We're with Rutherford: it's physics or it's stamp collecting!

You might imagine that women would find our monastic,

geeky life unattractive, but our Academy's crawling with coeds. A few are female physicists—the usual fraction—but the rest are poets, lit majors, anthropologists, and gender studies mavens. These gals showed up to condemn our reductionalist, instrumental male values, but they swiftly found out that our home is ideal for consciousness-raising, encounter groups, and performance art. Women now out-number us three to two. That's not a problem. We don't bother them with our weird obsessions, they don't bother us with theirs, and whatever happens between us after dark is nobody's business.

We have a beautiful, spiritual thing going on here. Feel free to join us. Please, no more atomic bomb fans. We know that atomic bombs are a dead simple, hundred-year-old technology, and anybody with a search engine, half a brain, and a lot of time could tinker one up. But really, why even bother? It's beneath us!

[*Nature* commissioned me to write a scenario about "the end of the world." So I obliged with this grimly plausible squib, which went unpublished until this appearance. I did, however, get a "kill fee" from *Nature* for destroying the world. The world of science is full of poetic justice!]

Message Found in a Bottle

To Whom It May Ever, Someday, Somehow Concern: Let me explain to you why you found these science magazines in a steel tank in the bottom of a Scottish lake.

This tank was once a library's hot water heater. The heater is no use to us now, because there's no fossil fuel. We survive in the library, because its walls are so thick, and we burn the books, not because we hate books, but because books pack a surprising amount of BTUs.

Besides, books from the past are not about today's experience, so they seem irrelevant to us. If they were about today's experience, they'd be too depressing to read.

Nobody moves during wintertime—when the wind pours over Britain from the frozen highlands of Germany, you can freeze in the space of a city block. In spring and autumn, survivors sometimes see the smoke and the glow of our burning books. If they survive our quarantine, we let them join our unhappy little tribe among the stacks here.

I could have let them burn these science magazines to keep us warm—heaven knows we've burned a lot of fossils —but I told them the ink would shed a toxic smoke. For once, they believed me on the subject of emissions, though, back when I was a climate scientist, they simply blinked like owls. They're simple folk, they didn't raise a fuss. There are still plenty of sci-fi and romance novels on the shelves— those should see us through to another summer.

We can move during the summers, but the summers are horrible. We've survived into a literal Dark Age, an epoch when the sky is blue maybe four times a year.

"A man gets a longing for a good gloom," as they used to say about Scotland, but when the sun never shines at all, when the blue sky is the color of gunmetal and stays that way, when you can't draw a clean breath anywhere, any time, and there's no prospect of that ever changing, for as long as you live—well, you don't much want to live. We were morally crushed, intellectually shredded, culturally wrecked by the extent of our calamitous folly. People are afraid of the sky now. The sensibility of these fatal times is a soul-killing superstitious dread.

We drew the black card in the climate change scenario— we drew the Queen of Spades, the Nightmare. We drew the Dirty Little Sister of Nuclear Holocaust. And yet, people still don't use the word "Greenhouse Effect." They're still pitifully unable to face the truth of atmospheric physics, they're in denial and just won't let themselves comprehend it. When they do understand it, they can't bear to speak it.

The Russians understood it. Somebody got the full extent of humanity's defeat across to them in words that they could grasp—some Russian poet, I think. She said something on television as Moscow was burning, and then, instead of losing half a million Russians a year, they lost half a million every day. Soon their transmissions stopped.

People talk about God now. And death. We seek divinity in our own annihilation. Bin Laden was our guru there.

We sinned, and God hates us, and we make amends by our dying, and there's a reward for all that somewhere, beyond that turgid, steel-gray sky. Having failed our civilization, we who were once in science still receive no credit for our insights; quite the contrary. Science is as dead as the glyptodon, a tender superstructure that fell like a tree and is reduced to nothing but seeds, like the magazines you just found in this watertight coffin.

Humanity stumbles in collapse, reduced to a tribalized scattering. We live on a wrecked and tattered planet that became one big Martyrdom Operation, a failed globe that strapped the gelignite to its obese belly and set itself alight.

Our heirs will wear shrouds and hoods. They'll follow the sheep from patch to patch of stubborn weeds. They will pray.

Spring will be here soon, because I can smell the intercontinental stench from the flames of Brazil. I'll break the gray ice on the lake with the heels of my rag-wrapped boot, tuck this note into the watertight bowels of the boiler, and heave this sarcophagus through the fracture and down to a bed in the sediments.

We were really onto something once. You should read these magazines I saved for you. Then for God's sake make a better use of your knowledge than we did.

⋆ IV ⋆

Architecture Fiction

(Architecture isn't science. But it's rigorous, challenging, influential, futuristic. . . . The work in an architecture and urban design magazine like *Metropolis* is easily as visionary and challenging to preconceptions as, say, the science fiction film called *Metropolis*, which is heavily dominated by imaginary architecture—"architecture fiction." This speculative, futuristic story was written for *Metropolis* and is set inside an imaginary work of architecture by Greg Lynn, the modern master of computer-designed "blobitecture." Given a stage set as remarkable as that, it was a pleasure to provide plot and characters.)

The Growthing

Milton's daughter sobbed aloud as she clutched the chaise longue. "But why can't I take the chair? I grew it myself from a bean!"

"Gretel, there's no room for that thing on your flight. Besides, a chaise longue isn't a 'chair.' "

Gretel flung herself in anguish on the biomorphic furnishing. In her frenzied teenage grip, the chaise gave a deep pneumatic moan and sentimentally changed color. "But I love my big bubbly sofa! And Mom's got the stupidest dead furniture in Jersey! My bed at home's made of *wood*, Dad! I'm your only daughter! How can you make me *sleep on wood?*"

Milton checked his wrist monitor. He knew that watching

his child's internal metabolism was a pretty cheap substitute for genuine fathering skills. However, Gretel was fourteen. Her hormonal storms were pegging the behavior meter. "Gret, you're hyperventilating. Let's walk around the Facility one last time before you go. A nice memento for you to take home, that's just no problemo, okay?"

Profoundly unmollified, Gretel lunged into her walking boots. A month in this Texan desert outpost had been quite the growthful experience for a girl from the megalopolis. She'd swiftly adopted Milton's mannerisms—his absent-minded hacker's stare, his habit of patting the red bark on the giant biomorphic cisterns. Milton would miss the kid dreadfully. The Facility was a majestic but lonely place, with its veiny dragonfly roofing and storage tanks shaped like swollen sequoias. It had taproots that went down to solid granite. It stored enough clean-power hydrogen to detonate Dubuque. The Facility fed and clothed Milton. It also lit itself, warmed itself, harnessed solar and wind power, and recycled every nutrient. The building had a baroque attention to design detail that rivaled Cinderella's midnight pumpkin. Still, it was basically a Texan energy refinery. Not quite the place for a gala soiree.

Every deer and javelina season, the Facility booked in some drunken hunters. Then the kitchen appliances would perk up and the food would taste more like real food. Most days, though, stuck on his patrol inside this high-biotech marvel, Milton was a lighthouse keeper. Just him, the Marooned Genius on the Forbidden Planet, and the maintenance software.

Gretel never seemed lonely. She liked her teenage friends much better when they were stuck behind computer-gaming screens. Gretel had a definite Mad Scientists' Beautiful Daughter riff. Stuck in some fashion spasm that was either total vanity or total despair (most likely both), she had been wearing the same dress every day. Each morning a fresh one emerged from a wall in a sheet from a slot, as dainty as Kleenex. Dirty clothes vanished down the composting toilets. The fashion choices available on the Facility's system were franchised direct from Milan and bounced in by Chinese satellite. But the sheer labor of those endless choices had bored or paralyzed Gretel. She was finally figuring out that mass-customized home manufacturing was way too much like work.

Occupation sensors popped to watchful life as the two of them left the manager's quarters. Milton spent most of his working days inside the Facility's office: the place was all skeins, screens, and thick paper panes, a little mossy and gooey here and there, but with a nice origami feel to it— very crisp, shoji, Shinto. They walked under the cabbagelike pergola, the dry, blistered floor popping like Bubblepak under their boot heels. Gummy zippers opened here and there in thick barky walls. Thoughtful gasps of flavored mist kept them cool in the insufferable Texan air.

"I'll miss this big wonderful place, Dad!"

"I'm glad you had a chance to witness some modern industry, honey. Someday the weird construction techniques they demo out here in the desert will become contemporary urban policy. Yes, even in pokey old New York. By the time you grow up to be my age, I'm sure you'll hate everything else."

"I'm ahead of the curve, Dad. I already hate everything else."

Life within the Facility had definite benefits, especially

considering the alternatives posed to Milton by the special prosecutor. Against his better judgment—well, mostly—Milton had been sucked into a massive city hall scandal involving phony revenue from automated traffic tickets. He'd made an unusual plea bargain, but any engineer who could manage the daily traffic flow across the Brooklyn Bridge had no problem administering a giant Texas fuel turnip. Once he'd done his time growing and pruning this place, Milton had plans to input some fresh biological juice into the Big Apple.

Some precious day he would return to his beloved Manhattan apartment. The place was sublet to a kindly magazine editor, a gentle civilized soul who worked eighty-hour weeks, surviving mostly on cold shrimp chow mein. Come Christmas 2045—or spring 2046 at the latest—he'd be cozying up again with his favorite classic Rashid blobjects. The top-end decor had been an endless source of friction with his ex-wife, who had no taste. The very thought of his own flesh and blood forced to live on Sears veneer colonials in some featureless brick condo in Jersey—man, that really stung.

Milton and his daughter walked together under the translucent arch of a giant veiny breezeway, grown in place to funnel the prevailing wind. West Texas was the Saudi Arabia of American native wind power. Unfortunately nobody lived in West Texas anymore because the aquifers were depleted and there was no drinkable water left. Yet somebody still had to mind the store. "Honey, you remember what you're supposed to tell Mom about those offshore accounts I kept?"

"Sure thing, Dad. Ooh look! A big solar barnacle! Can I take that home?"

"They die if you peel them loose, precious. They're kind of parasitic."

"How about some barnacle seeds, then? This one's flowering."

"They wouldn't do all that great in the New Jersey climate."

Gretel's face clouded in frustration. "Dad, just squeeze their stupid genetics till they can do New Jersey!"

"Well sure, if I broke copyright and hacked their gattaca, but . . ." Milton stopped. He was talking to a fourteen-year-old here. "You can have a solar barnacle, sweetie. Just send me e-mail as soon as you get home."

Fresh liquid reeking of praline, pepper sauce, and chocolate mole came from the double row of giant mushrooms outside the gate. Their vast waxy undersides bulged with captured rainwater from the last Greenhouse monsoon. As a value-added fillip, they fermented Tex-Mex flavoring agents within their giant bioactive cups. Twice a year guys from San Antonio came by in tanker trucks.

Gretel began to sniffle and wipe her eyes, in a rampant mix of sentiment and pepper sauce. "I'll miss this big growthing so much, Dad. The subterranean heat pipes, the hydrogenic bacteria. Those kids at Christie Whitman High just don't get this."

"I gotta admit, when Monsanto went into architecture, they really did it up brown. They've got it going on with that enigmatic spatial fluidity." It broke his heart when she stood there bravely on the Facility's windblown rubber launchpad, tethered to a kite and clutching her overstuffed pack. The passing zeppelin snagged her with a wire retrieval. Gretel shot into the sapphire Texas sky as if packed in a mime's invisible elevator. Goodbye, till the next time he got custody.

Milton pulled off his thick black glasses and rubbed both hands all over his close-cropped hair and beard. My God, reproduction was such a fantastic, terrifying business.

A week later another teenage girl showed up. She had tried to sneak up the Facility's drainpipes until stopped by the whooping intrusion alarms. She was thin, sunburned, covered in windblown dirt, and wore fringed buckskin leather and feathers.

"You'd better let me go," the girl advised Milton solemnly. "My dad's a desert war veteran. He's a SEAL. He's a Green Beret and Delta Force. He's got like lasers and daisy-cutters and stuff."

"What's your name, kid?"

"It's Janis. We're like Comanches. We've got tattoos. We're really scary and heavy. I've got an unmanned spy plane and a bazooka."

"So, you must be a native Texan, am I right?"

"Yeah, we-all are from Lubbock! Except there's no water left under the ground. So now we just live inside our pickup trucks. My dad's got a Howitzer and land mines, Mister. He could blow this whole place up just like that." Janis snapped her fingers.

"Look, Janis, this is a green renewable fuel-storage facility. We could blow this place up so hard that Taiwan would ring like a gong. But so what? There's nobody for miles around here but you, me, and our fellow enviro-disaster derelicts."

Janis's eyes darted from side to side. Then she faked a shrug. "Well, I got e-mail from a girl in New Jersey saying there was all kinds of fantastic cool stuff inside this place.

And boy, is there ever! It's like the Emerald City of Cabbage! And my tribe really needs water. Do you have, like, Perrier?"

"Does your dad ask for that? He sounds kind of picky."

"No, Abdullah says that. Abdullah's from Morocco. He's our appropriate technology advisor from the UN. Abdullah's teaching us how to make valuable trade goods from sheep." Janis brightened. " 'Cause sheep have this kind of cool hair that just grows on them! Like a Chia Pet! You can cut it off and weave it into stuff! It's great! You can even make tents!"

"Yeah, that sounds real advanced and bio-organic."

"Oh yes, it so much is! But you know, if you have sheep you have to water them."

Milton rubbed his chin. "So, uh, how many consumers are there in this big marauding desert tribe of yours?"

"About five hundred! Okay, three hundred. Two hundred. A hundred and eighty-eight."

"Are you guys in the market for cool furniture? Welcome to the future, kid. How would you like to live here?"

✱ V ✱

Design Fiction

(Designers are even cooler than architects and scientists. Given, this accomplishment is their stock in trade, but considering my own proclivities, this is a professional quality I deeply appreciate. I've hung out with design professors for many years now. I myself happen to be a design professor at the moment—I'm the "Visionary in Residence" at the Art Center College of Design in Pasadena, California. Hence the title of this story collection. I'm no designer, mind you. I'm not even much interested in becoming a designer—because I've got my own problem-solving challenges, and they're literary ones. However, as this story shows, I've become very, very interested indeed in how designers work and think. I particularly like their imaginative methods for working "outside the box" of previous definitions of the problem at hand, and their ways of directly engaging with the grain of the material. I admire these skills, and have taken them so much to heart that, although I don't design, I can teach it.)

User-Centric

From: Team Coordinator
To: "Design Team" [Engineer, Graphic Designer, Legal Expert, Marketer, Programmer, Social Anthropologist & Team Coordinator]
Subject: New Product Brainstorm

Another new product launch. Well, we all know what that means. Nobody ever said that they're easy. But I do believe the seven of us—given our unique backgrounds and our proven skills—are just the people to turn things around for this company.

Things aren't as bad as the last quarterly report makes them look. Despite what the shareholders may think, we've definitely bottomed out from that ultrasonic cleanser debacle. Sales in muscle-gel apps remain strong.

Plus, the buzz on our new product category just couldn't be hotter. People across our industry agree that locator tag microtechnology is a killer app in the intelligent-environment market. MEMS tech is finally out of the lab and bursting into the marketplace, and our cross-licenses and patents look very solid. As for the development budget—well, this is the biggest new product budget I've seen in eight years with this company.

My point is—we've got to get away from our old-fashioned emphasis on "technology for tech's sake." That approach is killing us in the modern marketplace. Yes, of course MEMS locator chips are a "hot, sweet" technology—and yes, "If you build it, they will come." Our problem is, we do build it, and they do come, but they *give all the money to somebody else.*

We can't live on our reputation as a cutting-edge engineering outfit. Design awards just don't pay the bills. That's not what our shareholders want, and it's not what the new management wants. No matter how we may grumble, this company has got to be competitive in the real world. That means that it's all about Return-On-Investment. It's about meeting consumer demand, and generating serious revenue.

So let's not start with the product qua product. Our product is not a "commodity" anymore, and the consumer is not a "user." The product is a point of entry for the buyer into a long-term, rewarding relationship.

So what we require here, people, is a story. That story has got to be a human story. It has to be a user-centric story—it's got to center on the user himself. It's all about the guy who's opening his wallet and paying up.

I want this character, this so-called "user," to be a real person with some real human needs. I want to know *who he is,* and *what we're doing for him, and why he's giving us money.* So we've got to know what he needs, what he wants, what he longs for, what he hopes for, what he's scared of. All about him.

If we understand him and his motivations, then we also understand our product. I want to know what we can do for this guy in his real life. How can we mold his thinking?

From: Design Engineer
To: Design Team
Subject: Re: New Product Brainstorm

FYI, User specs: Classic early adapter type. Male. Technically proficient. 18-35 age demographic. NAFTA/Europe. Owns lots of trackable, high-value-added, mobile hardware products: sporting goods, laptops, bicycles, luggage, possibly several cars.

From: Marketer
To: Design Team
Subject: User Specs

I just read the Engineer's email, and gee whiz, people. That is dullsville. That is marketing poison. Do you have any idea how burned out the Male-Early-Adapter thing is in today's competitive environment? These guys have digital toothbrushes now. They're nerd-burned, they've been consumer-carpet-bombed! There's nothing left of their demographic! They're hiding in blacked-out closets hoping their shoes will stop paging their belt buckles.

Nerds can't push this product into the high-volume category that we need for a breakeven. We need a housekeeping technology. I mean ultra-high volume, in the realm of soaps, mops, brooms, scrubbing brushes, latex gloves, lightbulbs. An impulse buy, but high-margin and everywhere.

From: Programmer

To: Design Team
Subject: [no subject]

I can't believe I agree with the Marketer. But really, I'd rather be dipped
in crumbs and deep-fried. Than grind out code for some lamer chip. That
tells you where your lawnmower is. I mean, if you don't know by now.
READ THE FRIENDLY MANUAL. I mean, how stupid are people out there
supposed to be? Don't answer that. Jeez.

From: the social anthropologist
To: Design Team
Subject: Creating Our Reality Model

People, forgive me for this, but I don't think you quite grasp what Fred,
our esteemed Team Leader, is suggesting to us approach-wise. We need
a solid story before we consider the specs on the technical MacGuffin. A
story just works better that way.

So: we need a compelling character. In fact, we need two characters.
One for the early-adoption contingent who appreciates technical sweet-
ness, and the other who is our potential mass-market household user.
To put a human face on them right away, I would suggest we call them
"Al" and "Zelda."

Al is a young man with disposable income who lives in a rather
complex household. (Perhaps he inherited it.) Al's not really at ease
with his situation as it stands—all those heirlooms, antiques, expensive furniture, kitchenware, lawn-care devices—it's all just a little out
of his control. Given Al's modern education, Al sees a laptop or
desktop as his natural means of control over a complex situation. Al
wants his things together and neat, and accessible, and searchable,
and orderly—just the way they are on his computer screen.

But what Al really needs is an understanding, experienced, high-tech housekeeper. That's where "Zelda" comes into the story. Zelda's in today's 65+ demographic, elderly but very vigorous, with some life-extension health issues. Zelda has smart pill-bottles that remind her of all her times and her dosages. She's got cognitive blood-brain inhalers, and smart orthopedic shoes. Zelda wears the customary, elder-demographic, biomaintenance wrist monitor. So I see Zelda as very up-to-speed with biomedical tech—so that her innate late-adapter conservatism has a weak spot that we might exploit. Is this approach working for the Team?

From: Coordinator
To: Design Team
Subject: All right!!

The Social Anthropologist knows just what we want: specificity. We're building a technology designed for these two characters—who are they, what do they need? How can we exceed their consumer expectations, make them go "Wow"?

And one other little thing—I'm not the "Leader." It's nice of Susan to say that, but my proper title is "Coordinator," and the new CEO insists on that across all divisions.

From: Graphics Gal
To: Design Team
Subject: My Turn

Okay, well, maybe it's just me, but I'm getting a kind of vibe from this guy "Albert." I'm thinking he's maybe, like, a hunter? Because I see him as, like, outdoors a lot? More than you'd think for a geek, anyway. Okay?
From: Engineer

To: Design Team
Subject: Story Time

Okay, I can play that way, too. "Albert Huddleston." He's the quiet type, good with his hands. Not a big talker. Doesn't read much. Not a ladies' man. But he's great at home repair. He's got the big house, and he's out in the big yard a lot of the time, with big trees, maybe a garden. A deer rifle wouldn't scare him. He could tie trout flies, if he were in the mood.

From: Marketer
To: Design Team
Subject: The Consumables within Al's Demographic

A bow saw, an extendible pruner. Closet full of extreme-sports equipment from college that he can't bear to get rid of.

From: Graphics Gal
To: Design Team
Subject: What is Albert really like?

So he's, like, maybe, a Cognition-Science major with a minor in environmental issues?

From: Marketer
To: Design Team
Subject: [none]

Albert's not smart enough to be a "cognition science major."
From: Legal Expert

To: Design Team
Subject: So-Called Cognition Science

In a lot of schools, "Cognition Science" is just the Philosophy Department in drag.

From: Team Coordinator
To: Design Team
Subject: Brainstorming

It's great to see you pitching in, Legal Expert, but let's not get too critical while the big, loose ideas are still flowing.

From: Legal Expert
To: Design Team
Subject: Critical Legal Implications

Well, excuse me for living. Forgive me for pointing out the obvious, but there are massive legal issues with this proposed technology. We're talking about embedding hundreds of fingernail-sized radio-chirping MEMS chips that emit real-time data on the location and the condition of everything you own. That's a potential Orwell situation. It could violate every digital-privacy statute on the books.

Let's just suppose that you walk out with some guy's chip-infested fountain pen. You don't even know the thing's bugged. So if the plaintiff's got enough bandwidth and big enough receivers, he can map you and all your movements, for as long as you carry the thing.

Legal issues must come first in the design process. It's not prudent to tack on anti-liability safeguards, somewhere down at the far end of the assembly line.

From: Engineer
To: Design Team
Subject: Correction

We don't use "assembly lines." Those went out with the twentieth century.

From: Marketer
To: Design Team
Subject: Getting Sued

Wait a minute. Isn't product-liability exactly what blew us out of the water with the ultrasonic cleanser?

From: the social anthropologist
To: Design Team
Subject: The Issues We Face as a Group

There are plenty of major issues here, no one's denying that. In terms of the story though—I'm very intrigued with the Legal Expert's views. There seems to be an unexamined assumption that a household control technology is necessarily "private."

But what if it's just the opposite? If Al has the location and condition of all his possessions cybernetically tracked and tagged in real time, maybe Al is freed from worrying about all his stuff. Why should Al fret about his possessions anymore? We've made them permanently safe. Why shouldn't Al loan the lawnmower to his neighbor? The neighbor can't lose the lawnmower, he can't sell it, because Al's embedded MEMS monitors just won't allow that behavior.

So now Al can be far more generous to his neighbor. Instead of being miserly and geeky, "labeling everything he possesses," obsessed with privacy—Al turns out to be an open-handed, open-hearted, very popular guy. He doesn't even need locks on his doors! Everything Al has is automatically theft-proof—thanks to us. He has big house parties, fearlessly showing off his home and his possessions. Everything that was once a personal burden to Al becomes a benefit to the neighborhood community. What was once Al's weakness and anxiety is now a source of emotional strength and community esteem.

From: Team Coordinator
To: Design Team
Subject: Wow

Right! That's it. That's what we're looking for. That's the "Wow" factor.

From: Graphics Gal
To: Design Team
Subject: Re: Wow

So here's how Al meets Zelda. 'Cause she's, like, living next door? And there's a bunch of Al's dinner plates in her house, kinda "borrowed"? Someone breaks a plate, there's an immediate screen prompt, Al rushes over.

From: Legal Expert
To: Design Team

Subject: Domestic Disputes

Someone threw a plate at Zelda. Zelda owns the home next door, and her son and daughter-in-law are living in it. But Zelda sold the home because she needs to finance her rejuvenation treatments. It's a basic cross-generational equity issue. Happens all the time nowadays, with the boom in life-extension. Granny Zelda comes home from the clinic looking 35. She's mortgaged the family wealth, and now the next generation can't afford to have kids. Daughter-in-law freaked because dear old mom suddenly looks better than she does. It's a soap-opera eruption of passion, resentment, and greed. Makes a child-custody case look like a traffic ticket.

From: Engineer
To: Design Team
Subject: Implications

Great. So listen. Zelda sells her house and moves in with Al. He's a nice guy, rescuing her from her family. She brings all her own stuff into Al's house—60 years' worth of tchotchkes. No problem. Thanks to us. Because Al and Zelda are getting everything out of her packing boxes and tagging it all with MEMS tags. Possessions are mixed up physically—and yet they're totally separate, virtually. With MEMS, unskilled labor can enter the house with handheld trackers, separate and re-pack everything in a few hours, tops. Al and Zelda never lose track of who belongs to what—that's a benefit we're supplying. They can live together in a new kind of way.

From: Graphics Gal
To: Design Team

Subject: A&Z Living Together

Okay, so Zelda's in the house cooking, right? Now Al can get to that yardwork he's been putting off. There's like squirrels and raccoons and out there, and they're getting in the attic? Only now Al's got some cybernetic live-traps, like the MuscleGel MistNet from our Outdoor Products Division. Al catches the raccoon, and he plants a MEMS chip under the animal's skin. Now he always knows where the raccoon is! It's like, Al hears this spooky noise in the attic, he goes up in the attic with his handheld, it's like, "Okay Rocky, I know it's you! And I know exactly where you're hiding. Get the hell out of my insulation."

From: Legal Expert
To: Design Team
Subject: Tagging Raccoons

Interesting. If Al really does track and catalog a raccoon, that makes the raccoon a property improvement. If Al wants to sell the house, he's got a market advantage. After all, Al's property comes with big trees, that's obvious, that's a given—but now it also comes with a legally verifiable raccoon.

From: Engineer
To: Design Team
Subject: Squirrels

They're no longer vermin. The squirrels in the trees, I mean. They're a wholly owned property asset.

From: Team Coordinator
To: Design Team
Subject: This Is Real Progress, People

I'm with this approach! See, we never would have thought of the rac-coon angle if we'd concentrated on the product as a product. But of course Al is moving his control-chips out of the house, into his lawn, and eventually into the whole neighborhood. Raccoons wander around all the time. So do domestic dogs and cats. But that's not a bug in our tracking technology—that's a feature. Al's cat has got a MEMS tag on its collar. Al can tag every cat's collar in the neighborhood and run it as a neighborhood service off his Web page. When you're calling Kitty in for supper, you just email Kitty's collar.

From: Programmer
To: Design Team
Subject: [no subject]

AWESOME! I am so with this! I got 8 cats myself, I want this product! I can smell the future here! And it smells like a winner!!

From: Engineer
To: Design Team
Subject: Current Chip Technology

That subcutaneous ID chip is a proven technology. They've been doing that for lab rats for years now. I could have a patent-free working model out of our Sunnyvale fab plant in 48 hours, tops.

The only problem Al faces is repeater technology, so he can cover the neighborhood with his radio locators. But a repeater net is a system admin-istration issue. That's a classic tie-in, service-provision opportunity. We're talking long-term contracts here, and a big buyer lock-in factor.

From: Marketer
To: Design Team
Subject: Buyer Lock-In Factor

That is hot! Of course! It's about consumer stickiness through market-segmentation upgrades. You've got the bottom-level, introductory, Household-Only tagging model. Then the midlevel Neighborhood model. Then, on to the Gold and Platinum service levels, with 24-hour tech support! AI can saturate the whole suburb. Maybe even the whole city! It's totally open-ended. We supply as many tags and as much monitoring and connectivity as the guy can pay for. The only limit is the size of his wallet!

From: Team Coordinator
To: Social Anthropologist
Subject: ***Private Message***

Susan, look at 'em go! I can't believe the storytelling approach works so well. Last week they were hanging around the lab with long faces, preparing their resumes and emailing headhunters.

From: the social anthropologist
To: Team Coordinator
Subject: Re: ***Private Message***

Fred, people have been telling each other stories since we were hominids around campfires in Africa. It's a very basic human cognition thing, really.

From: Team Coordinator
To: Social Anthropologist
Subject: ***Private Message Again***

We've gotta hit, Susan. I can feel it. I need a drink after all this, don't you? Let's celebrate. On my tab, ok? We'll make a night of it.

From: the social anthropologist
To: Team Coordinator
Subject: Our Relationship

Fred, I'm not going to deny there's chemistry between us. But I really have to question whether that's appropriate business behavior.

From: Team Coordinator
To: Social Anthropologist
Subject: ***Private Message***

We're grown-ups, Susan. We've both been around the block a few times. Come on, you don't have to be this way.

From: the social anthropologist
To: Team Coordinator
Subject: Re: ***Private Message***

Fred, it's not like this upsets me professionally—I mean, not in that oh-so-proper way. I'm a trained anthropologist. They train us to understand how societies work—not how to make people happy. I'm being very objective about this situation. I don't hold it against you. I know that I'm relationship poison, Fred. I've never made a man happy in my whole life.

From: Team Coordinator
To: Social Anthropologist
Subject: **Very Private Message**

Please don't be that way, Susan. That "you and me" business, I mean. I thought we'd progressed past that by now. We could just have a friendly cocktail down at Les Deux Magots. This story isn't about "you and me."

From: the social anthropologist
To: Team Coordinator
Subject: Your Unacceptable Answer

Then whose story is it, Fred? If this isn't our story, then whose story is it?

Albert's mouth was dry. His head was swimming. He really had to knock it off with those cognition enhancers—especially after 8 P.M. The smart drugs had been a major help in college —all those French philosophy texts, my God, Kant 301, that wasn't the kind of text that a guy could breeze through without serious neurochemical assistance—but he'd overdone it. Now he ate the pills just to keep up with the dyslexia syndrome— and the pills made him so, well, verbal. Lots of voices inside the head. Voices in the darkness. Bits and pieces arguing. Weird debates. A head full of yakking chemical drama.

Another ripping snore came out of Hazel. Hazel had the shape of a zaftig 1940s swimsuit model, and the ear-nose-and-throat lining of a sixty-seven-year-old crone. And what the hell was it with those hundred-year-old F. Scott Fitzgerald novels? Those pink ballet slippers. And the insistence on calling herself "Zelda."

Huddleston pulled himself quietly out of the bed. He lurched into the master bathroom, which alertly switched itself on as he entered. His hair was snow-white, his face a road-map of hard wear. The epidermal mask was tearing loose a bit, down at the shaving line at the base of his neck. He was a 25-year-old man who went out on hot dates with his own roommate. He posed as Zelda's fictional "70-year-old escort." When they were out in clubs and restaurants, he always passed as Zelda's sugar-daddy.

That was the way the two of them had finally clicked as a couple, somehow. The way to make the relationship work out. Al had become a stranger in his own life.

Al now knew straight-out, intimately, what it really meant to be old. Al knew how to pass for old. Because his girl-friend was old. He watched forms of media that were demo-graphically targeted for old people, with their deafened ears, cloudy eyes, permanent dyspepsia, and fading grip strength. Al was technologically jet-lagged out of the entire normal human aging process. He could visit "his '70s" the way you might buy a ticket and visit "France."

Getting Hazel, or rather "Zelda," to come across in the bedroom—the term "ambivalence" didn't begin to capture his feelings on that subject. It was all about fingernail-on-glass sexual tension and weird time-traveling flirtation mannerisms. There was something so irreparable about it. It was a massive transgressive rupture in the primal fabric of human relationships.

Not "love." It was a different arrangement. A romance

with no historical precedent, all beta pre-release, an early-adapter thing, all shakeout, with a million bugs and periodic crashes.

It wasn't love, it was "evol." It was "elvo." Albert was in elvo with the curvaceous bright-eyed babe who had once been the kindly senior citizen next door.

At least he wasn't like his dad. Stone dead of overwork on the stairsteps of his mansion, in a monster house with a monster coronary. And with three dead marriages: Mom One, Mom Two, and Mom Three. Mom One had the kid and the child support. Mom Two got the first house and the alimony. Mom Three was still trying to break the will.

How in hell had life become like this, thought Huddleston in a loud interior voice, as he ritually peeled dead pseudoskin from a mirrored face that, even in the dope-etched neural midnight of his posthuman soul, looked harmless and perfectly trustworthy. He couldn't lie to himself—because he was a philosophy major, he formally despised all forms of cheesiness and phoniness. He was here because he enjoyed it. It was working out for him. Because it met his needs. He'd been a confused kid with emotional issues, but he was so together now.

He had to give Zelda all due credit—the woman was a positive genius at home economics. A household maintenance whiz. Zelda was totally down with Al's ambitious tagging project. Everything in its place with a place for everything. Every single shelf and windowsill was spic and span. Al and Zelda would leaf through design catalogs together, in taut little moments of genuine bonding.

Zelda was enthralled with the new decor scheme and clung to her household makeover projects like a drowning woman grabbing life-rings. Al had to admit it: she'd been totally right about the stark necessity for new curtains. And the lamp thing—Zelda had amazing taste in lamps. You couldn't ask for a better garden-party hostess: the canapes, the Japanese lacquer trays, crystal swizzle sticks, stackable designer porch chairs, Chateau Neuf de Pape, stuff Al had never heard of, stuff he wouldn't have learned about for fifty years. Such great, cool stuff.

She was his high-maintenance girl. A fixer-upper. Like a part-time wife, sort of kind of, but requiring extensive repair work. A good-looking gal with a brand-new wardrobe, whose calcium-depleted skeletal system was slowly unhinging, requiring lots of hands-on foot rubs and devoted spinal adjustment. It was a shame about her sterility thing. But let's face it, who needed children? Zelda had children. She couldn't stand 'em.

What Al really wanted—what he'd give absolutely anything for—was somebody, something, somewhere, somehow, who would give him a genuine grip. To become a fully realized, fully authentic human being. He had this private vision, a true philosophy almost: Albert "Owl" Huddleston, as a truly decent person. Honest, helpful, forthright, moral. A modern philosopher. A friend to mankind. It was that Gesamtkunstwerk thing. No loose ends at all. No ragged bleeding bits. The Total Work of Design.

Completely *put together*, Al thought, carefully flushing his face down the toilet. A stranger in his own life, maybe, sure, granted, but so what, so were most people. Even a lame antimaterialist like Henry Thoreau knew that much. A tad dyslexic, didn't read all that much, stutters a little when he forgets his neuroceuticals, listens to books on tape about

Italian design theory, maybe a tad obsessive-compulsive about the $700 broom, and the ultra-high-tech mop with the chemical taggant system that Displays Household Germs in Real Time © ® ™. . . . But so what.

So what. So what is the real story here? Is Al a totally together guy, on top and in charge, cleverly shaping his own destiny through a wise choice of tools, concepts, and approaches? Or is Al a soulless figment of a hyperactive market, pieced together like a shattered mirror from a million little impacts of brute consumerism? Is Al his own man entire, or is Al a piece of flotsam in the churning surf of techno-revolution? Probably both and neither. With the gratifying knowledge that it's All Completely Temporary Anyway®. Technological Innovation Is An Activity, Not An Achievement (SM). Living On The Edge Is Never Comfortable ©.

What if the story wasn't about design after all? What if it wasn't about your physical engagement with the manufactured world, your civilized niche in historical development, your mastery of consumer trends, your studied elevation of your own good taste, and your hands-on struggle with a universe of distributed, pervasive, and ubiquitous smart objects that are choreographed in invisible, dynamic, interactive systems. All based, with fiendish computer-assisted human cleverness, in lightness, dematerialization, brutally rapid product cycles, steady iterative improvement, renewability, and fantastic access and abundance. What if all of that was at best a passing thing. A by-blow. A techie spin-off. A phase. What if the story was all about this, instead: What if you tried your level best to be a real-life, fully true human being, and it just plain couldn't work? It wasn't even possible. Period.

Zelda stirred and opened her glamorous eyes. "Is everything clean?"

"Yeah."

"Is it all put away?"

"Yep."

"Did you have another nightmare?"

"Uh. No. Sure. Kinda. Don't call them 'nightmares,' okay? I just thought I'd . . . you know . . . boot up and check out the neighborhood."

Zelda sat up in bed, tugging at the printed satin sheet. "There are no more solutions," Zelda said. "You know that, don't you? There are no happy endings. Because there are no endings. There are only ways to cope."

Mainstream Fiction

(This is a mainstream story; it's a tad mannered and quirky, but at heart it is simple, contemporary boy-meets-girl fiction. In 1975, though, most every plot twist, character trait, and even the setting in this story would have been science fictional. In 1950, this piece would have been blatantly mind-boggling, so far-out that the simplest details would have taken pages of exposition. So look what the passage of time can do to the nature of genre. That should inspire a sense of wonder, shouldn't it?)

Code

Even in death, Louis's bulk had wedged him firmly into his work chair.

Van felt swift, unthinking rage. How could Louis do this to him? Van had been working on a software patch all week, code that only Louis would appreciate.

But Louis's bearded face had gone slack, and his waxy hide was mottled and bluish. The little office—with its scrawled whiteboards, pinned wallboards, a host of colored Post-its—held the reek of a large dead animal. Van had entered a room with a corpse.

Van leaned across the body to the keyboard and punched up www.google.com.

<<Discover dead body proper legal procedures>>

The search engine spat up results. An exhumation carried out in Argentina by a human rights commission. A treatise on Jewish funerals. Frantic paranoia about the Global Traffic in Human Organs. Dizzy bullshit about extending the human lifespan.

Van needed immediate relevance. He surfed to www.Ask Jeeves.com.

<<I just found a dead body in the office. What should I do?>>

The response was broadband-swift.

"Where can I buy furniture for my office?" AskJeeves said, proffering a shiny blue e-commerce button.

Louis's office door opened and Julie the receptionist stepped in with a clipboard. "Hey, Louis, I need you to . . ." She stopped, and looked at the two of them, Van standing and fitfully typing, Louis fatally slumped. "What's wrong?"

"Louis is dead."

Julie raised her brows behind her rimless glasses. "No! Really?"

"Yeah. Really."

"So what are you doing?"

"I'm 'Asking Jeeves.' "

"Oh. Good idea." Julie stepped closer, shutting the door. Although Van saw Julie the receptionist without fail every working day, he did not know her last name. Julie seemed to have a ready smile for him, for pretty much every male geek infesting the building, really, but Van had merely managed a polite nod, the occasional howdy hey y'all. Since

Julie didn't write code, there was no real reason for her to ever register in Van's awareness.

"Has Vintelix ever had a workplace fatality before?" Van asked her. "You should know that, right?"

"Who, me?" said Julie, clutching the clipboard to her floppy-tied chest. She stared at the looming white cotton shoulder of Louis's XXXL T-shirt. "I've never *seen* a dead guy before! I mean, not all close and intimate."

"Well, we've got to take steps to deal with this."

"Oh sure," she said gamely, "I mean yeah, okay, whatever."

However, no immediate useful tactic came to Van's throbbing mind. He couldn't get over the fact that it was *Louis* that was dead. "Louis was such a good guy," Van offered painfully. "He got me this job."

"Oh sure, Louis hired me too! Louis and I used to play *Quest for Britannia* online together. He was 'Lord Melchior' and I was 'Dejah Thoris.' Hey, Van, shouldn't we call the cops?"

Van ran a hand through his hair. "Why bother? I'd bet the cops will show up here no matter *what* we do."

That was an evil thought. The two of them exchanged significant glances.

Soon the two of them were on their knees together, rummaging through Louis's desk.

Cigar-burned and boot-battered, Louis's desk was a relic from some long-dead Texan oil company with Texas-size notions of desktop real estate. The desk suited the spread of a longhaired three-hundred-pound hacker. Louis got away with this eccentricity because he was Vintelix Employee number three. Besides, it was an open secret that Louis kept all his drugs inside his private desk.

In the back of the left third drawer, Van and Julie discovered a brown cardboard box, taped over with ancient, peeling, underground cartoons. To judge by the rattling mess of pills, the dope habits of Louis's vanished youth had long since faded to a galaxy of painkillers, blood-pressure nostrums, and heart medicine. Louis had been eating these pills with the debonaire carelessness that was his signature: a relaxed contempt for the stuffy medical authorities, or utter, pigheaded, suicidal stupidity, you could pretty well take your pick.

Van lifted the battered cardboard box, a coffin of hopes. He put it on the desktop. It radiated FATAL ERROR in its fat-old-hippie defiance.

Louis's cardboard box also contained a folded sheet of paper. The sheet bore hundreds of tiny repeated motifs, perforated like postage stamps: little colorful dancing bears. A dozen of them had been neatly clipped from the blotter paper's lower edge, with something like toenail scissors.

Van nodded, his heart sinking. "That must be Louis's acid."

"Louis did *acid*?"

"Of course he did acid! He was a Deadhead!" Van turned on the corpse in exasperation, and realized he would never get a human response from Louis again. This time, the octopus of cold reality gripped him with crushing force. Because Louis was the *boss*. Louis was the *stud duck*. Louis was the guy in the company who *got it about code* and protected the coders from the suits. They hadn't even removed the poor guy's body yet, and already he was leaving a great big Louis-sized hole.

Julie, nothing daunted, whipped through Louis's wooden drawers and cubbyholes with a file clerk's determination, her bony elbows cranking like bike pedals. When she spoke again, she used her receptionist voice, as bright, phony, and cheery as injection-molded plastic. "This is the best we can do. Let's go now, okay? I'm getting creeped out."

"I'm just trying to protect the company," Van told her. "It would look bad for the company if somebody else found a lot of acid."

"Well, we'd better tell Darren that he's died," Julie said. "Because Darren gets mad in a hurry whenever he's, like, left out of the loop."

It made good sense to inform the CEO. Somebody had to do it, and with Louis dead, there wasn't any higher authority. "Okay," Van nodded. "I'll go tell Warren. You take care of the dope."

"Let *me* go tell Darren. *You* get rid of the dope."

Julie wasn't handling this logically. Frustrated in a noble ambition, Van felt a crazy urge to slug her, even though violence never solved anything around the office except in marathon Quake sessions. Keep a cool head, he thought. Just reason it out, there's a solution here. "Are we going to stand here and argue about dope?"

Julie lifted both her hands, stepping back, face pale. "Hey, I never even touched that dope! You're the guy holding the dope."

"Okay, I've got it." Van produced his Swiss Army knife, opened the scissors, and neatly bisected the sheet. "Now we'll *both* get rid of the dope. And we'll both tell Darren. How about that: you and me. Are you cool with that?"

Julie tucked her share of colored paper in the back of her clipboard. "I'm cool with it if you're cool with it."

The two of them jointly briefed the CEO. Darren quickly

alerted the Vintelix security guy, an ex-cop who usually hung out in a glass guard shack, pretending to study the video monitors. Thrilled to earn his salary for once, the security guy rumbled into action and appropriate steps took place.

Four medics in EMS jumpsuits took Louis away forever on a big sturdy medical roller-cart. They were quiet and tactful about it, as if they did this sort of thing every day, as Van rather imagined that they must.

A mournful hush fell over the Vintelix offices: long before the body left the premises, every last soul in the building knew the sad news through email.

People didn't confront sudden death every day, but there was scarcely an Austinite alive who hadn't held drugs and stayed cool at some point. Van and Julie had broken the awful news without a hitch. Carrying huge amounts of drugs on their persons had somehow chilled them out. Seeing their stony faces and unnatural calm, Darren, the Vintelix CEO, compassionately insisted that Van and Julie take the rest of the day off. Maybe, Darren urged, they might contemplate taking off a whole weekend.

Cold waves of disorientation had Van queasy. But he couldn't call the trauma a surprise. It had been obvious to him from day one that Louis was a waddling time-bomb. Van had been a fresh graduate in Computer Science when Louis had hired him. One look at his new boss in the private sector had sent Van scampering to join a gym. Guys of Louis's generation had never gotten it about the work hazards of using computers. They still thought that computers were cyber-magic, something like Day-Glo mushrooms, or maybe unicorns.

Now, three years later, Louis was freshly dead of a major

coronary, while Van could bench-press 180 pounds. Congratulating himself on his mature foresight didn't make Van feel any better about his own immediate future, though. Without Louis around to ride herd and grind code, Vintelix could easily slide straight off the edge into dot-bomb hell, and all Van's shares would be toilet paper.

Chased from the glass-and-limestone premises where he commonly spent eighty hours a week, Van walked home alone, brooding and shaken.

Van occupied an efficiency four blocks away from the Vintelix compound. The graceless little apartment suited his purposes, since it had a broadband DSL connection and was close to the gym. Van had no pets, no chairs, and no curtains. Lacking forks and knives, he commonly ate with plastic chopsticks from the Korean grocery next door. The utter bareness of his dwelling place had never bothered Van, for frills were of no relevance to him, and he commonly ate and slept at work anyway. Van owned only three primary possessions: a large couch, a large computer, and a large cable TV. He slept on a futon under his computer—a rather less cozy futon than the one he slept on at work.

Van came in, turned on the lights, killed a large roach, and logged on. He was too upset to do any coding work for Vintelix, so he thought he might amuse himself with his hobby, doing unpaid coding for a Linux project. First, of course, email. Van waded through the spam and found email from Julie. He discovered with vague interest that her full name was Julie Woertz. Julie's email offered an IRC channel. He found her waiting to chat.

"People around the office say you're cool," Julie typed cautiously. "They say you always bring beer to office parties."

"And???," Van parried. He brought the beer to the company's bashes because it was easier than making small talk. Van was Vintelix employee number twenty-six. If he cashed out some stock, he could bring a truckload of beer.

"And, so, you don't seem like a guy who needs to have two hundred hits of acid."

"143," Van corrected automatically.

"So I wanted to ask you. May I have it, please?"

Van logged into the Vintelix intranet, found the page for Julie Woertz, got her home phone number, and called her up voice. This took less than thirty seconds.

"First tell me why you want it."

"Do you still have it?"

"Yeah. I do."

"Well, why didn't you just trash it in the Dumpster like the rest of those pills and stuff?"

"I dunno," Van admitted. "A hundred and forty-three doses of acid is a whole lot. It's kind of impressive. I haven't seen that many drugs since I was in junior high school. "

"But you do really think it's LSD? This paper's all yellow and old. Some website says that LSD loses its potency."

"Could be."

"But if it's still okay, I got some people on eBay who sound really, really interested."

"Julie, why do you want to sell acid on eBay? Louis never sold anybody acid. It seems kind of, I dunno. Disrespectful."

"Hey, what's wrong with eBay?" Julie said defensively. "People love me on eBay! I got a great eBay reputation. But, you know, if they got some acid from me and it was just *no good,* then that would be *really humiliating.*"

"Well, what's the use of acid? I took ecstasy a couple of

times in high school. Maybe you want to dance, but you can't do anything worthwhile."

"Okay, fine, but it's sure dorky to just trash this paper when my Net-friends really want some. That just seems so . . . lame." She paused. "Hey wait a sec. My webcam's on. Why don't you use my webcam?"

Van courteously found his own webcam, blew gritty dust off the unit, untangled its cables, and set it up. Then he followed her instructions and clicked on to Julie's cam site. Soon they were gazing at blinky screen images of one another as they talked together on the phone.

Julie was wearing a sexy black wig. Small, polite, and efficient, Julie had always looked to Van like a grocery clerk. In her webcam getup, she looked like a grocery clerk in a sexy black wig.

"So, you have a lot of fans for this home webcam action?" Van speculated, studying her stained wallpaper and peeling anime posters.

"I usually forget that it's on," Julie admitted. "I just get used to it, since it's so much like being a receptionist." She smoothed her wig. "Mostly, I do a kind of role-playing game. I kind of write little fantasy skits and performances. Like a Cindy Sherman art thing. You know Cindy Sherman?"

"She's a big weblogger, right?"

"Well, no, not really." Julie plucked her sheet of acid paper from her purse. "So listen, Van: I had an idea. If I ate some of these to see if they still work, would you help me out? Like a quality test. I'm thinking that I could stay on the cam here, and you could just kind of watch over me."

"How many of those are you planning to eat?" he hedged.

"What do they call these little paper things, 'tabs'? They look really small. I was thinking maybe just four or five. Is that a big deal for you? You don't even have to get out of your chair, okay? You can just kind of click in on me and make sure that I'm, you know. Whatever."

Van sensed himself sliding gently into deep water. "Why are you picking on me for this?"

"Because nobody else knows that we have a ton of acid! You don't want me to *tell* anybody else, do you?"

Van gave himself a bump on the head with the flat of his hand. "Oh right! Sure. Sorry."

"So is that cool with you? Because if it's not cool with you, you can just say so. I'll understand."

"How about you eat just one."

"Okay! Don't worry! It'll be pretty boring. I mean, I'm not going to dress up and perform here, or do anything exciting." She sighed. "Even when I do that, nobody ever logs on."

"Well, I'm game." Van glanced at his sports watch. "I've gotta go do a few sets at the gym around 10 P.M., but that's like three hours from now. That should be plenty of time. I'll just put you on speakerphone now, and get in a little coding on my X-Windows while you're doing, you know, whatever."

Office doings gave them a natural topic of conversation, but Van lacked much interest in Julie's gossip about who was up, down, and in and out among the company's suits. Like the rest of the Vintelix coders, Van had always prided himself on the fact that he was technically indispensable.

Within an hour, Julie grew bright and elated and began to complain and unload. She told tales against her hippie roommate. She expressed deep dissatisfaction with her used car. She harkened back to her miserable childhood in a small West Texas town among some demented clan of Southern Baptists. Julie's well-meaning parents had committed the grave mistake of buying her a computer because she was making straight A's. A single day's exposure to the Internet had revealed to Julie that her parents knew absolutely nothing about anything that mattered. Some slow but terrific family rupture had occurred. Julie had ended up in Austin, the traditional destination for any Texan who was throughly shaken loose and not yet nailed down.

Two hours later, Julie was ranting like she'd gulped two Starbucks super-grandes. She kept losing track of the webcam, bolting and scampering out of camera range into the depths of her apartment, where she raided her closet for a tatty eBay finery of poodle skirts and feather boas.

To "keep him occupied," as she put it, she blasted MP3 files. Like many Austinites, Julie fancied herself quite the music aficionado. Julie and her pirate Net-club of World Music enthusiasts were into Congolese pygmy nose flutes and Bulgarian chorale classics. Van didn't care much for music, especially the kind requiring anthropological liner notes. Julie's "music collection" was a completely random jumble of global files. But as long as it sounded different from Texas radio, that seemed to be fine with her.

At 10 PM, Van went down to the gym for his customary workout, for Julie was nowhere in sight, and the death of Louis was weighing painfully on Van's mind. The gym had become a major emotional refuge for Van, although Van was not at all a fan of lifting weights, or even a fan of gyms. Van pumped a lot of iron because this was the only activity that made him stop thinking about code. Jogging and bicycling were far too dangerous for Van: in his abstracted haze, he could very easily fly off the limestone cliffs of Austin's hike and bike trails. But fifteen curls with a thirty-five-pound barbell were always enough to turn his arms to smoldering rubber, and to thoroughly empty his mind.

Van did not "keep in shape." The gym guys who were really shapely tended to be gay. Van wasn't particularly strong, either. Genuine weightlifters, those squinty, bearded guys who were seriously strong, were about eight feet around in the belly. Van wouldn't have minded looking sexy and picking up some women, but he simply had no time. Van was so busy coding that he didn't have time to pick up food, much less women. He didn't even have time to pick up his paychecks.

So the many full-length mirrors at Big Sam's showed him a silent geek, with thick glasses, a funny-looking nose, and cheap, infrequent haircuts. Van was pretty much content to look like what he was: a man that nobody ever took any trouble over.

After an hour and a shower, Van returned home with his gym bag. He found Julie wandering up and down the streetlit pavement, clutching an unopened Diet Coke. Julie had a fixed grin and her dilated eyes were as black and shiny as the buttons on a Sony boombox.

"I lost you, I lost you," she told him earnestly. "I got worried."

"What are you doing here?" he said.

"I got your address from the company website and drove over." She gestured glassily at her rusty Toyota. "But there's something wrong with my steering wheel now. It feels kind of . . . melty."

Van took the warm Coke from her hand, placed it in his

gym bag, and examined her with care. She was still in her work clothes, but she had put on flip-flops over her stocking feet and had yanked on a pullover, backward. Van felt that he was truly seeing Julie Woertz for the very first time. She was small, frail, vulnerable, and completely stoned.

"My apartment's kind of a mess," he told her. "But you better come up for a while."

"Is that cool with you?"

"Oh sure, I'm cool, we'll just hang out," he told her vaguely. "There's usually something good on the Nature channel this time of night."

He escorted Julie up the stairs and into his efficiency. "Wow," she said, her dinner-plate eyes examining the bare, constricting walls. "This is so . . . snug."

Van turned on the lights and pursued the vermin into hiding. He seated Julie carefully on the couch, which was nice, as it was the second most expensive choice at a local chain. He placed the remote control in her hands. He then fetched his laptop and sat down companionably.

"You shouldn't websurf when you have a guest," Julie told him, struggling to un-fix her stony grin. "That's against the rules."

"What rules?"

"That book, *The Rules*, by Sherrie Schneider?"

Van clicked up Amazon.com.

<<*The Rules: Time-Tested Secrets for Capturing the Heart of Mr. Right* by Ellen Fein, Sherrie Schneider
<<Customers who bought this book also bought:
<<*The Real Rules: How to Find the Right Man for the Real You* by Barbara De Angelis

<<*Secrets About Men Every Woman Should Know* by Barbara De Angelis
<<*The Rules II: More Rules to Live and Love By* by Ellen Fein, Sherrie Schneider
<<*The Code: Time-Tested Secrets for Getting What You Want from Women Without Marrying Them!* by Nate Penn, Lawrence Larose>>

Van clicked twice and immediately purchased both *The Rules* and *The Code* for overnight delivery.

"Hey Julie, what was that other one you were talking about? Cindy Sherman?"

But Julie had realized that the object in her grip was a remote control, and she was eagerly channel surfing.

"Ohmigod!" she squealed. "It's *The Barretts of Wimpole Street!* This is like my third-favorite movie! Ohmigod it's Norma Shearer! Look at her hair. I had a wig just like that once!"

Van did a movie search.

<<*The Barretts of Wimpole Street* (1934)

Starring: Fredric March, Norma Shearer
Director: Sidney Franklin
Synopsis: Poet Robert Browning successfully woos invalid writer Elizabeth Barrett in this glossy historical romance. Fans of old-fashioned Hollywood romance may find that handsome production values compensate for occasionally draggy story.

Julia was transfixed. Long, enraptured moments passed, broken only by her intakes of breath and the gentle clicking of Van's ThinkPad. "My God," Julie breathed at last. "I'm getting into this *so much!*"

With occasional glances upward, Van watched the movie enough to catch its drift. It was a period chick flick, about a sick girl stuck at home, whose situation turns around when some good-looking con artist shows up and hands her a line of artsy bullshit.

"How about some popcorn, Julie?"

"I don't think I'm hungry." She began to tremble.

Van went to his futon, fetched his musty blanket, and carefully wrapped her up.

"I'm afraid of dying, just like she was," she muttered. "I just don't want to die all alone."

"You're not dying. You're very alive and safe here."

"I saw a dead man today. If you hadn't been there, trying to fix it, I would have just completely freaked out. I just would have started screaming. I don't know how I would have ever stopped."

"Nice movie, huh? Handsome production values. How about a nice cup of Korean green tea?"

She hugged the blanket closer. "I'm having a really long day," she whispered, and began to sniffle.

He hadn't expected to see Julie crying. The crying thing turned him completely inside out. It hit him like a match on oil-soaked rags.

The darkest level of his psyche burst into sullen blue flames. Those tears meant she was helpless. Just like the handsome actor on the screen, he could hand this trapped, drug-addled girl any line he pleased, and she would have no choice but to nod and blink and hope for the best, and then he could do absolutely anything he wanted to her.

The crazy feeling subsided, as quick, sudden, and evil as a smash of glass and a midnight car alarm, but then there it was: she had come into focus for him. There was a woman in his life.

He sat down, picked up her hand, and patted it.

When they returned to work next morning, late, together, in her car, and with Julie still in yesterday's clothes, there could only be one logical conclusion. It was true that they had been sleeping together, since Van had bagged a couple of hours upright on the couch. Julie hadn't managed any sleeping. She claimed that she just felt "clear" and "kind of peaceful." Once in her workstation, she slipped right back into the routine. Although when word got out in email, absolutely everybody knew.

Warren called Van in for a conference. Warren was tall and handsome and probably gay, and got a lot of play in the Austin tech press. He was on the road all the time, selling the Vintelix vision to the distant venture-gods of Redmond and Silicon Valley. Warren was in a pinch because of Louis's sudden demise. The loss of a key programmer made it harder to meet shareholder expectations, keep up market momentum, and manage that special Vintelix buzz. So despite the fact that he was only twenty-six, Van found himself with most of Louis's code work, and a raise in salary.

Then came the obligatory "sandwich treatment," with hints that he dress more appropriately for his exalted managerial station. Inappropriate relationships with female Vintelix personnel were of particular concern to Darren. Van departed with a final lacquer of praise: a boost in stock options and a new and even more meaningless title.

Van spent the night going over Louis's code. The spaghetti ware was even worse than he'd imagined. Louis had always treated the Vintelix code like his own baby: in a way, the code *was* Louis's own baby. It was the only baby Louis had ever had.

By 1 AM Van had arrived at a game plan: outsource everything in sight. Louis had always hired people on instinct, but Louis was the kind of guy who would hire people he played Dungeons and Dragons with. Coders who really got it were worth twelve of anybody else. So even if they were upset by a reorg, all the hardcore guys would come around when they saw some real progress made. In sum, there was probably nothing wrong with Vintelix that a total and silent hacker revolution couldn't somehow cure behind the scenes.

Van was hauled from his bed at 8 AM to accept an express delivery of books. *The Rules* and *The Code* had arrived. While he moved out of his cubicle into an office suitable to a Senior Technology Coordinator, Van examined *The Code.* Unfortunately, this primer on exploiting women was merely a series of lame gags with no actual data or algorithms on exploiting women.

The Rules, by contrast, was a work of deadly seriousness. It was about life-and-death emotional survival tactics for the planet's majority gender. *The Rules* was bitter, life-and-death, stripped of all sentimentality. It was about surviving, and protecting children, among a race of large, brutal, half-blind creatures who would exploit you without conscience and could easily beat you to a pulp. Most everything in *The Rules* made plenty of sense to Van. The thing was more than a self-help book: basically, it was an operating system. The work fired his imagination and reset his agenda.

Van went home from work early—at a mere 7 P.M.—and picked up the phone. Then he put the phone back down and logged on to Julie's webcam instead. Much as he had expected, Julie had thoughtlessly left the camera plugged in. She was carefully painting her toenails, reading a woman's magazine, and almost literally hovering over her phone.

Van captured and froze a webcam frame and blew it up for closer study. Julie's magazine was *Cosmopolitan.* The magazine featured a shapely young blonde in a blue reptile bikini top. The cover text, though blurry on the screen, was still legible.

> <<Make Him All Yours: Play *Cosmo*'s Fantasy Game with Him
> Tonight and Win His Undying Love. Man-Melting Massage. 97
> Sexy Date Looks. The Confessions Issue!>>

Van dialed Julie's number. He saw it ring. She scrambled for it in a fury, upsetting her nail polish, her face alight with desperate hope.

"Hello, this is Van."

"Hello, Van," she said with polite indifference. "What's up?"

The previously unseen hippie roommate rushed into Julie's room. Julie emitted a silent scream of triumph, waving her fingers frantically. The roommate, enraptured, leapt up and down in sympathetic glee.

Van examined his stack of notes and cleared his throat. "Julie, listen. I need to ask a favor of you. I'm sure that you value your time and have a very crowded and fulfilling social life. However, I'd be truly grateful if you would join me tonight . . . *to shop for clothes.*"

"What did you just say?"

Had he overdone it? She seemed stunned.

"Julie, I need a new wardrobe. I just got a promotion. I feel uneasy about my new role, and I depend on your judgment and emotional support. I'm sure your unique insights will help me fit in among the top echelon of the company."

"You're not mad at me for freaking out on acid in your living room? Oh my God, I wish I'd never done that to you. I felt so embarrassed, I just could have died."

Van thumbed rapidly through his briefing cards. Here it was: the Self-Esteem Crisis. "Okay, maybe that was a little indiscreet of you. But frankly, I found it provocative and exciting. It was a bold move from a woman who knows what she wants from life." Van leaned back. "So, Patagonia closes at nine, right? Can you come and pick me up in your car? And bring us something to eat."

"Okay, sure, right! My God, Van, we'd better hurry."

"You're saving my life here, Julie. You're a treasure." As he hung up, a Net search hit paydirt in the browser window. It was some English-major site, dating back to the early 1990s, when the Web had still been full of academics. Public domain stuff, old poetry.

This Browning woman didn't seem to have much going on: a lot of thees and thous. Van spooled down the screen until something in the spinning text caught his eye.

> << A shadow across me. Straightway I was 'ware,
> So weeping, how a mystic Shape did move
> Behind me, and drew me backward by the hair:
> And a voice said in mastery, while I strove,—
> 'Guess now who holds thee?'—'Death,' I said. But, there,
> The silver answer rang,—'Not Death, but Love.' >>

He hit it with a bookmark. Plenty of time to decode that one later.

★ VII ★

Cyberpunk to Ribofunk

(When slashing one's way through the jungles of genre, it's good to have dependable help. No one knows better than a "cyberpunk" that the terms "cyber" and "punk" are both period coinages, now every bit as redolent of bygone times as "electro-," "atomic," "streamlined," or "jet-propelled." If being "cyber" becomes a job for your middle-aged uncle, what will the next techno-frontier look like? Something biological, that's a good guess . . . biomimetic . . . genetic . . . a world of "ribofunk," as my colleague Paul Di Filippo presciently described it. Maybe we could just hop a flight into genre futurity and raid the world of ribofunk . . . Come on, how hard could that be? Girls, gold, and glory! Pack a bag, Paul, let's go!)

The Scab's Progress
(with Paul Di Filippo)

The federal bio-containment center was a diatom the size of the Disney Matterhorn. It perched on fractal struts in a particularly charmless district of Nevada, where the waterless white sands swarmed with toxic vermin.

The entomopter scissored its dragonfly wings, conveying Ribo Zombie above the desert wastes. This was always the best part of the program: the part where Ribo Zombie lovingly checked out all his cool new gear before launching into action. As a top-ranking scab from the otaku-pirate underground, Ribo Zombie owned reactive gloves with slashproof ligaments and sandwiched Kevlar-polysaccharide. He owned a mother-of-pearl crash helmet, hung with daring insouciance on the scaled wall of the 'mopter's cockpit. And those Nevada desert boots—like something built by Tolkien orcs with day jobs at Nike.

Accompanying the infamous RZ was his legendary and much-merchandised familiar, Skratchy Kat. Every scab owned a familiar: they were the totem animals of the gene-pirate scene. The custom dated back to the birth of the scab subculture, when tree-spiking Earth Firsters and obsessive dog breeders had jointly discovered the benefits of outlaw genetic engineering.

With a flash of emerald eyes the supercat rose from the armored lap of the daring scab. Skratchy Kat had some much cooler name in the Japanese collectors' market. He'd been designed in Tokyo, and was a deft Pocket-Monster commingling of eight spliced species of felines and viverines, with the look, the collector cachet, and (judging by his stuffed-toy version) plenty of the smell of a civet cat. Ribo Zombie, despite frequent on-screen cameos by busty-babe groupies, had never enjoyed any steady feminine relationship. What true love there was in his life flowed between man and cat.

Clickable product-placement hot-tags were displayed on the 'mopter screens as Ribo Zombie's aircraft winged in for the kill. The ads sold magnums of cheap, post-Greenhouse Reykjavik Champagne. Ringside tix to a Celebrity Death-match (splatter-shields extra). Entomopter rentals in Vegas, with a rapid, low-cost divorce optional.

Then, wham! Inertia hit the settling aircraft, gypsum-sand flew like pulverized wallboard, and the entomopter's chitinous canopy accordioned open. Ribo Zombie vaulted to the glistening sands, clutching his cat to his armored bosom. He set the beast free with a brief, comradely exchange of meows, then sealed his facemask, pulled a monster pistol, and plucked a retro-chic pineapple grenade from his bandolier.

A pair of crystalline robot snakes fell to concussive explosions. Alluring vibrators disoriented the numerous toxic scorpions in the vicinity. Three snarling jackalopes fell to a well-aimed hail of dumdums. Meanwhile the dauntless cat, whose hide beneath fluffy fur was as tough as industrial Teflon, had found a way through the first hedge-barrier of barrel cacti.

The pair entered a maze of cholla. The famously vicious Southwestern cholla cactus, whose sausage-link segments bore thorns the size of fishhooks, had been rumored from time immemorial to leap free and stab travelers from sheer spite. A soupçon of Venus flytrap genes had turned this Pecos Pete tall-tale vaporware into grisly functionality. Ribo Zombie had to opt for brute force: the steely wand of a back-mounted flamethrower leapt into his wiry combat-gloves. Ignited in a pupil-searing blast, the flaming mutant cholla whipped and flopped like epileptic spaghetti. Then RZ and the faithful Skratchy were clambering up the limestone leg of the Federal cache.

Anyone who had gotten this far could be justly exposed to the worst and most glamorous gizmos ever cooked up by the Softwar Department's Counter-Bioterrorism Corps.

The ducts of the diatom structure yawned open and deployed a lethal arsenal of spore-grenade launchers, strangling vegetable bolas, and whole glittering clouds of hotwired fleas and mosquitos. Any scab worth his yeast knew that those insect vectors were stuffed to bursting with swift and ghastly illnesses, pneumonic plague and necrotizing fasciitis among the friendlier ones.

"This must be the part where the cat saves him," said Tupper McClanahan, all cozy in her throw rug on her end of the couch.

Startled out of his absorption, yet patiently indulgent, Fearon McClanahan froze the screen with a tapped command to the petcocks on the feedlines. "What was that, darling? I thought you were reading."

"I was." Smiling, Tupper held up a vintage Swamp Thing comic that had cost fully ten percent of one month's trust-fund check. "But I always enjoy the parts of this show that feature the cat. Remember when we clicked on those high-protein kitty treats, during last week's cat sequence? Weeble loved those things."

Fearon looked down from the ergonomic couch to the spotless bulk of his snoring pig, Weeble. Weeble had outgrown the size and weight described in his documentation, but he made a fine hassock.

"Weeble loves anything we feed him. His omnivorous nature is part of his factory specs, remember? I told you we'd save a ton on garbage bills."

"Sweetie, I never complain about Weeble. Weeble is your familiar, so Weeble is fine. I've only observed that it might be a good idea if we got a bigger place."

Fearon disliked being interrupted while viewing his favorite outlaw stealth download. He positively squirmed whenever Tupper sneakily angled around the subject of a new place with more room. More room meant a nursery. And a nursery meant a child. Fearon swerved to a change of topic.

"How can you expect Skratchy Kat to get Ribo Zombie out of this fix? Do you have any idea what those flying bolas do to human flesh?"

"The cat gets him out of trouble every time. Kids love that cat."

"Look, honey: kids are not the target demographic. This show isn't studio-greenlighted or even indie-syndicated, okay? You know as well as I do that this is outlaw media. Totally underground guerrilla infotainment, virally distributed. There are laws on the books—unenforced, sure, but still extant—that make it illegal for us even to watch this thing. After all, Ribo Zombie is a biological terrorist who's robbing a Federal stash!"

"If it's not a kid's show, why is that cute little cartoon in the corner of the screen?"

"That's his grafitti icon! The sign of his streetwise authenticity."

Tupper gazed at him with limpid spousal pity. "Then who edits all his raw footage and adds the special effects?"

"Oh, well, that's just the Vegas Mafia. The Mafia keeps up with modern times: no more Rat Pack crooners and gangsta rappers! Nowadays they cut licensing deals with freeware culture heroes like Ribo Zombie, lone wolf recombinants bent on bringing hot goo to the masses."

Tupper waved her comic as a visual aid. "I still bet the cat's gonna save him. Because none of that makes any difference to the archetypical narrative dynamics."

Fearon sighed. He opened a new window on his gelatinous screen and accessed certain data. "Okay, look. You know what runs security on Federal Biosequestration Sites like that one? Military-grade, laminated mouse brains. You know how smart that stuff is? A couple of cubic inches of murine brain has more processing power than every computer ever deployed in the twentieth century. Plus, mouse brain is unhackable. Computer viruses, no problem. Electromagnetic pulse doesn't affect it. No power source to disrupt, since neurons run on blood sugar. That stuff is indestructible."

Tupper shrugged. "Just turn your show back on."

Skratchy was poised at a vulnerable crack in the diatom's roof. The cat began copiously to pee.

When the trickling urine reached the olfactory sensors wired to the mouse brains, the controlling network went berserk. Ancient murine antipredator instincts swamped the cybernetic instructions, triggering terrified flight responses. Mis-aimed spore bomblets thudded harmlessly to the soil, whizzing bolas wreaked havoc through the innocent vegetation below, and vent ports spewed contaminated steam and liquid nitrogen.

Cursing the zany but dangerous fusillade, Ribo Zombie set to work with a back-mounted hydraulic can opener.

Glum and silent, Fearon gripped his jaw. His hooded eyes glazed over as Ribo Zombie crept through a surreal diorama of waist-high wells, HVAC systems, and plumbing. Every flick of Ribo Zombie's hand torch revealed a glimpse of some new and unspeakable mutant wonder, half concealed in ambient support fluids: yellow gruel, jade-colored hair gel, blue oatmeal, ruby maple syrup . . .

"Oh, honey," said Tupper at last, "don't take it so hard."

"You were right," Fearon grumbled. His voice rose. "Is that what you want me to say? You were right! You're always right!"

"It's just my skill with semiotic touchstones, which I've derived from years of reading graphic novels. But look, dear, here's the part you always love, when he finally lays his hands on the wetware. Honey, look at him stealing that weird cantaloupe with the big throbbing arteries on it. Now he'll go back to his clottage and clump, just like he does every episode, and sooner or later something really uptaking and neoteric will show up on your favorite auction site."

"Like I couldn't brew up stuff twice as potent myself."

"Of course you could, dear. Especially now, since we can afford the best equipment. With my inheritance kicking in, we can devote your dad's legacy to your hobby. All that stock your dad left can go straight to your hardware fetish, while my money allows us to ditch this creepy old condo and buy a new modern house. Duckback roof, slowglass windows, olivine patio. . . ." Tupper sighed deeply and dramatically. "Real quality, Fearon."

Predictably, Malvern Brakhage showed up at their doorstep in the company of disaster.

"Rogue mitosis, Fearon, my man. They've shut down Mixogen and called out the HazMat Squad."

"You're kidding? Mixogen? I thought they followed code."

"Hell no! The outbreak's all over downtown. Just thought I'd drop by for a newsy look at your high-bandwidth feed."

Fearon gazed with no small disdain on his bullet-headed fellow scab. Malvern had the thin fixed grin of a live medical student in a room full of cadavers. He wore his customary black leather lab coat and baggy cargo pants, their buttoned pockets bulging with Ziploc baggies of semi-legal jello.

"It's Malvern!" he yelled at the kitchen, where Tupper was leafing through catalogs.

"How about some nutriceuticals?" said Malvern. "Our mental edges require immediate sharpening." Malvern pulled his slumbering weasel, Spike, from a lab coat pocket and set it on his shoulder. The weasel—biotechnically speaking, Spike was mostly an ermine—immediately became the nicest-looking thing about the man. Spike's lustrous fur gave Malvern the dashing air of a Renaissance prince, if you recalled that Renaissance princes were mostly unprincipled bush-league tyrants who would poison anyone within reach.

Malvern ambled hungrily into the kitchen.

"How have you been, Malvern?" said Tupper brightly.

"I'm great, babe." Malvern pulled a clamp-topped German beer bottle from his jacket. "You up for a nice warm brewski?"

"Don't drink that," Fearon warned his wife.

"Brewed it personally," said Malvern, hurt. "I'll just leave it here in case you change your mind." Malvern plonked the heavy bottle onto the scarred Formica.

Raised a rich, self-assured, decorous girl, Tupper possessed the good breeding and manners to tolerate Malvern's flagrant transgressive behavior. Fearon remembered when he, too, had received adoring looks from Tupper—as a bright idealist who understood the true, liberating potential of biotech, an underground scholar who bowed to none in his arcane mastery of plasmid vectors. Unlike Malvern, whose scab popularity was mostly due to his lack of squeamishness.

Malvern was louche and farouche, so, as was his wont, he began looting Tupper's kitchen fridge. "Liberty's gutters are crawling!" Malvern declaimed, finger-snapping a bit to suit his with-it scab-rap. "It's a bug-crash of awesome proportions, and I urge forthwith we reap some peptides from the meltdown."

"Time spent in reconnaissance is never wasted," countered Fearon. He herded the unmannerly scab back to the parlor.

With deft stabs of his carpalled fingertips, Fearon used the parlor wallscreen to access Fusing Nuclei—the all-biomed news site favored by the happening hipsters of scabdom.

Tupper, pillar of support that she was, soon slid in with a bounty of hotwired snackfood. Instinctively, both men shared with their familiars, Fearon dropping creamy tidbits to his pig while Malvern reached salty gobbets up and back to his neck-hugging weasel.

Shoulder to shoulder on the parlor couch, Malvern and Fearon fixed their jittering attention on the unfolding urban catastrophe.

The living pixels in the electrojelly cohered into the familiar image of Wet Willie, FN's star business reporter. Wet Willie, dashingly clad in his customary splatterproof trenchcoat, had framed himself in the shot of a residential Miami skyscraper. The pastel Neo-Deco walls were sheathed in pearly slime. Wriggling like a nautch dancer, the thick, undulating goo gleamed in Florida's Greenhouse sunlight. Local bystanders congregated in their flowered shirts, sun hats, and sandals, gawking from outside the crowd-control pylons. The tainted skyscraper was under careful attack by truck-mounted glorp cannons, their nozzles channeling high-pressure fingers against the slimy pink walls.

"That's a major outbreak all right," said Fearon. "Since when was Liberty City clearstanced for wet production?"

"As if," chuckled Malvern.

Wet Willie was killing network lagtime with a patch of infodump. "Liberty City was once an impoverished slum. That was before Miami urbstanced into the liveliest nexus of the modern Immunosance, fueled by low-rent but ingenious Caribbean bioneers. When super-immune systems became the hottest somatic upgrade since osteojolt, Liberty City upgraded into today's thriving district of artlofts and hotshops.

"But today that immuconomic quality of life is threatened! The ninth floor of this building houses a startup named Mixogen. The cause of this rampaging outbreak remains speculative, except that the fearsome name of Ribo Zombie is already whispered by knowing insiders."

"I might have known," grunted Malvern.

Fearon clicked the RZ hotlink. Ribo Zombie's ninja-masked publicity photo appeared on the network's vanity page. "Ribo Zombie, the Legendary King of scabs—whose thrilling sub rosa exploits are brought to you each week by Fusing Nuclei, in strict accordance with the revised Freedom of Information Act and without legal or ethical endorsement! Click here to join the growing horde of cutting-edge bioneers who enjoy weekly shipments of his liberated specimens direct to their small office/home office wetware labs . . ."

Fearon valved off the nutrient flowline to the screen and stood abruptly up, spooking the sensitive Weeble. "That showboating scumbag! You'd think he'd invented scabbing! I hate him! Let's scramble, Mal."

"Yo!" concurred Malvern. "Let's bail forthwith, and bag something hot from the slop."

Fearon assembled his scab gear from closets and shelves throughout the small apartment, Weeble loyally dogging his heels. The process took some time, since a scab's top-end hardware determined his peer ranking in the demimonde of scabdom (a peer ranking stored by retrovirus, then collated globally by swapping saliva-laden tabs of blotter paper).

Devoted years of feral genetic hobbyism had brought Fearon a veritable galaxy of condoms, shrinkwrap, blotter kits, polymer resins, phase gels, reagents, femto-injectors, serum vials, canisters, aerosols, splat-pistols, whole bandoliers of buckybombs, padded cases, gloves, goggles, netting, cameras, tubes, cylinder dispensers of pliofilm—the whole assemblage tucked with a fly fisherman's neurotic care into an intricate system of packs, satchels, and strap-ons.

Tupper watched silently, her expression neutral shading to displeased. Even the dense and tactless Malvern could sense the marital tension.

"Lemme boot up my car. Meet you behind the wheel, Fearo my pard."

Tupper accompanied Fearon to the apartment door, still saying nothing as her man clicked together disassembled instruments, untelescoped his sampling staff, tightened buckles across chest and hips, and mated sticky-backed equipment to special patches on his vest and splashproof chaps.

Rigged out to his satisfaction, Fearon leaned in for a farewell kiss. Tupper merely offered her cheek.

"Aw, come on, honey, don't be that way! You know a man's gotta follow his bliss: which in my special case is a raw, hairy-eyed lifestyle on the bleeding edge of the genetic frontier."

"Fearon McClanahan, if you come back smeared with colloid, you're not setting one foot onto my clean rug."

"I'll really wash up this time, I promise."

"And pick up some fresh goat's-milk prestogurt!"

"I'm with the sequence."

Fearon dashed and clattered down the stairs, his nutraceutically enhanced mind already filled with plans and anticipations. Weeble barreled behind.

Malvern's algal-powered roadster sat by the curb, its fuel cell thrumming. Malvern emptied the tapering trunk, converting it into an open-air rumble seat for Weeble, who bounded in like a jet-propelled fifty-liter drum. The weasel Spike occupied a crash-hammock slung behind the driver's seat. Fearon wedged himself into the passenger's seat, and they were off with a pale electric scream.

After shattering a random variety of Miami traffic laws, the two scabs departed Malvern's street-smart vehicle to creep and skulk the last two blocks to the ongoing bio-Chernobyl. The federal swab authorities had thrown their usual cordon in place, enough to halt the influx of civilian lookyloos, but penetrating the perimeter was child's play for well-equipped scabs. Fearon and Malvern simply sprayed themselves and their lab animals with chameleon-shifting shrinkwrap, then strolled through the impotent ring of ultrasonic pylons. They then crept through the shattered glass, found the code-obligatory wheelchair access, and laboriously sneaked up to the ninth floor.

"Well, we're inside just fine," said Fearon, puffing for breath through the shredded shrinkwrap on his lips.

Malvern helped himself to a secretary's abandoned lunch. "Better check Fusing Nuclei for word on the fates of our rivals."

Fearon consulted his handheld. "They just collared Harry the Brewer. 'Impersonating a Disease-Control Officer.' "

"What a lack of gusto and panache. That guy's just not serious."

Malvern peered down streetward through a goo-dripping window. The glorp-cannon salvos had been supplemented by strafing ornithopter runs of uptake inhibitors and countermetabolizers. The battling federal defenders of humanity's physiological integrity were using combined-arms tactics. Clearly the forces of law and order were sensing victory. They usually did.

"How much of this hot glop you think we ought to kipe?" Malvern asked.

"Well, all of it. Everything Weeble can eat."

"You don't mind risking ol' Weeble?"

"He's not a pig for nothing, you know. Besides, I just upgraded his digestive tract." Fearon scratched the pig affectionately.

Malvern Velcroed his weasel Spike into the animal's crittercam. The weasel eagerly scampered off on point, as Malvern offered remote guidance and surveillance with his handheld.

"Out-of-Control Kevin uses video bees," remarked Fearon as they trudged forward with a rattle of sampling equipment. "Little teensy cameras mounted on their teensy insect backs. It's an emergent network phenomenon, he says."

"That's just Oldstyle Silicon Valley," Malvern dismissed. "Besides, a weasel never gets sucked into a jet engine."

The well-trained Spike had nailed the target, and the outlaw wetware was fizzing like cheap champagne. It was a wonder that the floor of the high-rise had withstood the sheer weight of criminal mischief. Mixogen was no mere R&D lab. It was a full-scale production facility. Some ingenious soul had purchased the junked remains of an Orlando aquasport resort, all the pumps, slides, and water-park sprinklers. Kiddie wading pools had been retrofitted with big gooey glaciers of serum support gel. The plastic fishtanks were filled to overflowing with raw biomass. Metastasizing cells had backed up into the genetic moonshine somehow, causing a violent bloom and a methane explosion as frothy as lemon meringue. The animal stench was indescribable.

"What stale hell is this?" said Malvern, gaping at a broken tub that brimmed with a demonic assemblage of horns, hoofs, hide, fur, and dewclaws.

"I take that to be widely variegated forms of mammalian epidermal expression." Fearon restrained his pig with difficulty. The rotting smell of the monstrous meat had triggered Weeble's appetite.

"Do I look like I was born yesterday?" snorted Malvern. "You're missing the point. Nobody can maintain a hybridoma with that gross level of genetic variety! Nothing with horns ever has talons! Ungulates and felines don't even have the same chromosome number."

Window plastic shattered. A wall-crawling police robot broke into the genetic speakeasy. It closed its gecko feet with a sound like venetian blinds and deployed a bristling panoply of lenses and spigots.

"Amscray," Malvern suggested. The duo and their animal familiars retreated from the swab machine's clumsy surveillance. In their absence came a loud frosty hiss as the police bot unleashed a sterilizing fog of Bose-Einstein condensate.

A new scent had Spike's attention, and it set Malvern off at a trot. They entered an office warren of glassblock and steel.

The Mixogen executive had died at her post. She sprawled before her desktop in her ergonomic chair, still in her business suit but reeking of musk and decay. Her swollen, veiny head was the size of a peach basket.

Fearon closed his dropped jaw and zipped up his Kevlar vest. "Jeez, Malvern, another entrepreneur-related fatality! How high do you think her SAT got before she blew?"

"Aw, man—she must have been totally off the IQ scale. Look at the size of her frontal lobes. She's like a six-pack of Wittgensteins."

Malvern shuddered as Spike the weasel tunneled to safety up his pants leg. Fearon wiped the sweat from his own pulsing forehead. The stench of the rot was making his head swim. It was certainly good to know that his fully modern immune system would never allow a bacteria or virus to live in his body without his permission.

Malvern crept closer, clicking flash-shots from his digicam. "Check out that hair on her legs and feet."

"I've heard about this," marveled Fearon. "Bonobo hybridoma. She's half chimp! Because that super-neural technique requires—so they say—a tactical retreat down the primate ladder before you can make that tremendous evolutionary rush for breakthrough extropian intelligence." He broke off short as he saw Weeble eagerly licking the drippy pool of ooze below the dead woman's chair. "Knock it off, Weeble!"

"Where'd the stiff get the stuff?"

"I'm as eager to know that as you are, so I'd suggest swiping her desktop," said Fearon craftily. "Not only would this seriously retard police investigation, but absconding with the criminal evidence would likely shelter many colleagues in the scab underground who might be righteously grateful to us and therefore boost our rankings."

"Excellent tactics, my man!" said Malvern, punching his fist in his open palm. "So let's just fall to sampling, shall we? How many stomachs is Weeble packing now?"

"Five, in addition to his baseline digestive one."

"Man, if I had your kind of money . . . Okay, lemme see . . . Cut a tendril from that kinesthetically active goo, snatch a sample from that wading-pool of sushi-barf . . . and, whoa, check the widget that the babe here is clutching."

From one contorted corpse-mitt peeked a gel-based pocket lab. Malvern popped the datastorage and slipped the honey-colored hockey puck into his capacious scabbing vest. With a murmured apology, Fearon pressed the tip of his sampling-staff to the woman's bloated skull and pneumatically shot a tracer into the proper cortical depths. Weeble fastidiously chomped the mass of gray cells. The prize slid safe into the pig's gullet, behind a closing gastric valve.

They triumphantly skulked from the reeking, cracking high-rise, deftly avoiding police surveillance and nasty street-spatters of gutter-goo. Malvern's getaway car rushed obediently to meet them. While Malvern slid through traffic, Fearon dispensed reward treats to the happy Spike and Weeble.

"Mal, you set to work dredging that gel-drive, okay? I'll load all these tissue samples into my code-crackers. I should have some preliminary results for us by, uhm . . . well, a week or so."

"Yeah, that's what you promised when we scored that hot jellyfish from those Rasta scabs in Key West."

"Hey, they used protein-encrypted gattaca! There was nothing I could do about that."

"You're always hanging fire after the coup, Fearon. If you can't unzip some heavy-duty DNA in your chintzy little bedroom lab, then let's find a man who can."

Fearon set his sturdy jaw. "Are you implying that I lack biotechnical potency?"

"Maybe you're getting there. But you're still no match for old Kemp Kingseed. He's a fossil, but he's still got the juice."

"Look, there's a MarthaMart!" Fearon parried.

They wheeled with a screech of tires into the mylar lot around the MarthaMart and handed the car to the bunny-suited attendant. The men and their animals made extensive use of the fully shielded privacy of the decon chambers. All four beings soon emerged as innocent of contaminants as virgin latex.

"Thank goodness for the local franchise of the goddess of perfection," said Fearon contentedly. "Tupper will have no cause to complain of my task-consequent domestic disorder! Wait a minute. . . . I think she wanted me to buy something."

They entered the brick-and-mortar retail floor of the MarthaMart, Fearon racking his enhanced memory for Tupper's instructions, but to no avail. In the end he loaded his wiry shopping basket with soda bottles, gloop cans, some recycled squip, and a spare vial of oven-cleaning bugs.

The two scabs rode home pensively. Malvern motored off to his scuzzy bachelor digs, leaving Fearon to trudge with spousal anxiety upstairs. What a bringdown from the heights of scab achievement, this husbandly failure.

Fearon faced an expectant Tupper as he reached the landing. Dismally, he handed over the shopping bag. "Here you go. Whatever it was you wanted, I'm sure I didn't buy it." Then he brightened. "Got some primo mutant brain-mass in the pig's innards, though."

Five days later, Fearon faced an irate Malvern. Fearon

hedged and backfilled for half an hour, displaying histo-printouts, some scanning-microscope cinema, even some corny artificial-life simulations.

Malvern examined the bloodstained end of his ivory toothpick. "Face defeat, Fearon. That bolus in the feedline was just pfisteria. The tendril is an everyday hybridoma of liana, earthworm, and slime mold. As for the sushi puke, it's just the usual chemosynthetic complex of abyssal tube-worms. So cut to the chase, pard. What's with those explosively ultra-smart cortical cells?"

"Okay, I admit it, you're right, I'm screwed. I can't make any sense of them at all. Wildly oscillating expression-inhibition loops, silent genes, jumping genes, junk DNA that suddenly reconfigures itself and takes control—I've never seen such a stew. It reads like a Martian road map."

Malvern squinched his batrachian eyes. "A confession of true scabbing lameitude. Pasting a 'Kick Me, I'm Blind' sign on your back. Have I correctly summarized your utter wussiness?"

Fearon kept his temper. "Look, as long as we're both discreet about our little adventure downtown, we're not risking any of our vital reputation in the rough-and-tumble process of scab peer review."

"You've wasted five precious days in which Ribo Zombie might radically beat us to the punch! If this news gets out, your league standings will fall quicker than an Italian government." Malvern groaned theatrically. "Do you know how long it's been since my groundbreaking investigative fieldwork was properly acknowledged? I can't even buy a citation."

Fearon's anger transmuted to embarrassment. "You'll get your quotes and footnotes, Malvern. I'll just shotgun those genetics to bits, and subcontract the sequences around the globe. Then no single individual will get enough of the big picture to know what we've been working on."

Malvern tugged irritably at the taut plastic wrapper of a Pynchonian British toffee. "Man, you've completely lost your edge! Everybody is just a synapse away from everybody else these days! If you hire a bunch of scabs on the Net, they'll just search-engine each other out and patch everything back together. It's high time we consulted Dr. Kingseed."

"Oh, Malvern, I hate asking Kemp for favors. He's such a bringdown billjoy when it comes to hot breakthrough technologies! Besides, he always treats me like I'm some website intern from the days of Internet slave labor."

"Quit whining. This is serious work."

"Plus, that cobwebby decor in Kemp's retrofunky domicile! All those ultra-rotten Hirst assemblages—they'd creep anybody out."

Malvern sighed. "You never talked this way before you got married."

Fearon waved a hand at Tupper's tasteful wallpaper. "Can I help it if I now grok interior decor?"

"Let's face some facts, my man: Dr. Kemp Kingseed has the orthogonal genius of the primeval hacker. After all, his startup companies pushed the Immunosance past its original tipping point. Tell the missus we're heading out, and let's scramble headlong for the Next New Thing like all true-blue scabs must do."

Tupper was busy in her tiny office at her own career, moderating her virtual agora on twentieth-century graphic narrative. She accepted Fearon's news with only half her attention. "Have fun, dear." She returned to her webcam.

"Now, Kirbybuff, could you please clarify your thesis on Tintin and Snowy as precursor culture heroes of the Immunosance?"

Weeble and Malvern, Spike, and Fearon sought out an abandoned petroleum distribution facility down by the waterfront. Always the financial bottom-feeder, the canny Kemp Kingseed had snapped up the wrecked facility after the abject collapse of the fossil-fuel industry. At one point in his checkered career, the reclusive hermit-genius had tried to turn the maze of steampipes and rusting storage tanks into a child-friendly industrial-heritage theme park. Legal problems had undercut his project, leaving the aged digital entrepreneur haunting the ruins of yet another vast, collapsed scheme.

An enormous spiderweb, its sticky threads thick as supertanker hawsers, hung over the rusting tanks like some Victorian antimacassar of the gods.

Malvern examined the unstable tangle of spidery cables. "We'd better leave Weeble down here."

"But I never, ever want to leave dear Weeble!"

"Just paste a crittercam on him and have him patrol for us on point." Malvern looked at the pig critically. "He sure looks green around the gills since he ate that chick's brain. You sure he's okay?"

"Weeble is fine. He's some pig."

The visitors began their climb. Halfway up the tank's curving wall, Kemp Kingseed's familiar, Shelob, scuttled from her lair in the black pipe of a giant smokestack. She was a spider as big as a walrus. The ghastly arachnid reeked of vinegar.

"It's those big corny spider-legs," said Malvern, hiding his visceral fear in a thin shroud of scientific objectivity. "You'd think old Kingseed had never heard of the cube-square law!"

"Huh?" grunted Fearon, clinging to a sticky cable.

"Look, the proportions go all wrong if you blow them up a thousand times life-size. For one thing, insects breathe through spiracles! Insects don't have lungs. An insect as big as a walrus couldn't even breathe!"

"Arachnids aren't insects, Malvern."

"It's just a big robot with some cheap spider chitin grown on it. That's the only explanation that makes rational sense."

The unspeakable monster retreated to her lair, and the climbers moved thankfully on.

Kemp Kingseed's lab was a giant hornet's nest. The big papery office had been grown inside a giant empty fuel tank. Kingseed had always resented the skyrocketing publication costs in academic research. So he had cut to the chase, and built his entire laboratory out of mulched back issues of *Cell* and *Nature Genomics.*

Kingseed had enormous lamp-goggle eyeglasses, tufts of snowy hair on his skull, and impressive white bristles in his withered ears. The ancient Internet mogul still wore his time-honored Versace labcoat over baggy green ripstop pants and rotting Chuck Taylor hightops.

"Africa," he told them, after examining their swiped goodies.

" 'Africa?' "

"I never thought I'd see those sequences again." Kingseed removed his swimmy lenses to dab at his moist red eyes with a swatch of lab paper. "Those were our heroic days. The world's most advanced technicians, fighting for the planet's environmental survival! Of course we completely failed, and the planet's ecosystem totally collapsed. But at least we didn't suck up to politicians."

Kingseed looked at them sharply. "Lousy, fake-rebel

pimps like that Ribo Zombie, turned into big phony pop stars. Why, in my generation, we were the real, authentic transgressive-dissident pop stars! Napster . . . Freenet . . . GNU/Linux . . . Man, that was the stuff!"

Kingseed beat vaguely at the air with his wrinkled fist. "Well, when the Greenhouse started really cooking us, we had to invent the Immunosance. We had no choice at that point, because it was the only way to survive. But every hideous thing we did to save the planet was totally UN-approved! Big swarms of rich-guy NGOs were backing us, straight out of the WTO and the Davos Forum. We even had security clearances. It was all for the public good!"

Malvern and Fearon exchanged wary glances.

Kingseed scowled at them. "Malvern, how much weasel flesh do you have in your personal genetic makeup?"

"Practically none, Dr. Kingseed!" Malvern demurred. "Just a few plasmids in my epidermal expression."

"Well, see, that's the vital difference between your decadent times and my heroic age. Back in my day, people were incredibly anxious and fussy about genetic contamination. They expected people and animals to have clean, unpolluted, fully natural gene lines. But then, of course, the greenhouse effect destroyed the natural ecosystem. Only the thoroughly unnatural and the totally hyped-up could thrive in that kind of crisis. Civilization always collapsed worst where the habitats were most nearly natural. So the continent of Africa was, well, pretty much obliterated."

"Oh, we're with the story," Fearon assured him. "We're totally with it heart-of-darkness-wise."

"Ha!" barked Kingseed. "You pampered punks got no idea what genuine chaos looks like! It was incredibly awful!

Guerrilla armies of African mercenaries grabbed all our state-of-the-art lab equipment. They were looting—burning—and once the narco-terror crowd moved in from the Golden Triangle, it got mondo bizarre!"

Malvern shrugged. "So how tough can it be? You just get on a plane and go look." He looked at Fearon. "You get on planes, don't you, Fearon?"

"Sure. Cars, sleds, waterskis, you bet I get on planes."

Kingseed raised a chiding finger. "We were desperate to save all those endangered species, so we just started packing them into anything that looked like it would survive the climate disruption. Elephant DNA spliced into cacti, rhino sequences tucked into fungi—and hey, we were the *good guys*. You should have seen what the *ruthless terrorists* were up to."

Malvern picked a fragment from his molars, examined it thoughtfully, and ate it. "Look Dr. Kingseed, all this ancient history's really edifying, but I still don't get it with the swollen, exploding brain part."

"That's also what Ribo Zombie wanted to know."

Fearon stiffened. "Ribo Zombie came here? What did you tell him?"

"I told that sorry punk nothing! Not one word did he get out of me! He's been sniffing around my crib, but I chased him back to his media coverage and his high-priced market consultants."

Malvern offered a smacking epidermal high-five. "Kemp, you are one uptaking guru! You're the Miami swamp yoda, Dad!"

"I kinda like you two kids, so let me cluetrain you in. Ever seen NATO military chimp brain? If you know how to tuck globs of digitally altered chimp brain into your own glial cells—and I'm not saying that's painless—then you can radically jazz your own cortex. Just swell your head up like a mushroom puffball." Kingseed gazed at them soberly. "It runs on DNA storage, that's the secret. Really, really long strands of DNA. We're talking like infinite Turing-tape strands of gattaca."

"Kemp," said Fearon kindly, "why don't you come along with us to Africa? You spend too much time in this toxic old factory with that big smelly spider. It'll do you good to get some fresh jungle air. Besides, we clearly require a wise native guide, given this situation."

"Are you two clowns really claiming that you wanna pursue this score to Africa?"

"Oh sure, Ghana, Guinea, whatever. We'll just nick over to the Dark Continent duty-free and check it out for the weekend. Come on, Kemp, we're scabs! We got cameras, we got credit cards! It's a cakewalk!"

Kingseed knotted his snowy eyebrows. "Every sane human being fled out of Africa decades ago. It's the dark side of the Immunosance. Even the Red Cross ran off screaming."

" 'Red Cross,' " said Malvern to Fearon. The two of them were unable to restrain their hearty laughter. " 'Red Cross.' What ineffectual lame-os! Man, that's rich."

"Okay, sure, have it your own way," Kingseed muttered. "I'll just go sherlock my oldest dead media and scare up some tech-specs." He retreated to his vespine inner sanctum. Antic rummaging noises followed.

Fearon patiently sank into a classic corrugated Gehry chair. Malvern raided Kingseed's tiny bachelor kitchen, appropriating a platter of honey-guarana snack cubes. "What a cool pad this rich geezer's got!" Malvern said, munching. "I am digging how the natural light piped in through fiber-optic channels renders this fuel-tank so potent for lab work."

"This place is a stinking dump. Sure, he's rich, but that just means he'll overcharge us."

Malvern sternly cleared his throat. "Let's get something straight, partner. I haven't posted a scab acquisition since late last year! And you're in no better shape, with married life putting such a crimp in your scabbing. If we expect to pull down big-time decals and sponsorships, we've just got to beat Ribo Zombie to a major find. And this one is definitely ours by right."

After a moment, Fearon nodded in grim commitment. It was impossible to duck a straight-out scab challenge like this one—not if he expected to face himself in the mirror.

Kingseed emerged from his papery attic, his glasses askew and the wild pastures of his hair scampering with dust bunnies. He bore a raven in a splintery bamboo cage, along with a moldy fistful of stippled paper strips.

"Candybytes! I stored all the African data on candybytes! They were my bonanza for the child educational market. Edible paper, tasty sugar substrate, info-rich secret ingredients!"

"Hey yeah!" said Malvern nostalgically. "I used to eat candybytes as a little kid in my Time-Warner-Disney Creche. So now one of us has to gobble your moldy old lemon drops?" Malvern was clearly nothing loath.

"No need for that, I brought old Heckle here. Heckle is my verbal output device."

Fearon examined the raven's cage. "This featherbag looks as old as a Victrola."

Kingseed set a moldy data strip atop a table, then

released Heckle. The dark bird hopped unerringly to the start of the tape and began to peck and eat. As Heckle's living readhead ingested and interpreted the coded candybytes, the raven jumped around the table like a fairy chess knight, a corvine Turing Train.

"How is a raven like a writing desk?" murmured Kemp.

Heckle shivered, stretched his glossy wings, and went Delphic. In a croaky, midnight-dreary voice, the neurally possessed bird delivered a strange tale.

A desperate group of Noahs and Appleseeds, Goodalls and Cousteaus, Leakeys and Fosseys had gathered up Africa's endangered flora and fauna, then packed the executable genetic information away into a most marvelous container: the Panspecific Mycoblastula. The Panspecific Mycoblastula was an immortal chimeric fungal ball of awesome storage capacity, a filamentously aggressive bloody tripe-wad, a motile Darwinian lights-and-liver battle-slimeslug.

Shivering with mute attention, Fearon brandished his handheld, carefully recording every cawed and revelatory word. Naturally the device also displayed the point of view of Weeble's crittercam.

Suddenly, Fearon glimpsed a shocking scene. Weeble was under attack!

There was no mistaking the infamous Skratchy Kat, who had been trying, without success, to skulk around Kingseed's industrial estate. Weeble's porcine war cry emerged tinnily from the little speakers. The crittercam's transmission whipsawed in frenzy.

"Sic him, Weeble! Hoof that feline spy!"

Gamely obeying his master's voice, the pig launched his bulk at the top-of-the-line postfeline. A howling combat ensued, Fearon's pig getting the worse of it. Then Shelob the multiton spider joined the fray. Skratchy Kat quickly saw the sense of retreat. When the transmission stabilized, the super-star's familiar had vanished. Weeble grunted proudly. The crittercam bobbed rhythmically as the potent porker licked his wounds with antiseptic tongue.

"You the man, Fearon! Your awesome pig kicked that cat's ass!"

Kingseed scratched his head glumly. "You had a crittercam channel open to your pig this whole time, didn't you?"

Fearon grimaced, clutching his handheld. "Well, of course I did! I didn't want my Weeble to feel all lonely."

"Ribo Zombie's cat was watergating your pig. Ribo Zombie must have heard everything we said up here. I hope he didn't record those GPS coordinates."

The possessed raven was still cackling spastically, as the last crackles of embedded data spooled through its post-corvine speech centers. Heckle was recaged and rewarded with a tray of crickets.

Suddenly, Fearon's handheld spoke up in a sinister basso. It was the incoming voice of Ribo Zombie himself. "So the Panspecific Mycoblastula is in Sierra Leone. It is a savage territory, ruled by the mighty bush soldier, Prince Kissy Mental. He is a ferocious cannibal who would chew you small-timers up like aphrodisiac gum! So, Malvern and Fearon, take heed of my street-wisdom. I have the top-line hardware, and now, thanks to you, I have the data as well. Save yourselves the trouble, just go home."

"Gumshoe on up here, you washed-up ponce!" said star-tled Malvern, dissed to the bone. "My fearsome weasel will go sloppy seconds on your big fat cat!"

Kingseed stretched forth his liver-spotted mitt. "Turn off those handhelds, boys."

When Fearon and Malvern had bashfully powered down their devices, the old guru removed an antique pager from his lab bench. He played his horny thumb across the rudimentary keypad.

"A pager?" Malvern goggled. "Why not, like, jungle drums?"

"Pipe down. You pampered modern lamers can't even manage elementary antisurveillance. While one obsolescent pager is useless, two are a secure link."

Kingseed read the archaic glyphs off the tiny screen. "I can see that my contact in Freetown, Dr. Herbert Zoster, is still operational. With his help, you might yet beat Zombie to this prize." Kingseed looked up. "After allowing Ribo Zombie to bug my very home, I expect no less from you. You'd better come through this time, or never show your faces again at the Tallahassee ScabCon. With your Dalkon shields or on them, boys."

"Lofty! We're outta here pronto! Thanks a lot, Gramps."

Tupper was very alarmed about Africa. After an initial tearful outburst, hot meals around Fearon's house became as rare as whales and pandas. Domestic conversation died down to apologetic bursts of dingbat-decorated e-mail. Their sex life, always sensually satisfactory and emotionally deep, became as chilly as the last few lonely glaciers of greenhouse Greenland. Glum but determined, Fearon made no complaint.

On the day of his brave departure—his important gear

stowed in two carry-on bags, save for that which Weeble wore in khaki-colored saddle-style pouches—Fearon paused at the door of their flat. Tupper sat morosely on the couch, pretending to surf the screen. For thirty seconds the display showed an ad from AT&T (Advanced Transcription and Totipotency) touting their latest telomere upgrades. Fearon was, of course, transfixed. But then Tupper changed channels, and he refocused mournfully for a last homesick look at his frosty spouse.

"I must leave you now, Tuppence honey, to meet Malvern at the docks." Even the use of her pet name failed to break her reserve. "Darling, I know this hurts your feelings, but think of it this way: my love for you is true because I'm true to my own true self. Malvern and I will be in and out of that tropical squalor in a mere week or two, with minimal lysis all around. But if I don't come back right away—or even, well, forever—I want you to know, without you, I'm nothing. You're the feminine mitochondrium in my dissolute masculine plasm, baby."

Nothing. Fearon turned to leave, hand on the doorknob. Tupper swept him up in an embrace from behind, causing Weeble to grunt in surprise. Fearon slithered around within the cage of her arms to face her, and she mashed her lips into his.

Malvern's insistent pounding woke the lovers up. Hastily, Fearon redonned his outfit, bestowed a final peck on Tupper's tear-slicked cheek, and made his exit.

"A little trouble getting away?" Malvern leered.

"Not really. You?"

"Well, my landlady made me pay the next month's rent in advance. Oh, and if I'm dead, she gets to sell all my stuff."

"Harsh."

"Just the kind of treatment I expect."

Still flushed from the fever-shots at US. Customs, the two globetrotting scabs watched the receding coast of America from the deck of their Cuba-bound ferry, *The Gloria Estefan*.

"I hate all swabs," said Malvern, belching as his innards rebooted.

Fearon clutched his squirming belly. "We could have picked better weather. These ferocious Caribbean hurricane waves . . ."

"What 'waves'? We're still in the harbor."

"Oh, my Lord . . ."

After a pitching, greenish sea-trip, Cuba hove into view. The City of Havana, menaced by rising seas, had been relocated up the Cuban coast through a massive levy on socialist labor. The crazy effort had more or less succeeded, though it looked as if every historic building in the city had been picked up and dropped.

Debarking in the fragrant faux-joy of the highly colored tropics, the eager duo hastened to the airfield—for only the cowboy Cubans still maintained direct air-flights to the wrecked and smoldering shell of the Dark Continent.

Mi Amiga Flicka was a hydrogen-lightened cargolifter of Appaloosa-patterned horsehide. The buoyant lift was generated by onboard horse stomachs, modified to spew hydrogen instead of the usual methane. A tanker truck, using a long boom-arm, pumped a potent microbial oatmeal into the tethered dirigible's feedstock reservoirs.

"There's a microbrewery on board," Malvern said with a

travel agent's phony glee. "Works off grain mash just like a horse does! *Cerveza muy potente*, you can bet."

A freestanding bamboo elevator ratcheted them up to the zeppelin's passenger module, which hung like a zippered saddlebag from the buoyant horsehide belly.

The bio-zep's passenger cabin featured a zebrahide mess hall that doubled as a ballroom, with a tiny bandstand and a touchingly antique mirrorball. The Cuban stewards, to spare weight and space, were all jockey-sized.

Fearon and Malvern discovered that their Web-booked "stateroom" was slightly smaller than a standard street toilet. Every feature of the tiny suite folded, collapsed, inverted, everted, or required assembly from scattered parts.

"I don't think I can get used to peeing in the same pipe that dispenses that legendary microbrew," said Fearon. Less finicky, Malvern had already tapped and sampled a glass of the golden boutique cerveza. "Life is a closed loop, Fearon."

"But where will the pig sleep?"

They found their way to the observation lounge for the departure of the giant gasbag. With practiced ease, the crew detached blimp-hook from mooring mast. The bacterial fuel cells kicked over the myosin motors, the props began to windmill and the craft surged eastward with all the verve and speed of a spavined nag.

Malvern was already deep into his third cerveza. "Once we get our hands on that wodge of extinct gene-chains, our names are forever golden! It'll be vino, gyno, and techno all the way!"

"Let's not count our chimeras till they're decanted, Mal. We're barely puttering along, and I keep thinking of Ribo Zombie and his highly publicized private entomopter."

"Ribo Zombie's a fat show-biz phony, he's all talk! We're heavy-duty street-level chicos from Miami! It's just no contest."

"Hmmph. We'd better vortal in to Fusing Nuclei and check out the continuing coverage."

Fearon found a spot where the zep's horsehide was thinnest and tapped an overhead satellite feed. The gel screen of his handheld flashed the familiar Fusing Nuclei logo.

"In his one-man supercavitating sub, Ribo Zombie and Skratchy Kat speed toward the grim no-man's land of sub-Saharan Africa! What weird and wonderful adventures await our intrepid lone-wolf scab and his plucky familiar? Does carnal love lurk in some dusky native bosom? Log on Monday for the realtime landing of RZ and Skratchy upon the sludge-sloshing shores of African doom! And remember, kids—Skratchy Kat cards, toys, and collectibles are available only through Nintendo-Benz. . . ."

"Did they say 'Monday'?" Malvern screeched. "Monday is tomorrow! We're already royally boned!"

"Malvern, please, the straights are staring at us. Ribo Zombie can't prospect all of Africa through all those old UN emplacements. Kingseed found us an expert native guide, remember? Dr. Herbie Zoster."

Malvern stifled his despair. "You really think this native scab has got the stuff?"

Fearon smiled. "Well, he's not a scab quite like us, but he's definitely our type! I checked out his online resume! He's pumped, ripped, and buff, plus he's wily and streets-mart. Herbie Zoster has been a mercenary, an explorer, an archaeologist, even the dictator of an offshore datahaven. Once we hook up with him, this ought to be a waltz."

In the airborne hours that followed, Malvern sampled a

foretaste of the vino, gyno and techno, while Fearon repeatedly wrote and erased apologetical e-mail to his wife. Then came their scheduled arrival over the melancholy ruins of Freetown— and a dismaying formal announcement by the ship's captain.

"What do you mean, you can't moor?" demanded Malvern.

Their captain, a roguish and dapper, yet intensely competent fellow named Luis Sendero, removed his cap and slicked back the two macaw feathers anchored at his temple. "The local caudillo, Prince Kissy Mental, has incited his people to burn down our trading facilities. One learns to expect these little setbacks in the African trade. Honoring our contracts, we shall parachute to earth the goods we bring, unless they are not paid for—in which case, they are dumped anyway, yet receive no parachute. As for you two Yankees and your two animals—you are the only passengers who want to land in Sierra Leone. If you wish to touch down, you must parachute just as the cargo."

After much blustering, whuffling, and whining, Fearon, Malvern, and Weeble stood at the open hatch of Mi Amiga Flicka, parachutes strapped insecurely on, ripcords wired to a rusty cable, while the exotic scents of the rainy African landscape wafted to their nostrils.

Wistfully, they watched their luggage recede to the scarred red earth. Then, with Spike clutched to his breast, Malvern closed his eyes and boldly tumbled overboard. Fearon watched closely as his colleague's fabric chute successfully bloomed. Only then did he make up his mind to go through with it. He booted the reluctant Weeble into airy space, and followed suit.

"Outsiders never bring us anything but garbage," mumbled Dr. Zoster.

"Is it Cuban garbage?" said Malvern, tucking into their host's goat-and-pepper soup with a crude wooden spoon. "Because if it is, you're getting ripped off even in terms of trash."

"No. They're always Cubans bringing it, but it's everybody's garbage that is dumped on Africa. Africa's cargo-cult prayers have been answered with debris. But perhaps any sufficiently advanced garbage is indistinguishable from magic."

Fearon surreptitiously fed the peppery cabrito to his pig. He was having a hard time successfully relating to Dr. Herbie Zoster. It had never occurred to him that elderly Kemp Kingseed and tough, sunburned Herbie Zoster were such close kin.

In point of fact, Herbie Zoster was Kingseed's younger clone. And it didn't require Jungian analysis to see that just like most clones Zoster bitterly resented the egotistical man who had created him. This was very clearly the greatest appeal of life in Africa for Dr. Herbie Zoster. Africa was the one continent guaranteed to make him as much unlike Kemp Kingseed as possible.

Skin tinted dark as mahogany, callused and wiry, dotted with many thorn scratches, parasites, and gunshot wounds, Zoster still bore some resemblance to Kingseed—about as much as a battle-scarred hyena to an aging bloodhound.

"What exactly do people dump around here?" said Malvern with interest.

Zoster mournfully chewed the last remnant of a baked yam and spat the skin into the darkness outside their thatched hut. Something with great glowing eyes pounced upon it instantly, with a rasp and a snarl. "You're familiar with the Immunosance?"

"Oh yeah, sure!" said Malvern artlessly, "we're from Miami."

"That new Genetic Age completely replaced the Nuclear Age, the Space Age, and the Information Age."

"Good riddance," Malvern offered. "You got any more of that *cabrito* stew? It's fine stuff!"

Zoster rang a crude brass bell. A limping, turbaned manservant dragged himself into their thatched hut, tugging a bubbling bucket of chow.

"The difficulty with massive technological advance," said Zoster, spooning the steamy goop, "is that it obsolesces the previous means of production. When the Immunosance arrived, omnipresent industries already covered all the advanced countries." Zoster paused to pump vigorously at a spring-loaded homemade crank, which caused the lightbulb overhead to brighten to its full thirty watts. "There simply was no room to install the new bioindustrial revolution. But a revolution was very necessary anyway. So all the previous junk had to go. The only major planetary area with massive dumping grounds was—and still is—Africa."

Zoster rubbed at his crank-stiffened forearm and sighed. "Sometimes they promote the garbage and sell it to us Africans. Sometimes they drop it anonymously. But nevertheless—no matter how we struggle or resist—the very worst always ends up here in Africa, no matter what."

"I'm with the sequence," said Malvern, pausing to belch. "So what's the 411 about this fabled Panspecific Mycoblastula?"

Zoster straightened, an expression of awe toughening his face below his canvas hat brim. "That is garbage of a very special kind. Because the Panspecific Mycoblastula is an entire, outmoded natural ecosystem. It is the last wild continent, completely wadded up and compressed by foreign technicians!"

Fearon considered this gnomic remark. He found it profoundly encouraging. "We understand the gravity of this matter, Dr. Zoster. Malvern and I feel that we can make this very worth your while. Time is of the essence. When can we start?"

Zoster scraped the dirt floor with his worn boot heel. "I'll have to hire a train of native bearers. I'll have to obtain supplies. We will be risking our lives, of course. . . . What can you offer us in return for that?"

"A case of soft drinks?" said Malvern.

Fearon leaned forward intently. "Transistor radios? Antibiotics? How about some plumbing?"

Zoster smiled for the first time, with a flash of gold teeth. "Call me Herbie."

Zoster extended a callused fingertip. It bore a single ant, the size and color of a sesame seed.

"This is the largest organism in the world."

"So I heard," Malvern interjected glibly. "Just like the fire ants invading America, right? They went through a Darwinian bottleneck and came out supercharged sisters, genetically identical even under different queens. They spread across the whole USA smoother than marshmallow fluff."

Zoster wiped his sweating stubbled jaw with a filthy bandanna. "These ants were produced four decades ago. They carry rhizotropic fungi, to fertilize crops with nitrogen. But their breeders overdesigned them. These ants cause tremendous fertile growth in vegetation, but they're also immune to insect diseases and parasites. The swabs finally wiped them out in America, but Africa has no swabs. We have no public health services, no telephones, no roads. So from Timbuktu to Capetown, cloned ants have spread in a massive wave, a single super-organism big as Africa."

Malvern shook his head in superior pity. "That's what you get for trusting in swabs, man. Any major dude could've told those corporate criminals that top-down hierarchies never work out. Now, the approach you Third Worlders need is a viral marketing, appropriate-technology pitch. . . ."

Zoster actually seemed impressed by Malvern's foolish bravado, and engaged the foreign scab in earnest jargon-laced discussion, leaving Fearon to trudge along in an unspeaking fug of sweat-dripping, alien jungle heat. Though Zoster was the only one armed, the trio of scabs boldly led their little expedition through a tangle of feral trails, much aided by their satellite surveillance maps and GPS locators.

Five native bearers trailed the parade, fully laden-down with scab-baggage and provisions. The bare-chested, bare-legged, dhoti-clad locals exhibited various useful bodily mods, such as dorsal water storage humps, toughened and splayed feet, and dirty grub-excavating claws that could shred a stump in seconds. They also sported less rational cosmetic changes, including slowly moving cicatrices (really migratory subepidermal symbiotic worms) and enlarged ears augmented with elephant musculature. The rhythmic flapping of the porters' ears produced a gentle creaking that colorfully punctuated their impenetrable sibilant language.

The tormented landscape of Sierra Leone had been

thoroughly reclaimed by a clapped-out mutant jungle. War, poverty, disease, starvation—the Four Landrovers of the African Apocalypse—had long since been and gone, bringing a drastic human population crash that beggared the Black Death, and ceding the continent to resurgent flora and fauna.

These local flora and fauna were, however, radically human-altered, recovering from an across-the-board apocalypse even more severe and scourging than the grisly one suffered by humans. Having come through the grinding hopper of a bioterror, they were no longer "creatures" but "evolutures." Trees writhed, leaves crawled, insects croaked, lizards bunny-hopped, mammals flew, flowers pinched, vines slithered, and mushrooms burrowed. The fish, clumsily reengineered for the surging greenhouse realities of rising seas, lay in the jungle trails burping like lungfish. When stepped upon, they almost seemed to speak.

The explorers found themselves navigating a former highway to some long-buried city, presumably Bayau or Moyamba, to judge by the outdated websites. Post-natural oddities lay atop an armature of ruins, revealing the Ozymandias lessons of industrial hubris. A mound of translucent jello assumed the outlines of a car, including a dimly perceived skeletal driver and passengers. Oil-slick-colored orchids vomited from windows and doors. With the descending dusk invigorating flocks of winged post-urban rats, the travelers made camp. Zoster popped up a pair of tents for the expedition's leaders and their animals, while the locals assembled a humble jungle igloo of fronds and thorns.

After sharing a few freeze-dried packets of slumgullion, the expedition sank into weary sleep. Fearon was so bone-tired that he somehow tolerated Malvern's nasal whistling and Zoster's stifled dream shouts.

He awoke before the others. He unseamed the tent flap and poked his head out into the early sunshine.

Their encampment was surrounded by marauders. Spindly scouts, blank-eyed and scarcely human, were watching the pop-tents and leaning on pig-iron spears.

Fearon ducked his head back and roused his compatriots, who silently scrambled into their clothes. Heads clustered like coconuts, the three of them peered through a fingernail's width of tent flap.

Warrior-reinforcements now arrived in ancient Jeeps, carrying antiaircraft guns and rocket-propelled grenades.

"It's Kissy Mental's Bush Army," whispered Zoster. He pawed hurriedly through a pack, coming up with a pair of mechanical boots.

"Okay, girls, listen up," Zoster whispered, shoving and clamping his feet in the piston-heavy footgear. "I have a plan. When I yank this overhead pull-tab, this tent unpops. That should startle the scouts out there, maybe enough to cover our getaway. We all race off at top speed just the way we came. If either of you survive, feel free to rendezvous back at my place."

Zoster hefted his gun, their only weapon. He dug the toe of each boot into a switch on the heel of its mate, and his boots began to chuff and emit small puffs of exhaust.

"Gasoline-powered seven-league boots," Zoster explained, seeing their stricken expressions. "South African Army surplus. There's no need for roads with these things, but with skill and practice, you can pronk along like a gazelle at thirty, forty miles an hour."

"You really believe we can outrun these jungle marauders?" Malvern asked.

"I don't have to outrun them; I only have to outrun you."

Zoster triggered the tent and dashed off at once, firing his pistol at random. The pistons of his boots gave off great blasting backfires, which catapulted him away with vast stainless-steel lunges.

Stunned and in terror, Malvern and Fearon stumbled out of the crumpling tent, coughing on Zoster's exhaust. By the time they straightened up and regained their vision, they were firmly in the grip of Prince Kissy Mental's troops.

The savage warriors attacked the second pop-tent with their machetes. They quickly grappled and snaffled the struggling Spike and Weeble.

"Chill, Spike!"

"Weeble, hang loose!"

The animals obeyed, though the cruel grip of their captors promised the worst.

The minions of the Prince were far too distanced from humanity to have any merely ethnic identity. Instead, they shared a certain fungal sheen, a somatype evident in their thallophytic pallor and exopthalmic gaze. Several of the marauders, wounded by Zoster's wild shots, were calmly stuffing various grasses and leaves into the gaping suety holes in their arms, legs, and chests.

A working squad now dismantled the igloo of the expedition's bearers, pausing to munch meditatively on the greenery of the cut fronds. The panic-stricken bearers gabbled in obvious terror but offered no resistance. A group of Kissy Mental's warriors, with enormous heads and great toothy jaws, decamped from a rusty Jeep. They unshouldered

indestructible Russian automatic rifles and decisively emptied their clips into the hut. Pathetic screams came from the
ruined igloo. The warriors then demolished the walls and
hauled out the dead and wounded victims, to dispassion-
ately tear them limb from limb.

The Army then assembled a new booty of meat, to bear
it back up the trail to their camp. Reeking of sweat and
formic acid, the inhuman natives bound the hands of
Fearon and Malvern with tough lengths of grass. They
strung Weeble and Spike to a shoulder-pole, where the terrified beasts dangled like pinatas.

Then the antmen forced the quartet of prisoners forward
on the quick march. As the party passed through the fetid
jungle, the Army paused periodically to empty their automatic weapons at anything that moved. Whatever victim fell
to earth would be swiftly chopped to chunks and added to
the head-borne packages of the rampaging mass.

Within the hour, Fearon and Malvern were delivered
whole to Prince Kissy Mental.

Deliberately, Fearon focused his attention on the Prince's
throne, so as to spare himself the sight of the monster
within it. The Army's portable throne was a row of three
first-class airplane seats, with the armrests removed to
accommodate the Prince's vast posthuman bulk. The throne
perched atop a mobile palanquin, juryrigged from rebar,
chipboard, and Astroturf. A system of crutches and tethers
supported and eased the Prince's vast, teratological skull.

The trophy captives were shoved forward at spearpoint
through a knee-deep heap of cargo-cult gadgets.

"Holy smallpox!" whispered Malvern. "This bossman's
half-chimp and half-ant!"

"That doesn't leave any percentage for human, Mal."

The thrust of a spear-butt knocked Fearon to his knees. Kissy Mental's coarse-haired carcass, barrel-chested to support the swollen needs of the head, was sketched like a Roquefort cheese with massive blue veins. The Prince's vast pulpy neck marked the transition zone to a formerly human skull whose sutures had long since burst under pressure, to be patched with big, red, shiny plates of antlike chitin. Kissy Mental's head was bigger than the prize-winning pumpkin at a 4-H Fair—even when "4-H" meant "Homeostasis, Haplotypes, Histogenesis, and Hypertrophy."

Fearon slitted his eyes, rising to his feet. He was terrified, but the thought of never seeing Tupper again somehow put iron in his soul. To imagine that he might someday be home again, safe with his beloved—that prospect was worth any sacrifice. There had to be some method to bargain with their captor.

"Malvern, how bright do you think this guy is? You suppose he's got any English?"

"He's got to be at least as intelligent as British royalty."

With an effort that set his bloated heart booming like a tribal drum, the Prince lifted both his hairy arms and beckoned. Their captors pushed Mal and Fear right up against the throne. The Prince unleashed a flock of personal fleas. Biting, lancing, and sucking, the tasters lavishly sampled the flesh of Fearon and Malvern, then returned to their master. After quietly munching a few of the blood-gorged familiars, the Prince silently brooded, the tiny bloodshot eyes in his enormous skull blinking like LEDs. He then gestured for a courtier to ascend into the presence. The bangled, headdressed ant-man hopped up and, well-trained, sucked a thin clear excretion from the Prince's rugose left nipple.

Smacking his lips, the lieutenant decrypted his proteinaceous commands, in a sudden frenzy of dancing, shouting, and ritual gesticulation.

Swiftly the Army rushed into swarming action, the ants trampling one another in an ardent need to lift the Prince's throne upon their shoulders. Once they had their entomological kingpin up and in lolling motion, the Army milled forward in a violent rolling surge, employing their machetes on anything in their path.

A quintet of burly footmen pushed Malvern and Fearon behind the bluish exhaust of an ancient military jeep. The flesh of the butchered bearers had been crudely wrapped in broad green leaves and dumped into the back of the vehicle.

Malvern muttered sullenly below the grumbles of the engine. "That scumbag Zoster. . . . All clones are inherently degraded copies. Man, if we ever get out of this pinch, it's no more Mr. Nice Guy."

"Uh, sure, that's the old scab spirit, Mal."

"Hey, look!"

Fearon followed Malvern's jerking head-nod. A split-off subdivision of the trampling Army had dragged another commensal organism from the spooked depths of the mutant forest. It was a large, rust-eaten, canary-yellow New Beetle, scribbled over with arcane pheremonal runes. Its engine long gone, the wreck rolled solely through the juggernaut heaving of the Army.

"Isn't that the 2015 New Beetle?" said Fearon. "The Sport Utility version, the one they ramped up big as a stretch HumVee?"

"Yeah, the Screw-the-Greenhouse Special! Looks like they removed the sunroof and moonroof and taped all the windows shut! But what the hell can they have inside? Whatever it is, it's all mashed up and squirmy against the glass. . . ."

A skinny Ant Army courtier vaulted and scrambled onto the top of the sealed vehicle. With gingerly care, he stuffed a bloody wad of meat in through the missing moonroof.

From out of the adjacent gaping sunroof emerged a hydralike bouquet of heterogenous animal parts: tails, paws, snouts, beaks, ears. Snarls, farts, bellows, and chitterings ensued.

At length, a sudden flow of syrupy exudate drooled out the tailpipe, caught by an eager cluster of Ant Army workers cupping their empty helmets.

"They've got the Panspecific Mycoblastula in there!"

The soldiers drained every spatter of milky juice, jittering crazily and licking one another's lips and fingers.

"I do wish I had a camera," said Fearon wistfully. "It's very hard to watch a sight like this without one."

"Look, they're feeding our bearers into that thing!" marveled Malvern. "What do you suppose it's doing with all that human DNA? Must be kind of a partially human genetic mole-rat thing going on in there."

Another expectant crowd hovered at the Beetle's tailpipe, their mold-spotted helmets at the ready. They had not long to wait, for a fleshy diet of protein from the butchered bearers seemed to suit the Panspecific Mycoblastula to a T.

Sweating and pale-faced, Malvern could only say, "If they were breakfast, when's lunch?"

Fearon had never envisioned such brutal slogging, so much sheer physical work in the simple effort of eating and staying alive. The Prince's Army marched well-nigh constantly, bull-dozing the landscape in a whirl of guns and knives. Anything they themselves could not devour was fed to the Mycoblastula. Nature knew no waste, so the writhing abomination trapped in the Volkswagen was a panspecific glutton, an always boiling somatic stewpot. It especially doted on high-end mammalian life, but detritus of all kinds was shoved through the sunroof to sate its needs: bark, leaves, twigs, grubs, and beetles. Especially beetles. In sheer number of species, most of everything living was always beetles.

Then came the turn of their familiars.

It seemed at first that those unique beasts had somehow earned the favor of Prince Kissy Mental. Placed onboard his rollicking throne, the trussed Spike and Weeble had been subjected to much rough cossetting and petting, their peculiar high-tech flesh particularly seeming to strike the Prince's fancy.

But such good fortune could not last. After noon of their first day of captivity, the bored Prince, without warning, snapped Spike's neck and flung the dead weasel in the path of the painted Volkswagen. Attendants snatched the weasel up and stuffed Spike in. The poor beast promptly lined an alimentary canal.

Witnessing this atrocity, Malvern roared and attempted to rush forward. A thorough walloping with boots and spear-butts persuaded him otherwise.

Then Weeble was booted meanly off the dais. Two hungry warriors scrambled to load the porker upside down onto a shoulder-carried spear. Weeble's piteous grunts lanced through Fearon, but at least he could console himself that, unlike Spike, his pig still lived.

But finally, footsore, hungry, and beset by migraines, his immune system drained by constant microbial assault, Fearon admitted despair. It was dead obvious that he and Malvern were simply doomed. There was just no real question that they were going to be killed and hideously devoured, all through their naive desire for mere fame, money, and professional technical advancement.

When they were finally allowed to collapse for the night on the edge of a marshy savannah, Fearon sought to clear his conscience.

"Mal, I know it's over, but think of all the good times we've had together. At least I never sold Florida real estate, like my dad. A short life and a merry one, right? Die young and leave a beautiful corpse. Hope I die before I get—"

"Fearon, I'm fed up with your sunnysided optimism! You rich-kid idiot, you always had it easy and got all the breaks! You think that rebellion is some kind of game! Well, let me tell you, if I had just one chance to live through this, I'd never waste another minute on nutty dilettante crap. I'd go right for the top of the food chain. Let me be the guy on top of life, let me be the winner, just for once!" Malvern's battered face was livid. "From this day forth, if I have to lie, or cheat, or steal, or kill. . . . aw, what's the use? We're ant meat! I'll never even get the chance!"

Fearon was stunned into silence. There seemed nothing left to say. He lapsed into a sweaty doze amid a singing mosquito swarm, consoling himself with a few last visions of his beloved Tupper. Maybe she'd remarry after learning of his death. Instead of following her sweet romantic heart, this time she'd wisely marry some straight guy, someone normal and dependable. Someone who would cherish her, and look after her, and take her rather large inheritance with the seriousness it deserved. How bitterly he regretted his every past unkindness, his every act of self-indulgence and neglect. The spouses of romantic rebels really had it rough.

In the morning, the hungry natives advanced on Weeble, and now it was Fearon's turn to shout, jump up, and be clouted down.

With practiced moves the natives slashed off Weeble's front limbs near the shoulder joints. The unfortunate Weeble protested in a frenzy of squealing, but his assailants knew all too well what they were doing. Once done, they carefully cauterized the porker's foreparts and placed him in a padded stretcher, which was still marked with an ancient logo from the Red Cross.

They then gleefully roasted the pig's severed limbs, producing an enticing aroma Fearon and Malvern fought to abhor. The crisped breakfast ham was delivered with all due ceremony to Prince Kissy Mental, whose delight in this repast was truly devilish to watch. Clearly the Ant Army didn't get pig very often, least of all a pig with large transgenic patches of human flesh. A pig that good you just couldn't eat all at once.

By evening, Fearon and Malvern were next on the menu. The two scabs were hustled front and center as the locals fed a roaring bonfire. A crooked pair of nasty wooden spits were prepared. Then Fearon and Malvern had their bonds cut through, and their clothes stripped off by a forest of groping hands.

The two captives were gripped and hustled and frog-marched as the happy Army commenced a manic dance around their sacred Volkswagen, ululating and keening in a thudding of drums. The evil vehicle oscillated from motion within, in time with the posthuman singing. Lit by the setting sun and the licking flames of the cannibal bonfire, big chimeric chunks of roiling Panspecific Mycoblastula tissue throbbed and slobbered against the glass.

Suddenly a brilliant klieg light framed the scene, with an eighty-decibel airborne rendition of "Ride of the Valkyries."

"Hit the dirt!" yelped Malvern, yanking free from his captor's grip and casting himself on his face.

Ribo Zombie's entomopter swept low in a strafing run. The cursed Volkswagen exploded in a titanic gout of lymph, blood, bone fragments, and venom, splattering Fearon—but not Malvern—from head to toe with quintessence of Mycoblastula.

Natives dropped and spun under the chattering impact of advanced armaments. Drenched with spew, Fearon crawled away from the Volkswagen, wiping slime from his face.

Dead or dying natives lay in crazy windrows, like genetically modified corn after a stiff British protest. Now Ribo Zombie made a second run, his theatrical lighting deftly picking out victims. His stagey attack centered, naturally, on the most dramatic element among the panicking Army, Prince Kissy Mental himself. The Prince struggled to flee the crimson targeting lasers, but his enormous head was strapped to his throne in a host of attachments. Swift and computer-sure came the next burst of gunfire. Prince Kissy Mental's abandoned head swung futilely from its tethers, a watermelon in a net.

Leaping and capering in grief and anguish, the demoralized Army scattered into the woods.

A swarm of mobile cameras wasped around the scene, carefully checking for proper angles and lighting. Right on cue, descending majestically from the darkening tropic sky came Ribo Zombie himself, crash-helmet burnished and gleaming, combat boots blazoned with logos.

Skratchy Kat leaped from Zombie's shoulder to strike a proud pose by the Prince's still-smoking corpse. The superstar scab blew nonexistent trailing smoke from the unused barrels of his pearl-handled sidearms, then advanced on the cowering Fearon and Malvern.

"Nice try, punks, but you got in way over your head." Ribo Zombie gestured at a hovering camera. "You've been really great footage ever since your capture, though. Now get the hell out of camera range, and go find some clothes or something. That Panspecific Mycoblastula is all mine."

Rising from his hands and knees with a look of insensate rage, Malvern lunged up and dashed madly into the underbrush.

"What's keeping you?" boomed Ribo Zombie at Fearon.

Fearon looked down at his hands. Miniature parrot feathers were sprouting from his knuckles.

"Interesting outbreak of spontaneous mutation," Ribo Zombie noted. "I'll check that out just as soon as I get my trophy shot."

Advancing on the bullet-riddled Volkswagen, Ribo Zombie telescoped a razor-pincered probe. As the triumphant conqueror dipped his instrument into the quivering mass, Malvern charged him with a leveled spear.

The crude weapon could not penetrate Ribo Zombie's armor, but the force of the rush bounced the superstar scab against the side of the car. Quick as lightning a bloodied briar snaked through a gaping bullet hole and clamped the super-scab tight.

Then even more viscous and untoward tentacles emerged from the engine compartment, and a voracious sucking, gurgling struggle commenced.

Malvern, still naked, appropriated the fallen crash helmet with the help of a spear haft. "Look, it liquefied him instantly and sucked all the soup clean out! Dry as a bone inside. And the readouts still work on the eyepieces!"

After donning the helmet, a suspiciously close fit, Malvern warily retrieved Ribo Zombie's armored suit, which lay in its high-tech abandonment like the nacreous shell of a hermit crab. A puzzled Skratchy Kat crept forward. After a despondent sniff at the emptied boots, the bereaved familiar let out a continuous yowl.

"Knock it off, Skratchy," Malvern commanded. "We're all hurting here. Just be a man."

Swiftly shifting allegiances, Skratchy Kat supinely rubbed against Malvern's glistening shins.

"Now to confiscate his cameras for a little judicious editing of his unfortunate demise." Malvern shook his helmeted head. "You can cover for me, right, Fearon? Just tell everybody that Malvern Brakhage died in the jungle. You should probably leave out the part about them wanting to eat us."

Fearon struggled to dress himself with some khaki integuments from a nearby casualty. "Malvern, I can't fit inside these clothes."

"What's your problem?"

"I'm growing a tail. And my claws don't fit in these boots." Fearon pounded the side of his head with his feathery knuckles. "Are you glowing, or do I have night vision all of a sudden?"

Malvern tapped his helmet with a wiry glove. "You're not telling me you're massively infected now, are you?"

"Well, technically speaking, Malvern, I'm the 'infection' in this situation, because the Mycoblastula's share of our joint DNA is a lot more extensive than mine is."

"Huh. Well, that development obviously tears it." Malvern backed off cautiously, tugging at the last few zips and buckles on his stolen armor to assure an airtight seal. "I'll route you some advanced biomedical help—if there's any available in the local airspace." He cleared his throat with a sudden rasp of helmet-mounted speakers. "In any case, the sooner I clear out of here for civilization, the better."

All too soon, the sound of the departing entomopter had died away. After searching through the carnage, pausing periodically as his spine and knees unhinged, Fearon located the still-breathing body of his beloved pig. Then he dragged the stretcher to an abandoned jeep.

"And then Daddy smelled the pollution from civilization with his new nose, from miles away, so he knew he'd reached the island of Fernando Po, where the UN still keeps bases. So despite the tragic death of his best friend, Malvern, Daddy knew that everything was going to be all right. Life would go on!"

Fearon was narrating his exploit to the embryo in Tupper's womb via a state-of-the-art fetal interface, the GestaPhone. Seated on the comfy Laura Ashley couch in their bright new stilt house behind the dikes of Pensacola Beach, Tupper smiled indulgently at her husband's oft-polished tale.

"When the nice people on the island saw Daddy's credit cards, Daddy and Weeble were both quickly stabilized. Not exactly like we were before, mind you, but rendered healthy enough for the long trip back home to Miami. Then the press coverage started and, well, son, someday I'll tell you about how Daddy dealt with the challenges of fame and fortune."

"And wasn't Mommy glad to see Daddy again!" Tupper chimed in. "A little upset at first about the claws and fur. But luckily, Daddy and Mommy had been careful to set aside sperm samples while Daddy was still playing his scab games. So their story had a real happy ending when Daddy finally settled down and Baby Boy was safely engineered."

Fearon detached the suction-cup terminal from Tupper's bare protuberant stomach. "Weeble, would you take these, please?"

The companionable pig reached up deftly, plucked the GestaPhones out of Fearon's grasp, and moved off with an awkward lope. Weeble's strange gait was due to his new forelimbs, a nifty pair of pig-proportioned human arms.

Tupper covered her womb with her frilled maternity blouse and glanced at the clock. "Isn't your favorite show on now?"

"Shucks, we don't have to watch every single episode. . . ."

"Oh, honey, I love this show, it's my favorite, now that I don't have to worry about you getting all caught up in it!"

They nestled on the responsive couch, Tupper stroking the fish-scaled patch on Fearon's cheek while receiving the absentminded caresses of his long tigerish tail. She activated the big wet screen, cohering a close-up of Ribo Zombie in the height of a ferocious rant.

"Keeping it real, folks, still keeping it real! I make this

challenge to all my fellow scabs, those who are down with the Zombie and those who dis him, those who frown on him and those who kiss him. Yes, you sorry posers all know who you are. But check this out. . . . Who am I?"

Fearon sighed for a world well lost. And yet, after all . . . there was always the next generation.

Glossary

4-H, noun: an amateurs' club, primarily for children, that focuses on homeostasis (bodily maintenance through negative feedback circuits), haplotypes (gamete amounts of DNA), histogenesis (cell differentiation from general to specific), and hypertrophy (gigantism).

billjoy, noun: a doomsayer; derived from Bill Joy, a fretful member of the twentieth-century digerati.

bioneer, noun: a bioengineering pioneer.

bio-zep, noun: a pseudo-living, lighter-than-air zeppelin.

Bose-Einstein condensate, noun: ultra-frigid state of matter.

buckybomb, noun: an explosive in a carbon buckminsterfullerene shell.

candybytes, noun: an educational nutriceutical.

clottage, noun: residence of a scab.

clump, verb: to enjoy meditative solitary downtime

crittercam, noun: small audio-video transmitter mounted on animals.

duckback, noun: a water-resistant building material.

entomopter, noun: a small flying vehicle whose wings employ elaborate, scissoring insectoid principles of movement, rather than avian ones; abbreviated as 'mopter.

evoluture, noun: an artificially evolved creature.

exopthalmic, adjective: pop-eyed.

extropian, noun, adjective: one who subscribes to a set of radical, wild-eyed optimistic prophecies regarding mankind's glorious high-tech future.

familiar, noun: the customary modified-animal partner of a scab.

femto-injector, noun: a delivery unit capable of perfusing substances through various membranes without making a macroscopic entry wound.

gattaca, noun: DNA; any substrate that holds genetic information.

gel-drive, noun: organic data-storage unit.

gloop, noun: a foodstuff.

glorp, noun: an antibiological sterilizing agent used by swabs.

HazMat, noun: hazardous materials.

hot-tag, noun: clickable, animated icons.

HVAC, noun: heating, ventilation, air-conditioning system.

Immunosance, noun: the Immunological Renaissance, the Genetic Age.

infodump, noun: large undigested portion of factoids.

jackalope, noun: the legendary antlered rabbit of Wyoming, now reified.

jello, noun: culture and transport medium.

lookyloo, noun: a gaping bystander at a public spectacle, usually the cause of secondary accidents.

lysis, noun: cell destruction.

neoteric, adjective: a term of scably approbation.

NGO, noun: nongovernmental organization.

nutriceutical, noun: a foodstuff modified with various synthetic compounds meant to enhance mental or physical performance.

olivine, noun: a naturally occuring gemstone used as a building material.

otaku, noun: Japanese term for obsessive nerds, trivia buffs.

Panspecific Mycoblastula, noun: a MacGuffin.

pliofilm, noun: all-purpose millipore wrap.

polysaccharide, noun: an organic polymer such as chitin.

prestogurt, noun: instant yogurt modified to be a nutriceutical.

ribo, adjective: all-purpose prefix derived from the transcriptive cellular organelle the ribosome; indicative of bioengineering.

scab, noun: a biohacker.

slowglass, noun: glass in which light moves at a radically different speed than it does elsewhere; term invented by Bob Shaw.

somatype, noun: the visible expression of gattaca.

squip, noun: a foodstuff.

supercavitation, noun: process of underwater travel employing leading air pockets.

swab, noun: governmental and private agents of bioregulation; the cops; antagonists to every scab.

thallophytic, adjective: mushroom-like.

uptaking, adjective: a term of scably approbation.

vortal, noun, verb: virtual portal.

wetware, noun: programmed organic components; software in living form.

WTO, noun: World Trade Organization.

[Rudy Rucker, mathematician, computer scientist, philosopher and fantasist, is a dear friend and colleague of mine. Every seven years or so, Rudy and I manage to write a story together. So far, there have been three of these collaborations: "Storming the Cosmos," "Big Jelly," and this third and most recent one, "Junk DNA." Oddly, despite the huge gaps of time and space in these works, these are closely related stories, with overlapping characters. If Professor Rucker and Professor Sterling can manage to grind their joint way through a contemporary male American life expectancy, there might conceivably be three more of these dual efforts. Maybe a postmortem Rucker-Sterling fixup novel is in the works.]

Junk DNA
(with Rudy Rucker)

Life was hard in old Silicon Valley. Little Janna Gutierrez was a native Valley girl, half Vietnamese, half Latino. She had thoughtful eyes and black hair in high ponytails.

Her mother, Shirley, tried without success to sell California real estate. Her father, Ruben, plugged away inside cold, giant companies like Ctenephore and Lockheed Biological. The family lived in a charmless bungalow in the endless grid of San Jose.

Janna first learned true bitterness when her parents broke up. Tired of her hard scrabble with a lowly wetware engineer, Shirley ran off with Bang Nguyen, the glamorous owner of an online offshore casino. Dad should have worked hard to win back Mom's lost affection, but, being an engineer, he contented himself with ruining Bang. He found and exploited every unpatched hole in Bang's operating system. Bang never knew what hit him.

Despite Janna's pleas to come home, Mom stubbornly stuck by her online entrepreneur. She bolstered Bang's broken income by retailing network porn. Jaded Americans considered porn to be the commonest and most boring thing on the Internet. However, Hollywood glamour still had a moldy cachet in the innocent Third World. Mom spent her workdays dubbing the ethnic characteristics of tribal Somalis and Baluchis onto porn stars. She found the work far more rewarding than real estate.

Mom's deviant behavior struck a damp and morbid echo in Janna's troubled soul. Janna sidestepped her anxieties by obsessively collecting Goob dolls. Designed by glittery-eyed comix freaks from Hong Kong and Tokyo, Goobs were wiggly, squeezable, pettable creatures made of trademarked Ctenephore piezoplastic. These avatars of ultra-cuteness sold off wire racks worldwide, to a generation starved for Nature. Thanks to environmental decline, kids of Janna's age had never seen authentic wildlife. So they flipped for the Goob menagerie: marmosets with butterfly wings, starfish that scuttled like earwigs, long, furry frankfurter cat-snakes.

Sometimes Janna broke her Goob toys from their mint-in-the-box condition and dared to play with them. But she quickly learned to absorb her parents' cultural values and to live for their business buzz. Janna spent her off-school hours on the Net, pumping-and-dumping collectible Goobs to younger kids in other states.

Eventually, life in the Valley proved too much for Bang Nguyen. He pulled up the stakes in his solar-powered RV and drove away, to pursue a more lucrative career retailing networked toilets. Janna's luckless mom, her life reduced to ashes, scraped out a bare living marketing mailing lists to mailing list marketers.

Janna ground her way through school and made it into UC Berkeley. She majored in computational genomics. Janna worked hard on software for hardwiring wetware, but her career timing was off. The latest pulse of biotech start-ups had already come and gone. Janna was reduced to a bottle-scrubbing job at Triple Helix, yet another subdivision of the giant Ctenephore conglomerate.

On the social front, Janna still lacked a boyfriend. She'd studied so hard she'd been all but dateless through school and college. In her senior year she'd moved in with this cute Korean boy who was in band. But then his mother had come to town with, unbelievable, a blushing North Korean bride for him in tow. So much the obvious advice-column weepie!

In her glum and lonely evenings, she played you-are-her interactives, romance stories, with a climax where Janna would lip-synch a triumphant, tear-jerking video. On other nights Janna would toy wistfully with her decaying Goob collection. The youth market for the dolls had evaporated with the years. Now fanatical adult collectors were trading the Goobs, stiff and dusty artifacts of their lost consumer childhood.

And so life went for Janna Gutierrez, every dreary day on the calendar foreclosing some way out. Until the fateful September when Veruschka Zipkinova arrived from Russia, fresh out of biohazard quarantine.

The zany Zipkinova marched into Triple Helix toting a

fancy briefcase with video display built into its piezoplastic skin. Veruschka was clear-eyed and firm-jawed, with black hair cut very short. She wore a formal black jogging suit with silk stripes on the legs. Her Baltic pallor was newly reddened by California sunburn. She was very thoroughly made up. Lipstick, eye shadow, nails—the works.

She fiercely demanded a specific slate of bio-hardware and a big wad of startup money. Janna's boss was appalled at Veruschka's archaic approach—didn't this Russski woman get it that the New Economy was even deader than Leninism? It fell to the luckless Janna to throw Veruschka out of the building.

"You are but a tiny cog," said Veruschka, accurately summing up Janna's cubicle. "But you are intelligent, yes, I see this in your eyes. Your boss gave me the brush-off. I did not realize Triple Helix is run by lazy morons."

"We're all quite happy here," said Janna lightly. The computer was, of course, watching her. "I wonder if we could take this conversation off-site? That's what's required, you see. For me to get you out of the way."

"Let me take you to a fine lunch at Denny's," said Veruschka with sudden enthusiasm. "I love Denny's so much! In Petersburg, our Denny's always has long lines that stretch down the street!"

Janna was touched. She gently counter-suggested a happening local coffee shop called the Modelview Matrix. Cute musicians were known to hang out there.

With the roads screwed and power patchy, it took forever to drive anywhere in California, but at least traffic fatalities were rare, given that the average modern vehicle had the mass and speed of a golf cart. As Janna forded the sunny moonscape of potholes, Veruschka offered her startup pitch.

"From Russia, I bring to legendary Silicon Valley a break-through biotechnology! I need a local partner, Janna. Someone I can trust."

"Yeah?" said Janna.

"It's a collectible pet."

Janna said nothing but was instantly hooked.

"In Russia, we have mastered genetic hacking," said Veruschka thoughtfully, "although California is the planet's legendary source of high-tech marketing."

Janna parked amid a cluster of plastic cars like colored seedpods. Inside, Janna and Veruschka fetched slices of artichoke quiche.

"So now let me show you," said Veruschka as they took a seat. She placed a potently quivering object on the tabletop. "I call him Pumpti."

The Pumpti was the size and shape of a Fabergé egg, pink and red, clearly biological. It was moist, jiggly, and veined like an internal organ with branching threads of yellow and purple. Janna started to touch it, then hesitated, torn between curiosity and disgust.

"It's a toy?" asked Janna. She tugged nervously at a fanged hairclip. It really wouldn't do to have this blob stain her lavender silk jeans.

The Pumpti shuddered, as if sensing Janna's hovering finger. And then it oozed silently across the table, dropped off the edge, and plopped damply to the diner's checkered floor.

Veruschka smiled, slitting her cobalt-blue eyes, and leaned over to fetch her Pumpti. She placed it on a stained paper napkin.

"All we need is venture capital!"

"Um, what's it made of?" wondered Janna.

"Pumpti's substance is human DNA!"

"Whose DNA?" asked Janna.

"Yours, mine, anyone's. The client's." Veruschka picked it up tenderly, palpating the Pumpti with her lacquered fingertips. "This one is made of me. Once I worked at the St. Petersburg Institute of Molecular Science. My boss—well, he was also my boyfriend . . ." Veruschka pursed her lips. "Wiktor's true obsession was the junk DNA—you know this technical phrase?"

"Trust me, Vero, I'm a genomics engineer."

"Wiktor found a way for these junk codons to express themselves. The echo from the cradle of life, evolution's roadside picnic! To express junk DNA required a new wetware reader. Wiktor called it the Universal Ribosome." She sighed. "We were so happy until the mafiya wanted the return on their funding."

"No National Science Foundation for you guys," mused Janna.

"Wiktor was supposed to tweak a cabbage plant to make opium for the criminals—but we were both so busy growing our dear Pumpti. Wiktor used my DNA, you see. I was smart and saved the data before the Uzbeks smashed up our lab. Now I'm over here with you, Janna, and we will start a great industry of personal pets! Wiktor's hero fate was not in vain. And—"

Janna found her grand Russian vision of user-based genomic petware infectious. Despite her natural skepticism, real hope began to dawn. The old Valley dreams had always been the best ones.

What an old-skool, stylin', totally trippy way for Janna to

shed her grind-it-out worklife! She and Veruschka Zipkinova would create a startup, launch the IPO, and retire by thirty! Then Janna could escape her life-draining servitude and focus on life's real rewards. Take up oil painting, go on a safari, and hook up with some sweet guy who understood her. A guy she could really talk to. Not an engineer, and especially not a musician.

Veruschka pitchforked a glob of quiche past her pointed teeth. For her pilgrimage to the source of the world's largest legal creation of wealth in history, the Russian girl hadn't forgotten to pack her appetite.

"Pumpti still needs little bit of—what you say here?—tweaking," said Veruschka. The prototype Pumpti sat shivering on its paper napkin. The thing had gone all goose-bumpy, and the bumps were warty: the warts had smaller warts upon them, topped by teensy wartlets with fine, waving hairs. Not exactly a magnet for shoppers.

Stuffed with alfalfa sprouts, Janna put her cutlery aside. Veruschka plucked up Janna's dirty fork and enthusiastically sucked it clean. She even scratched inside her cheek with the tines.

Janna watched this dubious stunt and decided to stick to business. "How about patents?"

"No one ever inspects Russian gene labs," said Veruschka with a glittery wink. "We Russians are the great world innovators in black market wetware. Our fetal stem cell research, especially rich and good. Plenty of fetus meat in Russia, cheap and easy, all you need! Nothing ever gets patented. To patent is to teach stupid people to copy!"

"Well, do you have a local lab facility?" pressed Janna.

"I have better," said Veruschka, nuzzling her Pumpti. "I

have pumptose. The super enzyme of exponential auto-catalysis!"

" 'Pumptose,' huh? And that means?" prompted Janna.

"It means the faster it grows, the faster it grows!"

Janna finally reached out and delicately touched the Pumpti. Its surface wasn't wet after all, just shiny like super-slick plastic. But—a pet? It seemed more like something little boys would buy to gross out their sisters. "It's not exactly cuddly," said Janna.

"Just wait till you have your own Pumpti," said Veruschka with a knowing smile.

"But where's the soft hair and big eyes? That thing's got all the shelf appeal of a scabby knee!"

"It's nice to nibble a scab," said Veruschka softly. She cradled her Pumpti, leaned in to sniff it, then showed her strong teeth and nipped off a bit of it.

"God, Veruschka," said Janna, putting down her coffee.

"Your own Pumpti," said Veruschka, smacking, "you are loving him like pretty new shoes. But so much closer and personal! Because Pumpti is you, and you are Pumpti."

Janna sat in wonderment. Then, deep within her soul, a magic casement opened. "Here's how we'll work it!" she exclaimed. "We give away Pumpti pets almost free. We'll make our money selling rip-off Pumpti-care products and accessories!"

Veruschka nodded, eyes shining. "If we're business partners now, can you find me a place to sleep?"

Janna let Veruschka stay in the spare room at her Dad's house. Inertia and lack of capital had kept Janna at home after college.

Ruben Gutierrez was a big, soft man with a failing spine, carpal-tunnel, and short, bio-bleached hair he wore moussed into a hedgehog's spikes. He had a permanent mirthless grin, the side effect of his daily diet of antidepressants.

Dad's tranquil haze broke with the arrival of Veruschka, who definitely livened up the place with her go-go arsenal of fishnet tights and scoop-necked Lycra tops. With Veruschka around, the TV blared constantly and there was always an open bottle of liquor. Every night the little trio stayed up late, boozing, having schmaltzy confessions, and engaging in long, earnest sophomore discussions about the meaning of life.

Veruschka's contagious warm-heartedness and her easy acceptance of human failing were a tonic for the Gutierrez household. It took Veruschka mere days to worm out the surprising fact that Ruben Gutierrez had a stash of half a million bucks accrued from clever games with his stock options. He'd never breathed a word of this to Shirley or to Janna.

Emotionally alive for the first time in years, Dad offered his hoard of retirement cash for Veruschka's long-shot crusade. Janna followed suit by getting on the Web and selling off her entire Goob collection. When Janna's Web money arrived freshly laundered, Dad matched it, and two days later, Janna finally left home, hopefully for good. Company ownership was a three-way split between Veruschka, Janna, and Janna's dad. Veruschka supplied no cash funding, because she had the intellectual property.

Janna located their Pumpti startup in San Francisco. They engaged the services of an online lawyer, a virtual realtor, and a genomics supply house and began to build the buzz that, somehow, was bound to bring them major-league venture capital.

Their new HQ was a gray stone structure of columns, arches, and spandrels, the stone decorated with explosive graffiti scrawls. The many defunct banks of San Francisco made spectacular dives for the city's genomics startups. Veruschka incorporated their business as Magic Pumpkin, Inc., and lined up a three-month lease.

San Francisco had weathered so many gold rushes that its real estate values had become permanently bipolar. Provisionary millionaires and drug-addled derelicts shared the very same neighborhoods, the same painted-lady Victorians, the same flophouses and anarchist bookstores. Sometimes millionaires and lunatics even roomed together. Sometimes they were the very same person.

Enthusiastic cops spewing pepper gas chased the last downmarket squatters from Janna's derelict bank. To her intense embarrassment, Janna recognized one of the squatter refugees as a former Berkeley classmate named Kelso. Kelso was sitting on the sidewalk amid his tattered Navajo blankets and a damp-spotted cardboard box of kitchen gear. Hard to believe he'd planned to be a lawyer.

"I'm so sorry, Kelso," Janna told him, wringing her hands. "My Russian friend and I are doing this genomics startup? I feel like such a gross, rough-shod newbie."

"Oh, you'll be part of the porridge soon enough," said Kelso. He wore a big sexy necklace of shiny junked cellphones. "Just hang with me and get colorful. Want to jam over to the Museum of Digital Art tonight? They're serving calamari, and nobody cares if we sleep there."

Janna shyly confided a bit about her business plans.

"I bet you're gonna be bigger than Pokemon," said Kelso. "I'd always wanted to hook up with you, but I was busy with my pre-law program and then you got into that pod thing with that Korean musician. What happened to him?"

"His mother found him a wife with a dowry from Pyongyang," said Janna. "It was so lovelorn."

"I've had dreams and visions about you, Janna," said Kelso softly. "And now here you are."

"How sweet. I wish we hadn't had you evicted."

"The wheel of fortune, Janna. It never stops."

As if on cue, a delivery truck blocked the street, causing grave annoyance to the local bike messengers. Janna signed for the tight-packed contents of her new office.

"Busy, busy," Janna told Kelso, now more than ready for him to go away. "Be sure and watch our Web page. Pumpti dot-bio. You don't want to miss our IPO."

"Who's your venture angel?"

Janna shook her head. "That would be confidential."

"You don't have one, then." Kelso pulled his blanket over his grimy shoulders. "And boy, will you ever need one. You ever heard of Revel Pullen of the Ctenephore Industry Group?"

"Ctenephore?" Janna scoffed. "They're just the biggest piezoplastic outfit on the planet, that's all! My dad used to work for them. And so did I, now that I think about it."

"How about Tug Mesoglea, Ctenephore's Chief Scientist? I don't mean to name-drop here, but I happen to know Dr. Tug personally."

Janna recognized the names, but there was no way Kelso could really know such heavy players. However, he was cute and he said he'd dreamed about her. "Bring 'em on," she said cheerfully.

"I definitely need to meet your partner," said Kelso,

making the most of a self-created opportunity. Hoisting his grimy blanket, Kelso trucked boldly through the bank's great bronze-clad door.

Inside the ex-bank, Veruschka Zipkinova was setting up her own living quarters in a stony niche behind the old teller counter. Veruschka had a secondhand futon, a moldy folding chair, and a stout refugees' suitcase. The case was crammed to brimming with the detritus of subsistence tourism: silk scarves, perfumes, stockings, and freeze-dried coffee.

After one glance at Kelso, Veruschka yanked a handgun from her purse. "Out of my house, *rechniki!* No room and board for you here, *maphiya bezprizorniki!*"

"I'm cool, I'm cool," said Kelso, backpedaling. Then he made a run for it. Janna let him go. He'd be back.

Veruschka hid her handgun with a smirk of satisfaction. "So much good progress already! At last we command the means of production! Today we will make your own Pumpti," she told Janna.

They unpacked the boxed UPS deliveries. "You make ready that crib vat," said Veruschka. Janna knew the drill; she'd done this kind of work at Triple Helix. She got a wet-ware crib vat properly filled with base-pairs and warmed it up to standard operating temperature. She turned the valves on the bovine growth serum, and a pink threading began to fill the blood-warm fluid.

Veruschka plugged together the components of an Applied Biosystems oligosynthesis machine. She primed it with a data-stuffed S-cube that she'd rooted out of a twine-tied plastic suitcase.

"In Petersburg, we have unique views of DNA," said Veruschka, pulling on her ladylike data gloves and staring into the synthesizer's screen. Her fingers twitched method-ically, nudging virtual molecules. "Alan Turing, you know of him?"

"Sure, the Universal Turing Machine," Janna core-dumped. "Foundations of Computer Science. Breaking the Enigma code. Reaction-diffusion rules; Turing wrote a paper to derive the shapes of patches on brindle cows. He killed himself with a poison apple. Alan Turing was Snow White, Queen, and Prince all at once!"

"I don't want to get too technical for your limited mathe-matical background," Veruschka hedged.

"You're about to tell me that Alan Turing anticipated the notion of DNA as a program tape that's read by ribosomes. And I'm not gonna be surprised."

"One step further," coaxed Veruschka. "Since the human body uses one kind of ribosome, why not replace that with another? The Universal Ribosome—it reads in its program as well as its data before it begins to act. All from that good junk DNA, yes, Janna? And what is junk? Your bottom drawer? My garbage can? Your capitalist attic and my startup garage!"

"Normal ribosomes skip right over the junk DNA," said Janna. "It's supposed to be meaningless to the modern genome. Junk DNA is just scribbled-over things. Like the crossed-out numbers in an address book. A palimpsest. Junk DNA is the half-erased traces of the original codes—from long before humanity."

"From before, and—maybe after, Wiktor was always saying." Veruschka glove-tapped at a long-chain molecule on the screen. "There is pumptose!" The gaudy molecule had seven stubby arms, each of them a tightly wound mass of smaller tendrils. She barked out a command in Russian. The S-cube-enhanced Applied Biosystems unit understood, and an amber bead of oily, fragrant liquid oozed from the output port. Veruschka neatly caught the droplet in a glass pipette.

Then she transferred it to the crib vat that Janna had prepared. The liquid shuddered and roiled, jolly as the gut of Santa Claus.

"That pumptose is rockin' it," said Janna, marveling at the churning rainbow oil-slick.

"We going good now, girl." Veruschka winked. She opened her purse and tossed her own Pumpti into the vat. "A special bath-treat for my Pumpti," she said. Then, with a painful wince, she dug one of her long fingernails into the lining of her mouth.

"Yow," said Janna.

"Oh, it feels so good to pop him loose," said Veruschka indistinctly. "Look at him."

Nestled in the palm of Veruschka's hand was a lentil-shaped little pink thing. A brand-new Pumpti. "That's your own genetics from your dirty fork at the diner," said Veruschka. "All coated with trilobite bile, or some other decoding from your junk DNA." She dropped the bean into the vat.

"This is starting to seem a little bent, Veruschka."

"Well . . . you never smelled your own little Pumpti. Or tasted him. How could you not bite him and chew him and grow a new scrap in your mouth? The sweet little Pumpti, you just want to eat him all up!"

Soon a stippling of bumps had formed on the tiny scrap of flesh. Soft little pimples, twenty or a hundred of them. The lump cratered at the top, getting thicker all around. It formed a dent and invaginated like a sea-squirt. It began pumping itself around in circles, swimming in the murky fluids. Stubby limbs formed momentarily, then faded into an undulating skirt like the mantle of a cuttlefish.

Veruschka's old Pumpti was the size of a grapefruit, and the new one was the size of a golf ball. The two critters rooted around the tank's bottom like rats looking for a drain hole.

Veruschka rolled up her sleeve and plunged her bare arm into the big vat's slimy fluids. She held up the larger Pumpti; it was flipping around like a beached fish. Veruschka brought the thing to her face and nuzzled it.

It took Janna a couple of tries to fish her own Pumpti out of the glass, as each time she touched the slimy thing she had to give a little scream and let it go. But finally she had the Pumpti in her grip. It shaped itself to her touch and took on the wet, innocent gleam of a big wad of pink bubblegum.

"Smell it," urged Veruschka.

And, Lord yes, the Pumpti did smell good. Sweet and powdery, like clean towels after a nice hot bath, like a lawn of flowers on a summer morn, like a new dress. Janna smoothed it against her face, so smooth and soft. How could she have thought her Pumpti was gnarly?

"Now you must squeeze him to make him better," said Veruschka, vigorously mashing her Pumpti in her hands. "Knead, knead, knead! The Pumpti pulls skin cells from the surface of your hands, you know. Then pumptose reads more of the junk DNA and makes more good tasty proteins." She pressed her Pumpti to her cheek, and her voice went up an octave. "Getting more of that yummy yummy wetware from me, isn't he? Squeezy-squeezy Pumpti." She gave it a little kiss.

"This doesn't add up," said Janna. "Let's face it, an entire human body only has like ten grams of active DNA. But this Pumpti, it's solid DNA like a chunk of rubber, and hey, it's almost half a kilo! I mean, where's that at?"

"The more the better," said Veruschka patiently. "It means that very quickly Pumpti code can be recombining his code. Like a self-programming Turing machine. Wiktor often spoke of this."

"But it doesn't even look like DNA," said Janna. "There's scraps of it all the labs at Triple Helix. I messed with that stuff every day. It looks like lint or dried snot."

"Pumpti is smooth because he's making nice old proteins from the ancient junk of the DNA. All our human predecessors from the beginning of time, amphibians, lemurs, maybe intelligent jellyfish saucers from Mars—who knows what. But every bit is my very own junk, of my very own DNA. So stop thinking so hard, Janna. Love your Pumpti."

Janna struggled not to kiss her pink glob. The traceries of pink and yellow lines beneath its skin were like the veins of fine marble.

"Your Pumpti is very eager," said Veruschka, reaching for it. "Now, into the freezer! We will store it, to show our financial backers."

"What?!" said Janna. She felt a sliver of ice in her heart. "Freeze my Pumpti? Freeze your own Pumpti, Vero."

"I need mine," snapped Veruschka.

To part from her Pumpti—something within her passionately rebelled. In a dizzying moment of raw devotion Janna suddenly found herself sinking her teeth into the unresisting flesh of the Pumpti. Crisp, tasty, spun cotton candy, deep-fried puffball dough, a sugared beignet. And under that a salty, slightly painful flavor—bringing back the memory of being a kid and sucking the root of a lost tooth.

"Now you understand," said Veruschka with a throaty laugh. "I was only testing you! You can keep your sweet Pumpti, safe and sound. We'll get some dirty street bum to make us a Pumpti for commercial samples. Like that stupid boy you were talking to before." Veruschka stood on tiptoe to peer out of the bank's bronze-mullioned window. "He'll be back. Men always come back when they see you making money."

Janna considered this wise assessment. Kelso was coming on pretty strong, considering that he'd never talked to her at school. "His name is Kelso," said Janna. "I went to Berkeley with him. He says he's always wanted me."

"Get some of his body fluid."

"I'm not ready for that," said Janna. "Let's just poke around in the sink for his traces." And, indeed, they quickly found a fresh hair to seed a Kelso Pumpti, nasty and testicular, suitable for freezing.

As Veruschka had predicted, Kelso himself returned before long. He made it his business to volunteer his aid and legal counsel. He even claimed that he'd broached the subject of Magic Pumpkin to Tug Mesoglea himself. However, the mysterious mogul failed to show up with his checkbook, so Magic Pumpkin took the path of viral marketing.

Veruschka had tracked down an offshore Chinese ooze farm to supply cheap culture medium. In a week, they had a few dozen Pumpti starter kits for sale. They came in a little plastic tub of pumptose-laced nutrient, all boxed up in a flashy little design that Janna had printed out in color.

Kelso had the kind of slit-eyed street smarts that came only from Berkeley law classes. He chose Fisherman's Wharf to hawk the product. Janna went along to supervise his retail effort.

It was the start of October now, a perfect fog-free day for the commercial birth of Magic Pumpkin. A visionary song of joy seemed to rise from the sparkling waters of San Francisco Bay, echoing from the sapphire dome of the California sky. Even the tourists could sense the sweetness of the occasion. They hustled cheerfully round Kelso's foldout table, clicking away with little biochip cameras.

Kelso spun a practiced line of patter while Janna publicly adored her Pumpti. She'd decked Pumpti out in a special sailor suit, and she kept tossing him high into the air and laughing.

"Why is this woman so happy?" barked Kelso. "She's got a Pumpti. Better than a baby, better than a pet, your Pumpti is all you! Starter kits on special today for the unbelievably low price of—"

Over the course of a long morning, Kelso kept cutting the offering price of the Pumpti kits. Finally a runny-nosed little girl from Olympia, Washington, took the bait.

"How do I make one?" she wanted to know. "What choo got in that kit?" And, praise the Holy Molecule, her parents didn't drag her away, they just stood there watching their little darling shop.

The First Sale. For Janna, it was a moment to treasure forever. The little girl with her fine brown hair blowing in the warm afternoon wind, the dazedly smiling parents, Kelso's abrupt excited gestures as he explained how to seed and grow the Pumpti by planting a kiss on a scrap of Kleenex and dropping into the kit's plastic jar. The feel of those worn dollar bills in her hand, and the parting wave of little Customer Number One. Ah, the romance of it!

Now that they'd found their price point, more sales followed. Soon, thanks to word-of-mouth, they began moving units from their site.

Janna's dad, Ruben, who had a legalistic turn of mind, had warned them to hold off any postal or private-carrier shipments until they had federal approval. Ruben took a sample Pumpti before the San Jose branch office of the Genomics Control Board. He argued that, since the Pumptis were neither self-reproducing nor infectious, they didn't fall under the strict provisions of the Human Heritage Home Security Act.

The consequent investigation made the Bay Area news shows. Then the right-wing religious crowd got in on it. An evangelist from Alameda appeared at one of the hearings—he'd confiscated a Pumpti from a young parishioner—and after his impassioned testimony he tore the Pumpti apart with pincers on the San Jose Federal Building's steps, calling the unresisting little glob the "spawn of Satan."

This was catnip for their business, of course. Magic Pumpkin's website gathered a bouquet of orders from eager early adopters.

But, paradoxically, Magic Pumpkin's flowering sales bore the slimy seeds of a smashing fiscal disaster. When an outfit started small, it didn't take much traffic to double production every week. This constant doubling brought on raging production bottlenecks and serious crimps in their cash flow. In point of fact, in pursuit of market establishment, they were losing money on each Pumpti sold. The eventual payback from all those Pumpti accessories was still well down the road.

Janna was bored by their practical difficulties, but she had a ball inventing high concepts for Pumpti care products and Pumpti collectibles. Kelso's many art-scene friends were happy to sign up. Kelso was a one-man recruiting whiz. Buoyed by his worldly success, he began to shave more often and even use deodorant. He was so pleased by his ability to sucker people into the Magic Pumpkin enterprise that he even forgot to make passes at Janna.

Every day-jobber in the startup was quickly issued his or her own free Pumpti. "Magic Pumpkin wants missionaries, not mercenaries," Janna announced from on high, and her growing cluster of troops cheered her on. Owning a personal Pumpti was an item of faith in the little company—the linchpin of their corporate culture. You couldn't place yourself in the proper frame of mind for Magic Pumpkin product development without your very own darling roly-poly.

Cynics had claimed that the male demographic would never go for Pumptis. Why would any guy sacrifice his computer gaming time and his weekend bicycling to nurture something? But once presented with their own Pumpti, men found that it filled some deep need in the masculine soul. They swelled up with competitive pride in their Pumptis and even became quite violent in their defense.

Janna lined up a comprehensive array of related products. First and foremost were costumes. Sailor Pumpti, Baby Pumpti, Pumpti Duckling, Angel Pumpti, Devil Pumpti, and even a Goth Pumpti dress-up kit with press-on tattoos. They shrugged off production to Filipina doll-clothes makers in a sweatshop in East LA.

Further up-market came a Pumpti Backpack for transporting your Pumpti in style, protecting it from urban pollution and possibly nasty bacteria. This one seemed like a sure hit, if they could swing the Chinese labor in Shenzhen and Guangdong.

The third idea, Pumpti Energy Crackers, was a no-brainer: crisp collectible cards of munchable amino-acid bases to fatten up your Pumpti. If the crackers used the "mechanically recovered meat" common in pet food and cattle feed, then the profit margin would be primo. Kelso had a contact for this in Mexico: they guaranteed their cookies would come crisply printed with the Pumpti name and logo.

Janna's fourth concept was downright metaphysical: a "Psychic Powers Pumpti Training Wand." Except for occasional oozing and plopping, the Pumptis never actually managed conventional pet tricks. But this crystal-topped gizmo could be hawked to the credulous as increasing their Pumpti's "empathy" or "telepathy." A trial mention of this vaporware on the Pumpti-dot-bio website brought in a torrent of excited New Age emails.

The final, sure-thing Pumpti accessory was tie-in books. Two of Kelso's many unemployed writer and paralegal friends set to work on the Pumpti User's Guide. The firm forecasted an entire library of guides, sucking up shelf space at chain stores and pet stores everywhere. The Moron's Guide to Computational Genomics. Pumpti Tips, Tricks and Shortcuts. Backing Up Your Pumpti. Optimize Your Pumpti for High Performance. The Three Week Pumpti Guide, the One Day Pumpti Guide, and the Ten Minute Pumpti Guide. The Pumpti Bible, with the quick-start guide, walk-through, lists, maps, and Pumpti model index. Pumpti Security

Threats: How to Protect Your Pumpti From Viral DNA Hacks, Trojan Goo Horses, and Unauthorized Genetic Access. And more, more, more!

But moving from high-vaporware to the street proved difficult. Janna had never quite realized that manufacturing real, physical products was so much harder than just thinking them up. Magic Pumpkin failed to do its own quality control, so the company was constantly screwed by fly-by-nighters. Subcontractors were happy to take their money, but when they failed to deliver, they had Magic Pumpkin over a barrel.

The doll costumes were badly sized. The Pumpti Backpacks were ancient Hello Kitty backpacks with their logos covered by cheap paper Pumpti stickers. The crackers were dog biscuits with the stinging misprint "Pupti." The "telepathic" wand sold some units, but the people nuts enough to buy it tended to write bad checks or have invalid credit card numbers. As for the User's Guides, the manuscripts were rambling and self-indulgent, long on far-fetched jokes yet critically short on objective scientific facts.

One ugly roadblock was finally removed when the Genomics Control Board came through with their blessing. The Pumptis were deemed harmless, placed in the same schedule-category as home gene-testing kits. Magic Pumpkin was free to ship throughout the nation!

But now that their production lines were stabilized, now that their catalogs were finally proofed and printed, now that their ad campaign was finally in gear, their fifteen minutes of ballroom glamour expired. The pumpkin clock struck midnight. The public revealed its single most predictable trait: fickleness.

Instantly, without a whimper of warning, Magic Pumpkin was deader than pet rocks. They never shipped to the Midwest or the East Coast, for the folks in those distant markets were sick of hearing about the Pumptis before they ever saw one on a shelf.

Janna and Veruschka couldn't make payroll. Their lease was expiring. They were cringing for cash.

A desperate Janna took the show on the road to potential investors in Hong Kong, the toy capital of the world. She emphasized that Magic Pumpkin had just cracked the biggest single technical problem: the fact that Pumptis looked like slimy blobs. Engineering-wise, it all came down to the pumptose-based Universal Ribosome. By inserting a properly tweaked look-up string, you could get it to express the junk DNA sequences in customizable forms. Programming this gnarly cruft was, from an abstract computer-science perspective, "unfeasible," meaning that, logically speaking, such a program could never be created within the lifetime of the universe.

But Janna's dad, fretful about his investment, had done it anyway. In two weeks of inspired round-the-clock hacking, Ruben had implemented the full OpenAnimator graphics library, using a palette of previously unused rhodopsin-style proteins. A whiff of the right long-chain molecule could give your Pumpti any mesh, texture, color-map, or attitude matrix you chose. Not to mention overloaded frame-animation updates keyed into the pumptose's ribosomal time-steps! It was a techie miracle!

Dad had even flown along to Hong Kong to back Janna's pitch, but the Hong Kong crowd had no use for software jargon in American English. The overwrought Ruben killed the deal by picking fights over intellectual property—no way to build partnerships in Hong Kong.

Flung back to San Francisco, Janna spent night after night frantically combing the Web, looking for any source of second-round venture capital, no matter how far-fetched.

Finally she cast herself sobbing into Kelso's arms. Kelso was her last hope. Kelso just had to come through for them: he had to bring in the seasoned business experts from Ctenophore, Inc., the legendary masters of jellyfish A-Life.

"Listen, babe," said Kelso practically, "I think you and the bio-Bolshevik there have already taken this concept just about as far as any sane person oughta push it. Farther, even. I mean, sure, I recruited a lot of my cyberslacker friends into your corporate cult here, and we promised them the moon and everything, so I guess we'll look a little stupid when it Enrons. They'll bitch and whine, and they'll feel all disenchanted, but come on, this is San Francisco. They're used to that here. It's genetic."

"But what about my dad? He'll lose everything! And Veruschka is my best friend. What if she shoots me?"

"I'm thinking you, me, and Mexico," said Kelso dreamily. "Way down on the Pacific coast—that's where my mother comes from. You and me, we've been working so hard on this start-up that we never got around to the main event. Just dump those ugly Pumptis in the Bay. We'll empty the cash box tonight and catch a freighter blimp for the South. I got a friend who works for Air Jalisco."

It was Kelso's most attractive offer, maybe even sincere, in its way. Janna knew full well that the classic dot-com move was to grab that golden parachute and bail like crazy before the investors and employees caught on. But Magic

Pumpkin was Janna's own brain-child. She was not yet a serial entrepreneur, and a boyfriend was only a boyfriend. Janna couldn't walk away from the green baize table until that last, final spin of the wheel.

It had been quite some time since Ctenephore Inc. had been a cutting-edge startup. The blazing light of media tech-hype no longer escaped their dense, compact enterprise. The firm's legendary founders, Revel Pullen and Tug Mesoglea, had collapsed in on their own reputations. Not a spark could escape their gravity. They had become twin black holes of biz weirdness.

Ctenophore's main line of business had always been piezoplastic products. Ctenephore had pumped this protean, blobject material into many crazy scenes in the California boom years. Bathtub toys, bondage clothing, and industrial-sized artificial-jellyfish transport blimps—and Goob dolls as well! GoobYoob, creator of the Goob dolls, had been one of Ctenephore's many Asian spin-offs.

As it happened, quite without Janna's awareness, Ctenephore had already taken a professional interest in the workings of Magic Pumpkin. GoobYoob's manufacturing arm, Boogosity, had been the Chinese ooze-farm supplier for Pumpti raw material. Since Boogosity had no advertising or marketing expenses, they'd done much better by the brief Pumpti craze than Magic Pumpkin itself.

Since Magic Pumpkin was going broke, Boogosity faced a production glut. They'd have to move their specialty goo factories back into the usual condoms and truck tires. Some kind of corporate allegiance seemed written in the stars.

Veruschka Zipkinova was transfixed with paranoia about Revel Pullen, Ctenephore's chairman of the board. Veruschka considered major American capitalists to be sinister figures—this conviction was just in her bones, somehow—and she was very worried about what Pullen might do to Russia's oil.

Russia's black gold was the life-blood of its pathetic, wrecked economy. Years ago Revel Pullen, inventively manic as always, had released gene-spliced bacteria into America's dwindling oil reserves. This fatal attempt to increase oil production had converted millions of barrels of oil into (as chance would have it) raw piezoplastic. Thanks to the powerful Texas lobby in Washington, none of the lawsuits or regulatory actions against Ctenophore had ever succeeded.

Janna sought to calm Veruschka's jitters. If the company hoped to survive, they had to turn Ctenophore into Magic Pumpkin's fairy godmother. The game plan was to flatter Pullen, while focusing their persuasive efforts on the technical expert of the pair. This would be Ctenophore's chief scientist, a far-famed mathematician named Tug Mesoglea.

It turned out that Kelso really did know Tug Mesoglea personally, for Mesoglea lived in a Painted Lady mansion above the Haight. During a protracted absence to the Tweetown district of Manchester (home of the Alan Turing Memorial), Tug had once hired Kelso to baby-sit his jellyfish aquarium.

Thanks to San Francisco's digital grapevine, Tug knew about the eccentric biomathematics that ran Pumptis. Tug was fascinated, and not by the money involved. Like many mathematicians, Mesoglea considered money to be one boring, merely bookkeeping subset of the vast mental universe of general computation. He'd already blown a fortune endowing chairs in set theory, cellular automata, and higher-dimensional topology. Lately, he'd published widely on the holonomic attractor space of human dreams, producing a remarkable proof that dreams of flight were a mathematical inevitability for a certain fixed percentage of the dreams—this fixed percentage number being none other than Feigenbaum's chaos constant, 4.6692.

Veruschka scheduled the meet at a Denny's near the Moffat Field blimp port. Veruschka had an unshakeable conviction that Denny's was a posh place to eat, and the crucial meeting had inspired her to dress to the nines.

"When do they want to have sex with us?" Veruschka fretted, paging through her laminated menu.

"Why would they want to do that?" said Janna.

"Because they are fat capitalist moguls from the West, and we are innocent young women. Evil old men with such fame and money, what else can they want of us? They will scheme to remove our clothing!"

"Well, look, Tug Mesoglea is gay." Janna looked at her friend with concern. Veruschka hadn't been sleeping properly. Stuck on the local grind of junk food and eighty-hour weeks, Veruschka's femme-fatale figure was succumbing to Valley hacker desk-spread. The poor thing barely fit in her designer knockoffs. It would be catty to cast cold water on her seduction fantasies, but really, Veruschka was swiftly becoming a kerchiefed babushka with a string-bag, the outermost shell of some cheap nest of Russian dolls.

Veruschka picked up her Pumpti, just now covered in baroque scrolls like a *fin-de-siècle* picture frame. "Do like this," she chirped, brushing the plump pet against her fluffy marten-fur hat. The Pumpti changed its surface texture to give an impression of hairiness and hopped onto the crown.

"Lovely," said Veruschka, smiling into her hand mirror. But her glossy smile was tremulous.

"We simply must believe in our product," said Veruschka, pep-talking to her own mirror. She glanced up wide-eyed at Janna. "Our product is so good a fit for their core business, no? Please tell me more about them, about this Dr. Tug and Mr. Revel. Tell me the very worst. These gray-haired, lecherous fat-cats, they are world-weary and cynical! Success has corrupted them and narrowed their thinking! They no longer imagine a brighter future, they merely go through the rote. Can they be trusted with our dreams?"

Janna tugged fitfully at the floppy tie she'd donned to match her dress-for-success suit. She always felt overwhelmed by Veruschka's fits of self-serving corn. "It's a biz meeting, Vero. Try to relax."

Just as the waitress brought them some food, the glass door of the Denny's yawned open with a ring and a squeak. A seamy, gray-haired veteran with the battered look of a broncobuster approached their table with a bowlegged scuff.

"I'm Hoss Jenks, head o' security for Ctenophore." Jenks hauled out a debugging wand and a magnetometer. He then swept his tools with care over the pair of them. The wand began beeping in frenzy.

"Lemme hold on to your piece for you, ma'am," Jenks suggested placidly.

"It's just a sweet little one," Veruschka demurred, handing over a pistol.

Tug Mesoglea tripped in moments later, sunburned and querulous. The mathematician sported a lavender dress shirt and peach-colored ascot, combined with pleated khaki trail shorts and worn-out piezoplastic Gripper sandals.

Revel Pullen followed, wearing a black linen business

suit, snakeskin boots, and a Stetson. Janna could tell there was a bald pate under that high hat. Jenks faded into a nearby booth, where he could shadow his employers and watch the door.

Mesoglea creaked into the plastic seat beside Veruschka and poured himself a coffee. "I phoned in my order from the limo. Where's my low-fat soy protein?"

"Here you go, then," said Janna, eagerly shoving him a heaped plate of pseudo-meat.

Pullen stared as Mesoglea tucked in, then fastidiously lit a smokeless cigarette. "I don't know how the hell this man eats the food in a sorry-ass chain store."

"I believe in my investments," Mesoglea said, munching. "You see, ladies, this soy protein derives from a patented Ctenophore process." He prodded at Veruschka's plate. "Did you notice that lifelike, organic individuality of your waffle product? That's no accident, darling."

"Did we make any real foldin' money off that crap?" said Revel Pullen.

"Of course we did! You remember all those sintered floating gel rafts in the giant tofu tanks in Chiba?" Mesoglea flicked a blob of molten butter from his ascot.

"Y'all don't pay no never mind to Dr. Mesoglea here," Revel counter-advised. "Today's economy is all about diversity. Proactive investments. Buying into the next technical wave, before you get cannibalized." Revel leered. "Now as for me, I get my finger into every techno-pie!" His lipless mouth was like a letter-slot, bent slightly upward at the corners to simulate a grin.

"Let me brief you gentlemen on our business model," said Janna warily. "It's much like your famous Goob dolls, but the hook here is that the Pumpti is made of the user's very own DNA. This leads to certain, uh, powerful consumer bonding effects and . . ."

"Oh good, let's see your Pumptis, girls," crooned Tug, with a decadent giggle. "Whip out your Pumptis for us."

"You've never seen our product?" asked Janna.

"Tug's got a mess of 'em," said Revel. "But y'all never shipped to Texas. That's another thing I just don't get." Pullen produced a sheaf of printout and put on his bifocals. "According to these due-diligence filings, Magic Pumpkin's projected on-line capacity additions were never remotely capable of meeting the residual in-line demand in the total off-line market that you required for breakeven." He tipped back his Stetson, his liver-spotted forehead wrinkling in disbelief. "How in green tarnation could you gals overlook that? How is that even possible?"

"Huh?" said Janna.

Revel chuckled. "Okay, now I get it. Tug, these little gals don't know how to do business. They've never been anywhere near one."

"Sure looks that way," Tug admitted. "No MBAs, no accountants? Nobody doing cost control? No speakers-to-animals in the hacker staff? I'd be pegging your background as entry-level computational genomics," he said, pointing at Janna. Then he waggled his finger at Veruschka, "And you'd be coming from—Slavic mythology and emotional blackmail?"

Veruschka's limpid eyes went hard and blue. "I don't think I want to show you men my Pumpti."

"We kind of have to show our Pumptis, don't we?" said Janna, an edge in her voice. "I mean, we're trying to make a deal here."

"Don't get all balky on the bailout men," added Revel, choking back a yawn of disdain. He tapped a napkin to his wrinkled lips, with a glint of diamond solitaire. He glanced at his Rolex, reached into his coat pocket, and took out a little pill. "That's for high blood pressure, and I got it the hard way, out kickin' ass in the market. I got a flight back to Texas in less than two hours. So let's talk killer app, why don't we? Your toy pitch is dead in the water. But Tug says your science is unique. So the question is: where's the turnaround?"

"They're getting much prettier," Janna said, swiftly hating herself.

"Do y'all think Pumptis might have an app in home security?"

Janna brightened. "The home market?"

"Yeah, that's right, Strategic Defense for the Home." Pullen outlined his scheme. Ever the bottom-feeder, he'd bought up most of the patents to the never-completed American missile defense system. Pullen had a long-cherished notion of retrofitting the Star Wars shield into a consumer application for troubled neighborhoods. He had a hunch that Pumptis might meet the need.

Revel's proposal was that a sufficiently tough-minded, practical Pumpti could take a round to the guts, fall to earth, crawl back to its vat in the basement, and come back hungry for more. So if bullets were fired at a private home from some drug-crazed drive-by, then a rubbery unit of the client's Pumpti Star Wars shield would instantly fling itself into the way.

Veruschka batted her eyes at Pullen. "I love to hear a strong man talk about security."

"Security always soars along with unemployment," said Pullen, nodding his head at his own wisdom. "We're in a major downturn. I seen this before, so I know the drill. Locks, bolts, Dobermans, they're all market leaders this quarter. That's Capitalism 301, girls."

"And you, Ctenephore, you would finance Magic Pumpkin as a home-defense industry?" probed Veruschka.

"Maybe," said Pullen, his sunken eyes sly. "We'd surely supply you a Washington lobbyist. New public relations. Zoning clearances. Help you write up a genuine budget for once. And of course, if we're on board, then y'all will have to dump all your crappy equipment and become a hunnert-percent Ctenephore shop, technologically. Ctenephore sequencers, PCRs, and bioinformatic software. That's strictly for your own safety, you understand: stringent quality assurance, functional testing and all."

"Uhm, yeah," nodded Tug. "We'd get all your intellectual property copyrighted and patented straight with the World Intellectual Property Organization. The lawyer fees, we'll take care of that. Ctenephore is downright legendary for our quick response times to a market opportunity."

"We gonna help you youngsters catch the fish," said Pullen smugly. "Not just give you a damn fish. What'd be the fun in that? Self-reliance, girls. We wanna see your little outfit get up and walk, under our umbrella. You sign over your founder's stock, put in your orders for our equipment—and we ain't gonna bill for six months—then my men will start to shake the money tree."

"Wait, they still haven't shown us their Pumptis," said Tug, increasingly peevish. "And, Revel, you need to choke it back to a dull roar with those Star Wars lawn jockeys. Because I can grok ballistic physics, dude, and that crap never flies." Tug muffled a body sound with his napkin. "I ate too many waffles."

Janna felt like flipping the table over into their laps. Veruschka shot her a quick, understanding glance and laid a calming hand on her shoulder. Veruschka played a deep game.

Veruschka plucked the Pumpti from her furry hat and set it on the table.

Tug did a double take and leaned forward, transfixed.

Veruschka segued into her cuddly mode. "Pumpti was created in a very special lab in Petersburg. In the top floor of old Moskfilm complex, where my friends make prehistoric amber jewelry. You can see the lovely River Neva while you hunt for dinosaur gnats—"

As she put the squeeze on their would-be sponsors, Veruschka compulsively massaged her Pumpti. She was working it, really getting into it finger and thumb, until suddenly a foul little clot of nonworking protein suddenly gave way inside, like popping bubble pack.

"Stop it, Vero," said Janna.

Tug daintily averted his gaze as Veruschka sucked goo from her fingers.

"Look at mine," offered Janna. She'd programmed her Pumpti to look rubbery and sleek, like a top-end basketball shoe.

"Hey, any normal kid would kill to have one of those," said Revel cheerily. "I'm getting me another product brainstorm! It's risin' in me like a thunderhead across Tornado Alley!"

"The junk DNA is the critical aspect," put in Tug, forestalling another windy bout of Revel's visions. "Those are traces of early prehuman genomics. If we can really express those primordial codons, we might—"

"Those globbies suck the DNA right off people's fingers, right?" demanded Revel.

"Well, yes," said Janna.

"Great! So that's my Plan B. Currency! You smash 'em out flat and color 'em pretty. As they daisy-chain from hand to hand, they record the DNA of every user. Combine those with criminal DNA files, and you got terrorist-proof cash!"

"But the mafiya always wears gloves," said Veruschka.

"No problem, just turn up the amps," said Pullen. "Have 'em suck DNA fragments out of the dang air." He wiggled his lower jaw to simulate deep thought. "Those little East European currencies, they're not real cash money anyways! That user base won't even know the difference!"

Mesoglea blinked owlishly. "Bear with us, ladies. Revel's always like this right after he takes his medicine."

"Now, Tug, we gotta confront the commercial possibilities! You and I, we could hit the lab and make some kind of money that only works for white males over fifty. If anybody else tries to pass it, it just, like—bites their dang hands off!" Pullen chuckled richly, then had another drag off his cig. "Or how about a hunnert-dollar bill that takes your DNA and grows your own face on the front!"

Mesoglea sighed, looked at his watch, and shook it theatrically.

"But this is such pure genius!" gushed Veruschka, leaning toward Revel with moistening eyes. "We need your veteran skills. Magic Pumpkin needs grown men in the boardroom. We wasted our money on incompetent artists and profiteers! We had great conceptual breakthroughs, but—"

"Can it with the waterworks and cut to the chase, ptista," said Pullen. "It's high time for you amateurs to hand over."

"Make us the offer," said Janna.

"Okay, cards on the table," said Pullen, fixing her with his hard little eyes. "You'll sign all your founder's stock over to us. I'll take your stock, chica, and Tug'll take your pretty

Russian friend's. That'll give us controlling interest. As for your dad's third, he might as well keep it since he's too maverick to deal with. Dad's in clover. Okay?"

"Where's the cash?" said Janna. "I don't believe this. The Pumpti was our original idea!"

"You sign on with us, you get a nice salary," said Pullen. Then he broke into such cackles that he had to sip ice water and dab at his eyes with a kerchief.

"You two kids really are better off with a salary," added Tug in a kindly tone. "It won't be anything huge, but better than your last so-called jobs. We already checked into your histories. You'll get some nice vague titles, too. That'll be good experience for your next job or, who knows, your next start-up."

"The sexy Russki can be my Pumpti Project Manager," said Pullen. "She can fly down to my ranch tomorrow. I'll be waitin'. And what about the other one, Tug? She's more the techie type."

"Yes, yes, I want Janna," said Tug, beaming. "Executive Assistant to the Chief Scientist."

Janna and Veruschka exchanged unhappy glances.

"How—how big of a salary?" asked Janna, hating herself.

After the fabled entrepreneurs departed the Denny's in the company of a watchful Hoss Jenks, Veruschka dropped her glued-on smile and scrambled for the kitchen. She was just in time to save the abandoned forks before they hit the soapy water.

Shoving a busboy aside, Veruschka wrapped the DNA-soiled trophies in a sheet of newspaper and stuffed them into her purse.

"Veruschka, what do you think you're doing?"

"I'm multiplying our future options. I am seizing the future imperfectly. Visualize, realize, actualize," Veruschka recited, her lower lip trembling. "Leap, and the Net will appear."

Stuck in the clattering kitchen of Denny's, feeling sordid and sold-out, Janna felt a moment of true sorrow for herself, for Vero, and even for the Latin and Vietnamese busboys. Poor immigrant Veruschka, stuck in some foreign country, with an alien language—she'd seen her grandest dreams seized, twisted up, and crushed by America, and now, in her valiant struggle to rise from ash heap to princess, she'd signed on to be Pullen's marketeer droid. As for Janna— she'd be little more than a lab assistant.

At least the business was still alive. Magic Pumpkin was still a market player. Even if it wasn't her business anymore.

When they returned to their San Francisco lair, they discovered that Hoss Jenks had arrived with a limo full of men in black suits and mirrorshades. They had seized the company's computers and fired everyone. To make things worse, Jenks had called the police and put an APB out for Kelso, who had last been seen departing down a back alley with a cardboard box stuffed with the company's petty cash.

"I can't believe that horrible old cowboy called the cops on Kelso," Janna mourned, sitting down in the firm's very last cool, swoopy Blobular Concepts chair. "I'm glad Kelso stole that money, since it's not ours anymore. I hope he'll turn up again. I never even got to make out with him."

"He's gay, you know."

"Look, Kelso is *not gay*," yelled Janna. "He is so totally not gay. There's a definite chemistry between us. We were just too incredibly busy, that's all."

Veruschka sniffed and said nothing. When Janna looked up, her eyes brimming, she realized that Veruschka was actually feeling sorry for her. This was finally it for Janna; it was too much for flesh and blood to bear; she bent double in her designer chair, racked with sobs.

"Janna, my dear, don't surrender to your grief. I know things look dark now, but the business cycle, always, it turns around. And California is the Golden State."

"No it isn't. We've got a market bear stitched right on our flag. We're totally doomed, Veruschka! We've been such fools!"

"I hate those two old men," said Veruschka, after the two of them had exhausted half a box of Kleenex. "They're worse than their reputations. I expected them to be crazy, but not so—greedy and rude."

"Well, we signed all their legal papers. It's a little late to fuss now."

Veruschka let out a low, dark chuckle. "Janna, I want revenge."

Janna looked up. "Tell me."

"It's very high-tech and dangerous."

"Yeah?"

"It's completely illegal, or it would be, if any court had the chance to interpret the law in such a matter."

"Spill it, Vero."

"Pumpti Gene Therapy."

Janna felt a twinge, as of seasickness. "That's a no-no, Vero."

"Tell me something," said Veruschka. "If you dose a man with an infectious genomic mutagen, how do you keep him from knowing he's been compromised?"

"You're talking bioterrorism, Vero. They'd chase us to the ends of the earth in a rain of cruise missiles."

"You use a Pumpti virus based on your victim's own DNA," said Veruschka, deftly answering her own rhetorical question. "Because nobody has an immune response to their own DNA. No matter how—how very strange it might be making their body."

"But you're weaponizing the human genome! Can't we just shoot them?"

Veruschka's voice grew soft and low. "Imagine Tug Mesoglea at his desk. He feels uneasy, he begins to complain, his voice is like a rasping locust's. And then his eyeballs—his eyeballs pop out onto his cheeks, driven from his head by the pressure of his bursting brain!"

"You call that gene therapy?"

"They need it! The shriveled brains of Pullen and Mesoglea are old and stiff! There is plenty of room for new growth in their rattling skulls. You and I, we create the Pumpti Therapy for them. And then they will give us money." Veruschka twirled on one heel and laughed. "We make Pumptis so tiny like a virus! Naked DNA with Universal Ribosome and a nine-plus-two microtubule apparatus to rupture the host's cell walls! One strain for Pullen, and one for Mesoglea. The Therapy is making them smarter, so they are grateful to shower money upon us. Or else"—her eyes narrowed—"the Therapy is having some unpleasant effects and they are begging on their knees to purchase an antidote."

"So it's insanity and/or blackmail, in other words."

"These men are rotten bastards," said Veruschka.

"Look, why don't we give a fighting chance to the home defense Pumptis?" asked Janna. "Or the money Pumptis?

They're nutty ideas but not all that much crazier than your original scheme about pets. Didn't I hear you call Revel Pullen a marketing genius?"

"Don't you know me yet even a little bit?" said Veruschka, her face frank and open. "Revel's ideas for my Pumptis were like using a beautiful sculpture for a hammer. Or like using a silk scarf to pick up dog doo."

Janna sighed. "Too, too true. Get the forks out of your purse and let's start on those nanoPumptis."

To begin with, they grew some ordinary kilogram-plus Pumptis from Revel and Tug's fork-scrapings, each in its own little vat. Veruschka wanted to be sure they had a whopping big supply of their enemies' DNA.

For fun, Janna added OpenAnimator molecules to shade Revel's Pumpti blue and Tug's red. And then, for weirdness, Vero dumped a new biorhythm accelerator into the vats. The fat lumps began frantically kneading themselves, each of them replicating, garbage-collecting, and decoding their DNA hundreds of times per second. "So perhaps these cavemen can become more highly evolved," remarked Veruschka.

By three in the morning, they'd made their first nanoPumpti. Janna handled the assembly, using the synthesizer's datagloves to control a molecular probe. She took the body of a cold virus and replaced its polyhedral head with a Universal Ribosome and a strand of hyper-evolved DNA from the Pullen Pumpti. And then she made a nanoPumpti for Tug. Veruschka used her hands-on wetware skills to quickly amplify the lone Tug and Revel nanPumptis into respectable populations.

When the first morning sunlight slanted in the lab window it lit up two small stoppered glass vials: a blue one for Revel, a red one for Tug.

Veruschka rooted in the cornucopia of her tattered suitcase. She produced a pair of cheap-looking rings, brass things with little chrome balls on them. "These are Lucrezia Borgia rings. I bought them in a tourist stall before I left St. Petersburg." Practicing with water, Veruschka showed Janna how to siphon up a microliter through the ring's cunningly hidden perforations and how—with the crook of a finger— to make the ring squirt the liquid back out as a fine mist.

"Load your ring with Mesoglea's nanoPumptis," said Veruschka, baring her teeth in a hard grin. "I want see you give Mesoglea his Therapy before my flight to Texas. I'll load my ring for Pullen and when I get down there, I'll take care of him."

"No, no," said Janna, stashing the vials in her purse. "We don't load the rings yet. We have to dose both the guys at the exact same time. Otherwise, the one will know when the other one gets it. They've been hanging together for a long time. They're like symbiotes. How soon are you and Pullen coming back from Texas anyway?"

"He says two weeks," said Veruschka, pulling a face. "I hope it is less time."

And then Hoss Jenks was there with a limo to take Veruschka to the airport. Janna cleaned up the lab and stashed the vials of nanoPumptis in her office. Before she could lie down to sleep there, Tug Mesoglea arrived for his first day of work.

The first day was rough, but Tug turned out to be a pleasant man to work for. Not only did he have excellent taste in office carpeting and window treatments, but he was a whiz at industrial R&D. Under his leadership, the science of the Pumptis made great strides: improvements in the mechanism of the Universal Ribosome, in the curious sets of proteins encoded by the junk DNA, even in the looping strangeness of Ruben Gutierrez's genomic OpenAnimator graphics library. And then Tug stumbled onto the fact that the Pumptis could send and receive a certain gigahertz radio frequency. Digital I/O.

"The ascended master of R&D does not shoehorn new science into yesterday's apps," the serenely triumphant Tug told Janna. "The product is showing us what it wants to do. Forget the benighted demands of the brutish consumers: we're called to lead them to the sunlit uplands of improved design!"

So Janna pushed ahead, and under Tug's Socratic questioning, she had her breakthrough: why stop at toys? Once they'd managed to tweak and evolve a new family of forms and functions for the Pumptis, they would no longer be mere amusements but personal tools. Not like Pokemons, not like Goob dolls, but truly high-end devices: soft uvvy phones, health monitors, skin-interfaced VR patches, holistic gene maintenance kits, cosmetic body-modifiers! Every gadget would be utterly trustworthy, being made of nothing but you!

As before, they would all but give away the pretty new Pumptis, but this time they'd have serious weight for the after market: "Pumpti Productivity Philtres" containing the molecular codes for the colors, shapes, and functionalities of a half dozen killer apps. Get 'em all! While they last! New Philtres coming soon!

Veruschka's stay in Texas lasted six weeks. She phoned daily to chat with Janna. The laid-back Texan lifestyle on the legendary Pullen spread was having its own kind of seduction.

Vero gave up her vodka for blue agave tequila. She surrendered her high heels for snakeskin boots. Her phone conversations became laced with native terms such as "darlin' " and "sugar" as she gleefully recounted giant barbecues for politicians, distributors, the Ctenophore management, and the Pullen Drilling Company sales force.

By the time Revel and Veruschka came back to San Francisco, Magic Pumpkin had the burn-rate under firm control and was poised for true market success. But, as wage slaves, Janna and Veruschka would share not one whit of the profit. So far as Janna knew, they were still scheduled to poison their bosses.

"Do we really want to give them the Pumpti Therapy?" Janna murmured to Veruschka. They were in Janna's new living quarters, wonderfully carpentered into the space beneath the bank's high dome. It had proved easier to build an apartment than to rent one. And Tug had been very good about the expenses.

Veruschka had a new suitcase, a classy Texas item clad in dappled calfskin with the hair still on. As usual, her bag had disgorged itself all over the room. "Mesoglea must certainly be liquidated," she said, cocking her head. Tug's voice was drifting up from the lab below, where he was showing Revel around. "He is fatuous, old, careless. He has lost all his creative fire."

"But I like Tug now," said Janna. "He taught me amazing things in the lab. He's smart."

"I hate him," said Veruschka stubbornly. "Tonight he meets the consequences of his junk DNA."

"Well, your Revel Pullen needs Pumpti Therapy even more," said Janna crossly. "He's a corrupt, lunatic bully—cram-full of huckster double-talk he doesn't even listen to himself."

"Revel and I are in harmony on many issues," allowed Veruschka. "I begin almost to like his style."

"Should—should we let them off the hook?" pleaded Janna.

Veruschka gave her a level stare. "Don't weaken. These men stole our company. We must bend them to our will. It is beyond personalities."

Janna sighed, feeling doomed. "Oh, all right. You poison Tug and I'll poison Revel. It'll be easier for us that way."

The four of them were scheduled to go out for a celebratory dinner, this time to Popo's, a chichi high-end gourmet establishment of Tug's choosing. Pullen's voice could now be heard echoing up from the lab, loudly wondering what was "keeping the heifers." Janna swept downstairs to distract the men while Veruschka loaded her ring. Then Veruschka held the floor while Janna went back up to her room to ready her own ring.

The two little vials of nanoPumpti sat in plain sight amid the clutter of the women's cosmetics. They could have been perfume bottles, one red, one blue.

As Janna prepared to fill her Borgia ring, she was struck by a wild inspiration. She'd treat Revel Pullen with Tug's Pumptized DNA. Yes! This would civilize the semi-human Pullen, making him be more like Tug—instead of, horrors, even more like himself! There might be certain allergic effects—but the result for the Magic Pumpkin company would be hugely positive. To hell with the risk. No doubt the wretched Pullen would be happy with the change.

It went almost too easily. The old men guzzled enough wine with dinner to become loose and reckless. When the cappuccinos arrived, Janna and Veruschka each found a reason to reach out toward their prey. Veruschka adjusted

* 207 *

Pullen's string tie. Janna dabbed a stain of prawn sauce from Tug's salmon-colored lapel. Then each woman gently misted the contents of her ring onto the chocolate-dusted foam of her victim's coffee. And the old men, heavy-lidded with booze and digestion, took their medicines without a peep.

Soon after, Pullen retired to his hotel room, Tug caught a cab back to his house in the Haight, and the two women walked the few blocks back to the Magic Pumpkin head-quarters, giggling with relief. Janna didn't tell Veruschka about having given Pullen the red Tug Treatment. Better to wait and see how things worked out. Better to sleep on it.

But sleep was slow in coming. Suppose Pullen swelled up horribly and died from toxic Tug effects? The Feds would find the alien DNA in him, and the law would be on Janna right away. And what if the Therapies really did improve the two old men? Risen to some cold, inhuman level of intelligence, they'd think nothing of wiping out Janna and Veruschka like ants.

Janna rubbed her cellphone nervously. Maybe she could give poor old Tug some kind of anonymous warning. But she sensed that Veruschka was still awake, over on the other side of Janna's California King bed.

Suddenly the phone rang. It was Kelso.

"Yo babe," he said airily. "I'm fresh back from sunny Mexico. The heat's off. I bought myself a new identity and an honest-to-God law license. I'm right outside, Janna. Saw you and Vero go jammin' by on Market Street just now, but I didn't want to come pushing up at you like some desperado tweaker. Let me in. Nice new logo you got on the Magic Pumpkin digs, by the way, good font choice, too."

"You're a lawyer now? Well, don't think we've forgotten about that box of petty cash, you sleaze."

Kelso chuckled. "I didn't forget you either, *mi vida!* As for that money—hey, my new ID cost as much as what I took. Paradoxical, no? Here's another mind-bender: even though we're hot for each other, you and me have never done the deed."

"I'm not alone," said Janna. "Veruschka's staying with me."

"For God's sake will you two at last get it over?" said Veruschka, sleepily burying her head under her pillow. "Wake me up when you're done and maybe the three of us can talk business. We'll need a lawyer tomorrow."

The next morning Tug Mesoglea arrived at Magic Pumpkin and started acting—like Revel Pullen.

"Git along little dogies," he crooned, leaning over the incubator where they were keeping their dozen or so new-model Pumptis. And then he reached over and fondled Janna's butt.

Janna raced out of the lab and cornered Veruschka, who was noodling around at her desk trying to look innocent. "You gave Tug the Pullen potion, didn't you? Bitch!"

Before Veruschka could answer, the front door swung open, and in sashayed Pullen. He was dressed, unbelievably, in a caftan and striped Capri pants. "I picked these up in the hotel shop," he said, looking down at one of his spindly shanks. "Do you think it works on me, Janna? I've always admired your fashion sense."

"Double bitch!" cried Veruschka, yanking at Janna's hair. Janna grabbed back, knocking off the red cowboy hat that Vero was sporting today.

"Don't think we haven't already seen clear through your little game," said the altered Pullen with a toss of his head.

"You and your nanoPumptis. Tug and I had a long heart-to-heart talk on the phone this morning. Except we didn't use no phone. We can hear each other in our heads."

"Shit howdy!" called Tug from the lab. "Brother Revel's here. Ready to take it to the next level?"

"Lemme clear out the help," said Revel. He leaned into the guard-room and sent Hoss Jenks and his mirrorshades assistants out for a long walk. To Jenks's credit, he didn't bat an eye at Revel's new look.

"Let's not even worry about that Kelso boy up in Janna's room," said Tug. "He's still asleep." Tug gave Janna an arch look. "Don't look so surprised, we know everything. Thanks to the Pumpti Therapy you gave us. We've got, oh, a couple of million years of evolution on you now. The future of the race, that's us. Telepathy, telekinesis, teleportation, and shape-shifting, too."

"You're—you're not mad at us?" said Janna.

"We only gave the Therapy to make you better," begged Veruschka. "Don't punish us."

"I dunno about that," said Revel. "But I do know I got a powerful hankerin' for some Pumpti meat. Can you smell that stuff?"

"Sure can," sang Tug. "Intoxicating, isn't it? What a seductive perfume!"

Without another word, the two men headed for the lab's vats and incubators. Peeping warily through the open lab doors, Janna and Veruschka saw a blur of activity. The two old men were methodically devouring the stock, gobbling every Pumpti in sight.

There was no way that merely human stomachs could contain all that mass, but that wasn't slowing them down much. Their bodies were puffing up and—just as Veruschka had predicted, the eyeballs were bulging forward out of their heads. Their clothes split and dropped away from their expanding girths. When all the existing Pumptis were gone, the two giants set eagerly to work on the raw materials. And when Tug found the frozen kilograms of their own personal Pumptis, the fireworks really began.

The two great mouths chewed up the red and blue Pumpti meat, spitting, drooling, and passing the globs back and forth. Odd ripples began moving up and down along their bodies like ghost images of ancient flesh.

"What's that a-comin' out of your rib cage, Tuggie?" crowed Revel.

"Cootchy-coo," laughed Tug, twiddling the tendrils protruding from his side. "I'm expressing a jellyfish. My personal best. Feel around in your genome, Revel. It's all there, every species, evolved from our junk DNA right along with our super duper futuristic new bodies." He paused, watching. "Now you're keyin' it, bro. I say—are those hooves on your shoulder?"

Revel palpated the twitching growth with professional care. "I'd be reckoning that's a quagga. A prehistoric zebra-type thing. And, whoa, Nellie, see this over on my other shoulder? It's an eohippus. Ancestor of the horse. The cowboys of the Pullen clan got a long relationship with horse-flesh. I reckon there was some genetic bleedover when we was punchin' cattle up the Goodnight-Loving Trail; that's why growin' these ponies comes so natural to me."

"How do you like it now, ladies?" asked Tug, glancing over toward Janna and Veruschka.

"Ask them," hissed Veruschka in Janna's ear.

"No you," whispered Janna.

Brave Vero spoke up. "My friend is wondering now if you will sign those Magic Pumpkin founder's shares back over to us? And the patents as well, if you please."

"Groink," said Revel, hunching himself over and deforming his mouth into a dinosaur-type jaw.

"Squonk," said Tug, letting his head split into a floppy bouquet of be-suckered tentacles.

"You don't need to own our business anymore," cried Janna. "Please sign it back to us."

The distorted old men whooped and embraced each other, their flesh fusing into one. The meaty mass seethed with possibilities, bubbled with the full repertoire of zoological forms—with feelers, claws, wings, antennae, snouts; with eyes of every shape and color winking on and off; with fleeting mouths that lingered only long enough to bleat, to hiss, to grumble, to whinny, screech, and roar. It wasn't exactly a "no" answer.

"Kelso," shouted Janna up the stairs. "Bring the papers!"

A high, singing sound filled the air. The Pullen-Mesoglea mass sank to the floor as if melting, forming itself into a broad, glistening plate. The middle of the plate swelled like yeasty bread to form a swollen dome. The fused organism was taking on the form of—a living UFO?

"The original genetic Space Friend!" said Veruschka in awe. "It's been waiting in their junk DNA since the dawn of time!"

As Kelso clattered down the stairs, the saucer came for the three of them, far too fast to escape. Kelso, Janna, and Veruschka were absorbed into the saucer's ethereal bulk.

Everything got white, and in the whiteness, Janna saw a room, a round space expressing wonderful mathematical proto-design: a vast Vernor Panton 1960s hashish den, languidly and repeatedly melting into a Karim Rashid all-plastic lobby.

The room's primary inhabitants were idealized forms of Tug Mesoglea and Revel Pullen. The men's saucer bodies were joyous, sylphlike forms of godlike beauty.

"I say we spin off the company to these girls and their lawyer," intoned the Tug avatar. "Okay by you, Revel? You and I, we're more than ready to transcend the material plane."

"There's better action where we're going," Revel agreed. "We gotta stake a claim in the subdimensions, before the yokels join the gold rush."

A pen appeared in Tug's glowing hand. "We'll shed the surly bonds of incorporation."

It didn't take them long to sign off every interest in Magic Pumpkin. And then the floor of the saucer opened up, dropping Janna, Veruschka, and Kelso onto the street. Over their awestruck heads, the saucer briefly glowed and then sped away, though not in any direction that a merely human being could specify. It was more as if the saucer shrank. Reorganized itself. Corrected. Downsized. And then it was gone from all earthly ken.

And that's how Janna Gutierrez and Veruschka Zipkin got rich.

★ VIII ★

The Past Is a Future That Already Happened

(History is not a science. One can't experiment with history. But all true futurists are historians. If you are truly interested in how societies change, you will come to understand that the roots of the future are not in the thin and narrow moments of the present. Those roots are sunk deep in the 13.7 billion-year legacy of the past. The future is a kind of history that hasn't happened yet. The future is already here—it's just not well distributed. And the present—it's made out of mulch.)

(I wrote this very brief story for UNESCO, whose task it is to guard humanity's monuments. It was originally published in Italian. It's about the effect of future shock on a historian.)

The Necropolis of Thebes

Father and son rolled together into the valley of death. "This sad neglect and ruin that you see, this is all the fault of those wicked foreigners," said Apepi to his son. His fatherly counsel was almost lost in the squeak and rumble of their wheels. "When I was your age, my boy, this city of death was the center of the world. Then, from blighted regions beyond all decency, came many coarse invaders of obscure lineage. Unfairly possessed of awesome vehicles, they conquered our time-honored land. With wheels and sharp iron arrows they overpowered the gentlemen of the Pharaoh. Thus we were forced to abandon sacred Thebes and eat the bitter bread of Hyksos bondage."

Apepi's son feigned attention, flicking the leather reins.

The boy doted on the family's chariot. He also excelled in commanding horses. When not assisting his father in his work, he spent hours polishing and oiling the vehicle's rigging, yoke, and wheels.

By trade, training, and conviction, Apepi was a master carver of shabti figures. Shabtis were the small, enchanted wooden servitors placed inside the royal tombs of Thebes. In order to properly create these sacred figurines, Apepi had been taught about the useful work of every trade in the land. Without some shabti present in his tomb, a god-king's afterlife would lack vital human services. Apepi therefore knew about the actions, services, rituals, and prayers of courtiers, priests, scribes, boatmen, bakers, butchers, huntsmen, animal tamers, goatherds, brewers, dancing girls, and even wigmakers, barbers, and masseurs.

However, Apepi had never in his working life carved a chariot or a charioteer. Chariots were the creations of the Hyksos. Due to their Hyksos occupation regime, there were now hundreds of new chariots in Egypt. Every Egyptian of substance wanted a chariot, and to be without one was a keenly felt demerit. So even if the evil Hyksos invaders were all killed—and many direly wished this to be so—their chariots would never go away. These innovations were permanent additions to Egypt. This much was clear.

The Necropolis of Thebes sheltered many ancient tombs of Egyptian kings. Not a single tomb contained a shabti chariot or shabti charioteer. The silent, sacred dead in their sarcophagi would therefore be deprived of chariots until the end of time. They would have to walk on foot through the afterlife, even though they were dead gods. Apepi found this an awful, deeply confusing thought.

Apepi gazed morosely at the stricken, stony landscape of the Valley of Thebes. The stark decline of his beloved necropolis tore at his heart. The place of death seemed so silent, empty, and deprived of vitality. Once this valley had been lavishly crowded with eager labor gangs. The peasants had prayed of death, worshipped death, told old-fashioned death stories, and sang glorious funeral songs. The people had such simple, honest faces. It was such a good time.

They were all serfs of course, but they knew their place in the universe. When properly fed on thick barley beer and fine onions, the peasants excelled at the movement of stone. Sun-blackened and naked but for their loincloths, these indomitable men of the soil would find raw chunks of flint, crack them with their hands, mount the sharpened blades on hoe handles, and dig fearlessly straight into the face of the native limestone. They would discover more flint buried within the limestone, and turn those flints into fresh digging tools as well. They would chip, chop, haul, sledge, and burrow, serenely singing, deep into the stony flesh of the Theban earth. During the Nile's flood seasons they left their fields to excavate royal tombs the size of boatyards.

Apepi, as an expert in every facet of Egyptian trade and labor, knew that there was nothing more entirely decent and praiseworthy than this tomb-digging activity. The peasants were eager to fulfill their necropolitan duties. They might seem humble folk, but they and they alone were digging the spectacular posthumous palaces that would shelter Pharaohs through all eternity, godlike and untouchable. If their betters thought to bring them a haunch of gazelle meat or some dancing girls, the laborers felt a gratitude that knew no bounds.

But not anymore.

The Hyksos had no words for such sacred practices. Their alien jabber was stupefying, narrow-minded, and bitterly practical. The Hyksos bluntly dumped their dead into simple holes like dogs. Their dead kings were not rewarded with so much as a single wooden shabti butler or maidservant.

Egypt's docile peasants were of course eager to create the tombs for their new Hyksos overlords. Given one word of encouragement, they would tackle naked rock and create splendid mastabas with lavish colonnades. But all they got from the Hyksos for such offers were beatings and a raise in their taxes.

Apepi sat in the bottom of the chariot as his teenaged son stood and clicked his tongue at the horses. Apepi had never learned to control horses—large, dirty, hay-gobbling beasts—but he could no longer travel on foot. Seeing that Apepi knew so much about the inner workings of the nation, the local Hyksos nomarch, satrap of the Theban demesne, had appointed Apepi as a tax collector. Apepi loathed this tax job. However, when Apepi failed to fill his master's hands with wealth, the Hyksos boss beat Apepi on the soles of his feet with a long iron rod. Apepi pointed out that these cruel injuries made his tax-collection duties impossible. The Hyksos agreed, gave Apepi an official chariot, and then walloped his broken feet twice as hard.

Stimulated by these agonies, Apepi had bent to the tax work and wrung his beloved people dry of their hard-won barley, spelt, dates, and salt. Wigmakers had to use a cheaper, coarser horsehair, and even the dancing girls were often forced to dance until morning. Apepi's fine hands, which had once carved sacred wood and chiselled the holy cartouches, were reduced to scribbling the sordid records of the conqueror's financial exactions. Though his family ate well, Apepi knew that he was hated, and his bold sons were feared.

The Necropolis, spirit of the nation, suffered just as the soul of Egypt did. The funereal gardens had died unwatered. The paint was peeling from the statuary. It was awful to see how bleak and inhuman the dead god-kings looked when their stone was left without proper cosmetics. It was as if these giant rulers of the universe had never been anything but carved rocks.

His son pulled the chariot to a stop. They would walk henceforth, with their sandaled feet wrapped in rags to blur their guilty tracks. None were to know the exigencies to which Apepi had been forced by Hyksos tyranny.

"Our fathers built for their kings deep houses adorned with gold," Apepi quoted, as he trudged, each step a wince. "Their ceiling were of lapis lazuli, their walls of silver, the doors of copper, and the door bolts of bronze. We built them for eternity, and we prepared them for the everlasting."

The two of them prepared to further plunder the looted tomb. Having offended everyone living, Apepi knew that there was no one left to tax but the dead. The tomb's gold adornments had been the first to go. The walls of silver had slowly been stripped, year by year. Apepi and his son were now working to remove the door bolts of valuable bronze. They were saving the lapis lazuli for the sake of the grandchildren.

Stripped of its precious metal casings, the dessicated mummy lay on an impromptu bed of rushes. "It's a terrible sin we are committing, my son. No gesture of atonement can be deep enough for this."

"Yeah, dad, sure."

"This was a god-king. He made the whole land open to our oxen. The great and the small alike rejoiced in Him. Men cheered at His coming! He shone, and all the river lands exulted. Every belly was rich with joy, every creature was nourished, and every human jaw was given food. The skull wrapped within those dark bandages—it once spoke to me with its own lips."

The boy sighed as he filled a linen bag in the flickering torchlight. "Dad, a dead king can't hit your feet with an iron stick."

They had turned the place upside down, hunting gold. Only the wooden shabti remained undisturbed and loyal. There was no need or reason to rob the Pharaoh of their sacred services. The small army of wooden servitors stood in ranks in their torch light. They stood were just as Apepi had created them: sailors, dancing maidens, royal butlers, and accountants. The Hyksos put no value on shabti—they considered them mere "dolls," unfit even for children.

So the mummy was still served by a loyal and useful people. The rest, the metal and the precious goods, that was mere dross.

"I can carve Him a chariot, father. I've been practicing. I know a lot about chariots. I'll do it for Him after you are dead."

Apepi nodded. Then he opened his own linen bag. He placed a new wooden figure among the silent, dusty crowd.

Within all the tombs of Egypt, there had never been a shabti model for a man who made the shabti. He was the artist of all, yet he remained invisible. Now the wooden maker sat among his own creations, one among many, forever alert, crosslegged and staring-eyed, a tiny wooden block and gleaming copper chisel in his hands.

Apepi had given himself the same calm gaze as all his other figurines. All the little faces, lost in endless blackness deep within the Theban stone, were pure, and eager to serve, and without reproach.

(This story is about encountering aliens. Everyone is alien to someone. And the past is alien to all of us.)

The Blemmye's Stratagem

A messenger flew above the alleys of Tyre, skirting the torn green heads of the tallest palm trees. With a flutter of wings, it settled high on a stony ledge. The pigeon was quickly seized by a maiden within the tower. She gratefully kissed the bird's sleek gray head.

Sir Roger of Edessa, the maiden's lover, roamed the Holy Land on his knight errantry. Thanks to the maiden herself, Sir Roger possessed one precious cage of homing pigeons. Roger's words winged it to her, straight to her tender hands, soaring over every obstacle in a Holy Land aflame. The birds flapped over drum-pounding, horn-blaring Seljuk marauders and evil mamelukes with faces masked in chainmail. They flitted over Ismaili fedayeen bent on murder and utterly careless of life.

An entire, busy network of messenger pigeons moved over the unknowing populace. These birds carried news through Jerusalem, Damascus, Cairo, and Beirut. They flitted over cavaliers from every cranny of Christendom, armed pilgrims who were starving, sweating, flea-bitten, and consumed with poxes. Birds laden with script flew over sun-burned, ax-wielding Vikings. Over fanatical Templars and cruel, black-clad Teutonic Knights, baking like armored lob-sters in the blazing sun. Over a scum of Greek peltasts and a scrim of Italian condottiere.

With trembling, ink-stained fingers, the maiden untied the tidy scroll from the bird's pink leg. There was a pounding ache within her bosom. Would it be another poem? She often swooned on reading Roger's poems.

No. This bird had not come from Roger of Edessa. She had been cruelly misled by her own false hopes. The mes-senger bird was just another tiresome commercial bird. It carried nothing but a sordid rush of text.

Salt. Ivory. Tortoiseshell. Saffron. Rice. Frankincense. Iron. Copper. Tin. Lead. Coral. Topaz. Storax. Glass. Realgar. Anti-mony. Gold. Silver. Honey. Spikenard. Costus. Agate. Car-nelian. Lycium. Cotton. Silk. Mallow. Pepper. Malabathrum. Pearls. Diamonds. Rubies. Sapphires.

Every good in this extensive list was followed by its price.

The girl locked the pigeon into its labeled wooden cage, along with dozens of other birds, her fellow captives within the gloomy tower. Using cuttlefish ink and a razor-trimmed feather, the girl copied the message into an enormous dusty ledger. If she ever failed in her duty to record, oh the woe she would receive at the hands of the Mother Superior. Bread and water. Endless kneeling, many rosaries.

The pigeon clerk rubbed at her watery eyes, harshly afflicted by fine print and bad lighting. She returned to lean her silken elbows on the cool, freckled stone, to contemplate the sparkling Mediterranean and a black swarm of profiteering Italian galleys. Perhaps Sir Roger of Edessa was dead. Poor Roger had been slain by a cruel Muslim champion, or else he was dead of some plague. Roger would never write a poem to her again. At the age of seventeen, she was abandoned to her desolate fate.

How likely all this seemed. Her doom was so total and utter. If Roger failed to rescue her from this miserable life tending pigeons, she would be forced to take unwelcome vows.

She would have to join the Little Sisters of the Hospitallers below the tower of birds, in that ever-swelling crowd of the Holy Land's black widows, another loveless wretch of a girl amid that pitiful host of husbandless crones and fatherless orphans, all of them bottled up behind tall, rocky walls, hopelessly trapped without any lands or dowries. The pale brides of Christ, moody and distracted, waiting in itchy torment for some fatal pagan horde of dark-eyed Muslim fiends to conquer Tyre and ravage their fortress of chastity.

Another bird appeared in flight. The maiden's heart rose to beat in her throat. This was a strong bird, a swift one. When he arrived, his legs were clasped by two delicate bands of gold. His feathers smelled of incense.

The writing, though very tiny, was the most beautiful the girl had ever seen. The ink was blood-red, and it glittered.

DEAREST HUDEGAR

With the tip of my brush I give you the honey of good news

Our Silent Master has summoned us both

So prepare yourself quickly

For I hasten to you with a caravan of many strong men to take you to his Paradise

    (signed) THE OLD MAN OF THE MOUNTAIN

The maiden began to weep, for her name was not Hudegar. She had never heard of any woman named Hudegar.

Whether Christian or Muslim, hamlets in the Holy Land were always much the same: a huddle of dusty cottages around a well, a mill, and an oven. The Abbess Hildegart rode demurely into the plundered village, escorted by the heavily armed caravan of the Grand Assassin.

This hapless little village had been crushed with particular gusto. Vengeful marauders had hacked down the olive groves, set fire to the vineyard, and poisoned the well. Since they were still close to Tyre, the strongest city yet held by the reeling Crusader forces, Hildegart rather suspected the work of Hospitallers.

This conclusion disturbed her. Hildegart herself had founded the Hospitaller Order. She had created and financed a hospital corps in order to heal the sick, to run a chain of inns, and to give peace, comfort, and money-changing services to the endless sun-dazed hordes of holy European pilgrims.

Hildegart's idea had been a clever one, and was much appreciated by her patron, the Silent Master. However, some seventy years had passed since this invention of hers, and Hildegart had been forced to see her brilliant scheme degenerating. Somehow the Hospitaller corps, this kindly order of medical monks, had transformed itself into the most violent, fanatical soldiery in the Crusader forces. It seemed that their skills in healing injured flesh and bone also gave them a special advantage in chopping men apart. Even the Templars were scared of the Hospitallers, and the Templars frightened Assassins so badly that the Assassins often paid them for protection.

Some of the barns in the smashed village were still defensible. Sinan, the Old Man of the Mountain and the Ayatollah of Assassins, ordered his caravan to put up for the night. The caravan men made camp, buried several abandoned corpses, set up sentries, and struggled to water the horses with the tainted murk from the well.

The Abbess and the Assassin settled down to eat and chat behind their armed sentries. Hildegart and Sinan had known each other for much longer than most people would ever live. Despite the fact that they both labored loyally for the Silent Master, their personal relations were rather strained. There had been times in her long, long life when Hildegart had felt rather safe and happy with Sinan. Sinan was an ageless Muslim wizard and therefore evil incarnate, but Sinan had once sheltered her from men even more dangerous than himself.

Those pleasant years of their history, unfortunately, were long behind both of them. At the age of one hundred seventeen, Sinan could not possibly protect Hildegart from any man more dangerous than himself, for Sinan the Assassin had become the most dangerous man in the world. The number of Crusaders who had fallen to his depredations

was beyond all reckoning, though Hildegart shrewdly esti-
mated it at somewhere over four thousand.

Underlit by red flames from his dainty iron camp stove,
Sinan ate his roasted kabobs and said little. He offered her
a warm, dark, gazelle-eyed look. Hildegart stirred uneasily
in her dark riding cloak, hood, and wimple. Although Sinan
was very intelligent and had learned a great deal about
inflicting terror, Sinan's heart never changed much with the
passing decades. He was always the same. Sinan was
simple, direct, and devout in his habits, and he prayed five
times every day, which (by Hildegart's reckoning) would
likely make some two hundred thousand acts of prayer,
every one of them involving a fervent hope that Crusaders
would perish and burn in Hell.

Hildegart warmed one chilly hand at the iron brazier.
Nearby, the homing pigeons cooed in their portable cribs.
The poor pigeons were cold and unhappy, even more anx-
ious to return to Tyre than she was. Perhaps they sensed that
Sinan's mercenaries longed to pluck and eat them.

"Sinan, where did you find this horrible band of cut-
throats?"

"I bought them for us, my dear," Sinan told her politely.
"These men are Khwarizmian Turks from the mountains far
beyond Samarkand. They are quite lost here in Palestine,
without any land or loyalties. Therefore they are of use to
me, and to our Silent Master, and to his purposes."

"Do you trust these bandy-legged fiends?"

"No, I don't trust them at all. But they speak only an
obscure dialect, and unlike you and me, they are not People of
the Book. So they cannot ever reveal what they may see of our
Silent Master. Besides, the Khwarizmian Turks were cheap to

purchase. They flee a great terror, you see. They flee the Great Khan of the Mongols."

Hildegart considered these gnomic remarks. Sinan wasn't lying. Sinan never lied to her; he was just grotesquely persistent in his pagan delusions. "Sinan, do I need to know more about this terrible Great Khan?"

"Better not to contemplate such things, my pearl of wisdom. Let's play a game of chess."

"Not this time, no."

"Why be coy? I'll spot you an elephant rook!"

"My markets for Chinese silk have been very disturbed these past ten years. Is this so-called Great Khan the source of my commercial difficulty?"

Sinan munched thoughtfully at his skewer of peppered mutton. Her remarks had irritated him. Brave men killed and died at Sinan's word, and yet she, Hildegart, was far richer than he was. Hildegart was the richest woman in the world. As the founder, accountant, banker, and chief moneylender of the Hospitaller order, Hildegart found her greatest joy in life managing international markets. She placed her money into goods and cities where it would create more money, and then she counted that money with great and precise care, and she placed it again. Hildegart had been doing this for decades, persistently and secretly, through a network of nameless agents in cities from Spain to India, a network linked by swift birds and entirely unsuspected by mankind.

Sinan knew how all this counting and placing of money was done, but as an Ayatollah of Assassins, he considered it boring and ignoble labor. That was why he was always sending her messenger birds and begging her for loans of cash.

"Dear, kind, sweet Hudegar," the Assassin said coaxingly. Hildegart blushed. "No one calls me Hudegar. Except for you, they all died ages ago."

"Dear Hudegar, how could I ever forget my sweet pet name for you?"

"That was a slave girl's name."

"We're all the slaves of God, my precious! Even our Silent Master." Sinan yanked the metal skewer from his strong white teeth. "Are you too proud to obey his summons now, blessed Mother Superior? Are you tired of your long life, now that your Christian Franks are finally chased back into the sea by the warriors of righteousness?"

"I'm here with you, aren't I?" said Hildegart, avoiding his eyes. "I could be tending the wounded and doing my accounts. Why did you write to me in French? The whole convent's chattering about your mysterious bird and its message. You know how women talk when they've been cloistered."

"You never answer me when I write to you in Arabic," Sinan complained. He mopped at his fine black beard with a square of pink silk. "I write to you constantly! You know the cost of shipping these homing pigeons! Their flesh is more precious than amber!" The Assassin waved away the thickening smoke from the coals of his cookstove.

Hildegart lit the sesame oil at the spout of a small brass lamp. "I do write to you, dear Sinan, with important financial news, but in return, you write to me of nothing but your evil boasting and your military mayhem."

"I'm composing our history there!" Sinan protested. "I am putting my heart's blood into those verses, woman! You of all women should appreciate that effort!"

"Oh, very well then." Hildegart switched to Arabic, a language she knew fluently, thanks to her years as a captive concubine.

" 'With the prodigies of my pen I express the marvel of the fall of Jerusalem,' " she quoted at him. " 'I fill the towers of the Zodiac with stars, and the caskets with my pearls of insight. I spread the joyful news far and wide, bringing perfume to Persia and conversation to Samarkand. The sweetness of holy victory surpasses candied fruits and cane sugar.' "

"How clever you are, Hudegar! Those were my finest verses, too." Sinan's dark, arching brows knotted hopefully. "That's some pretty grand stuff there, isn't it?"

"You shouldn't try to be a poet, Sinan. Let's face it, you are an alchemist."

"But I've learned everything there is to know about chemistry and machinery," Sinan protested. "Those fields of learning are ignoble and boring. Poetry and literature, by contrast, are fields of inexhaustible knowledge! Yes, I admit it, I do lack native talent for poesy—for when I began writing, my history was a dry recital of factual events! But I have finally found my true voice as a poet, for I have mastered the challenge of narrating great deeds on the battlefield!"

Hildegart's temper rose. "Am I supposed to praise you for that? I had investments in Jerusalem, you silly block of wood! My best sugar presses were there . . . my favorite cotton dyes . . . and you can bet I'll tell the Blemmye all about those commercial losses!"

"You may quote me even further, and recite to him how Christian Jerusalem fell to the Muslims in flames and screams," said Sinan tautly. "Tell him that every tribe of Frank will be chased back into the ocean! Eighty-nine long years since these unbathed wretches staggered in from Turkey to steal our lands, looking like so many disinterred corpses! But at last, broken with righteous fire and sword, the occupiers flee the armies of Jihad like whipped dogs. Never to return! I have lived through all of that humiliation, Hudegar. I was forced to witness every sorrowful day of my people's long affliction. At last, in this glorious day of supreme justice, I will see the backs of those alien invaders. Do you know what I just heard Saladin say?"

Hildegart ate another salted olive. She had been born in Germany and had never gotten over how delicious olives were. "All right. What did Saladin say?"

"Saladin will build ships and sail after the retreating Christians to Europe." Sinan drew an amazed breath. "Can you imagine the stern qualities of that great soldier, who would trust to the perils of the open ocean to avenge our insulted faith? That's the greatest tribute to knightly bravery that I can imagine!"

"Why do you even bother with lowborn scum like Saladin? Saladin is a Kurd and a Shi'ite."

"Oh, no. Saladin is the chosen of God. He used the wealth of Egypt to conquer Syria. He used the wealth of Syria to conquer Mesopotamia. The wealth of Mesopotamia will finally liberate Palestine. Saladin will die with exhausted armies and an empty treasury. Saladin is very thin, and he suffers from bellyaches, but thanks to him Palestine will be ours again. Those outlaw Crusader states of Christian Outremer will cease to be. That is the divine truth of history and, yes, I will bear witness to divine truth. I must bear witness, you know. Such things are required of a scholar."

Hildegart sighed, at a loss for words. Hildegart knew so many words, reams and reams of words. She knew low German, French, Arabic, much Turkish, some Greek. Proper history was written in Latin, of course. Having successfully memorized the Old and New Testaments at the age of fourteen, Hildegart could manage rather well in Latin, but she had given up her own attempts to write any kind of history during the reign of Baldwin the Leper.

The Crusader King of Jerusalem had a loathsome Middle Eastern disease, and Hildegart found herself chronicling Baldwin's incessant defeats in a stale, stilted language that smelled of death. "King Baldwin the Leper suffered this crushing setback, King Baldwin the Leper failed at that diplomatic initiative. . . ." The Leper seemed to mean well, and yet he was so stupid. . . . One stormy morning Hildegart had pulled years of secret records from her hidden cabinets and burned every one of them. It felt so good to destroy such weary knowledge that she had sung and danced.

Sinan gazed on her hopefully. "Can't you say just a bit more about my glamorous poetic efforts, Hudegar?"

"You are improving," she allowed. "I rather liked that line about the candied fruits. Those jongleurs of Eleanor of Aquitaine, they never write verse half so luscious as you do."

Sinan beamed on her for a moment and returned to gnawing his mutton. However, he was quick to sense a left-handed compliment. "That Frankish queen, she prefers the love poems made by vagrants for women. All Frankish ladies enjoy such love poems. I myself can write very sweetly about women and love. But I would never show those poems of mine to anyone, because they are too deeply felt."

"No doubt."

Sinan narrowed his eyes. "I can remember every woman who ever passed through my hands. By name and by face!"

"All of them? Could that be possible?"

"Oh come now, I never married more than four at a time! I can remember all of my wives very vividly. I shall prove it to you now, my doubting one! My very first wife was the widow of my older brother; she was Fatima, the eldest, with the two sons, my nephews. Fatima was dutiful and good. Then there was the Persian girl that the Sultan gave me: she was Bishar. She had crossed eyes, but such pretty legs. When my fortunes prospered, I bought the Greek girl Phoebe to cook for my other two."

Hildegart shifted uneasily.

"Then there was you, Hudegar the Frankish girl, my gift from the Silent Master. What splendid flesh you had. Hair like wheat and cheeks like apples. How you thrived in my courtyard and my library. You wanted kisses more than the other three combined. We had three daughters and the small son who died nameless." Sinan sighed from the depth of his heart. "Those are all such songs of loss and sorrow, my sweet songs of all my dear wives."

Hildegart's early years had been tangled and difficult. She had left Germany as a teenaged nun in the massive train of Peter the Hermit, a tumbling migration of thousands of the wildly inspired, in the People's Crusade. They walked down the Rhine, they trudged down the Danube, they stumbled starving across Hungary, Byzantium, and the Balkans, asking at every town and village if the place might perhaps be Jerusalem.

The People's Crusade killed most of its participants, but a crusade was the only sure way that Hildegart, who was the humble daughter of a falconer, could guarantee the remission of her sins. Hildegart marched from April to October of 1096. She was raped, starved, survived typhus, and arrived pregnant on an obscure hilltop in Turkey. There every man in her dwindling band was riddled with Seljuk arrows by the troops of Kilij Arslan.

Hildegart was purchased by a Turkish speculator, who took her infant for his own purposes and then sold her to the aging Sultan of Mosul. The Sultan visited her once for form's sake, then left her to her own devices within his harem. The Mosul harem was a quiet, solemn place, very much like the convent she had left in Germany, except for the silks, the dancing, and the eunuchs. There Hildegart learned to speak Turkish and Arabic, to play a lute, to embroider, and to successfully manage the considerable administrative overhead involved in running the palace baths.

After the Sultan's murder, she was manumitted and conveyed to a Jewish merchant, by whom she had a son.

The Jew taught her accounting, using a new system of numeration he had learned from colleagues in India. He and the son then vanished on an overly daring business expedition into Christian-held Antioch. Hildegart was sold to meet his business debts. Given her skills and accomplishments, though, she was quickly purchased by a foreign diplomat.

This diplomat traveled extensively through Islam, together with his train of servants, in a slow pilgrimage from court to court. It was a rewarding life, in its way. Muslim courts competed in their lavish hospitality for distinguished foreigners.

Foreign merchants and envoys, who lacked local clan ties, often made the most honest and efficient court officials. The Blemmye profited by this.

Literate scholars of the Islamic courts had of course heard tell of the exotic Blemmyae people. The Blemmyae were men from the land of Prester John, the men whose heads grew beneath their shoulders.

The Blemmye had no head; he was acephalous. Across his broad, barren shoulders grew a series of horny plates. Where a man might have paps, the Blemmye had two round black eyes, and he had a large, snorting nose in his chest. Where a navel might have been was his mouth. The Blemmye's mouth was a round, lipless, speechless hole, white and pink and ridged inside, and cinching tight like a bag. The Blemmye's feet, always neatly kept in soft leather Turkish boots, were quite toeless. He had beautiful hands, however, and his dangling, muscular arms were as round and solid as the trunks of trees.

The Blemmye, although he could not speak aloud, was widely known for his courteous behavior, his peaceable demeanor, and his generous gifts. In the troubled and turbulent Damascene court, the Blemmye was accepted without much demur.

The Blemmye was generally unhappy with the quality of his servants. They lacked the keen intelligence to meet his exacting requirements. Hildegart was a rare find for him, and she rose rapidly in her Silent Master's estimation.

The Blemmye wrote an excellent Arabic, but he wrote it in the same way he read books: entire pages at once, in one single comprehensive glance. So rather than beginning at the top of a page and writing from right to left, as any Arab scholar would, the Blemmye dashed and dotted his black markings across the paper, seemingly at random. Then he would wait, with unblinking eyes, to see if enough ink had arrived for his reader's comprehension.

If not, then he would dabble in more ink, but the trial annoyed him.

Hildegart had a particular gift for piecing out the Blemmye's fragmentary dabblings. For Hildegart, Arabic was also a foreign language, but she memorized long texts with ease, and she was exceedingly clever with numbers. Despite her master's tonguelessness, she also understood his moods, mostly through his snorts and his nervous hand-wringing gestures. The Blemmye became reliant on her services, and he rewarded her well.

When his business called him far from Damascus, the Blemmye conveyed Hildegart to the care of his chief agent within the Syrian court, an Iraqi alchemist and engineer. Rashid al-din Sinan made his living from *Naphth*, a flaming war-product that oozed blackly from the reedy marshes of his native Tigris.

Like most alchemists, Sinan had extensive interests in hermetic theology, as well as civil engineering, calligraphy, rhetoric, diplomacy, and the herbarium. As a canny and gifted courtier, living on his wits, Sinan was quick to serve any diplomat who could pay for his provisions with small but perfect diamonds, as the Blemmye did. Sinan gracefully accepted Hildegart as his new concubine and taught her the abacus and the tally-stick.

The Blemmye, being a diplomat, was deeply involved in international trade. He tirelessly sought out various rare oils, mineral salts, glasses, saltpeter, sulfur, potash, alchemical acids, and limes. He would trade in other goods to obtain the substances he prized, but his means were always subordinated to those same ends.

The Blemmye's personal needs were rather modest. However, he lavished many gifts on his mistress. The Blemmye was pitifully jealous of this female Blemmye. He kept her in such deep, secluded purdah that she was never glimpsed by anyone.

Hildegart and Sinan became the Blemmye's most trusted servants. He gave them his alchemical philters to drink, so that their flesh would not age in the mortal way of men and women. Many years of energetic action transpired, led by the pressing needs of their Silent Master. As wizard and mother abbess, Sinan and Hildegart grew in age and cunning, wealth and scholarship. Trade routes and caravans conveyed the Blemmye's goods and agents from the far reaches of Muslim Spain as far as the Spice Islands.

When Crusader ships appeared in the Holy Land and linked the Muslim world with the distant commercial cities of the Atlantic and the Baltic, the Blemmye was greatly pleased.

Eventually, Sinan and Hildegart were forced to part, for their uncanny agelessness had aroused suspicion in Damascus. Sinan removed himself to a cult headquarters in Alamut, where he pursued the mystic doctrines and tactics of the Ismaili Assassins. Hildegart migrated to the Crusader cities of Outremer, where she married a wise and all-accepting Maronite. She had three more children by this union.

Time ended that marriage as it had all her other such relations. Eventually, Hildegart found that she had tired of men and children, of their roughness and their importunities. She resumed the veil as the female Abbess of a convent stronghold in Tyre. She became the wealthy commander of a crowd of cloistered nuns, busy women with highly lucrative skills at weaving, adorning, and marketing Eastern fabrics.

The Abbess Hildegart was the busiest person that she knew. Even in times of war, she received many informations from the farthest rims of the world, and she knew the price and location of the rarest of earthly goods. Yet there was a hollowness in her life, a roiling feeling that dark events were unfolding, events beyond any mastery.

Assuming that all her children had somehow lived . . . and that her children had children, and that they had lived as well . . . and that those grandchildren, remorseless as the calendar, had further peopled the Earth . . . Hildegart's abacus showed her as a silent Mother Superior to a growing horde of over three hundred people. They were Christians, Jews, Muslims, a vast and ever-ramifying human family, united in nothing but their ignorance of her own endlessly spreading life.

The Dead Sea was as unpleasant as its name. Cursed Sodom was to the south, suicidal Masada to the middle, and a blood-stained River Jordan to the north. The lake gave pitch and bitumen, and mounds of gray, tainted salt. Birds that bathed in its water died and were crusted with minerals.

Arid limestone hills and caves on the Dead Sea shores had gone undisturbed for centuries.

Within this barren wilderness, the Blemmye had settled himself. Of late, the Silent Master, once so restless in his worldly quests for goods and services, moved little from his secretive Paradise, dug within the Dead Sea's barren hills.

Sometimes, especially helpful merchants from Hildegart's pigeon network would be taken there, or Assassins would be briefed there on one last self-sacrificing mission. It was in the Blemmye's Paradise that Sinan and Hildegart drank the delicious elixirs that lengthened their lives.

There were gardens there, and stores of rare minerals. The Blemmye's hidden palace also held an arsenal. It concealed the many sinister weapons that Sinan had built.

No skill in military engineering was concealed from the cunning master of Assassins. Sinan knew well the mechanical secrets of the jarkh, the zanbarak, the qaws al-ziyar, and even the fearsome manjaniq, a death machine men called "The Long-Haired Bride." With the Blemmye's aid and counsel, Sinan had built sinister crossbows with thick twisted skeins of silk and horsehair, capable of firing great iron beams, granite stones, red-hot bricks, and sealed clay bombs that splattered alchemical flames. Spewing, shrieking rockets from China were not beyond Sinan's war skills, nor was the Byzantine boiler that spewed ever-burning Greek Fire. Though difficult to move and conceal, these massive weapons of destruction were frighteningly potent. In cunning hands, they had shaped the fates of many a quarrelsome emirate. They had even hastened the fall of Jerusalem.

In his restless travels, the Blemmye had collected many rare herbs for the exquisite pergolas of his Paradise. He carefully collected the powder from within their flowers, and strained and boiled their saps for his marvelous elixirs. The Blemmye had forges and workshops full of curious instruments of metal and glass. He had struggled for years to breed superior camels for his far-ranging caravans. He had created a unique race of peculiar beasts, with hairless, scaly hides and spotted necks like cameleopards.

The choicest feature of the Blemmye's Paradise was its enormous bath. Sinan led his caravan men in a loud prayer of thanksgiving for their safe arrival. He commended their souls to his God, then he ushered the dusty, thirsting warriors within the marbled precincts.

Pure water gushed there from many great brass nozzles. The men eagerly doffed their chainmail armor and their filthy gear. They laughed and sang, splashing their tattooed limbs in the sweet, cleansing waters. Delicate fumes of incense made their spirits soar to the heavens.

Very gently, their spirits left their bodies.

The freshly washed dead were carried away on handcarts by the Blemmye's house servants. These servants were eunuchs, and rendered tongueless.

Through her long and frugal habit, Hildegart carefully sorted through the effects of the dead men. The Muslim and Christian women who haunted the battlefields of the Holy Land, comforting the wounded and burying the slain, generally derived more wealth from dead men than they ever did from their live protectors. Female camp followers of various faiths often encountered one another in the newly strewn fields of male corpses. They would bargain by gesture and swap the dead men's clothes, trinkets, holy medals, knives, and bludgeons.

Sinan sought her out as Hildegart neatly arranged the dead men's dusty riding boots. He was unhappy. "The Silent One has written his commands for us," he told her. He frowned over his freshly inked instructions. "The eunuchs are to throw the bodies of the men into the mine shaft, as usual. But then we are to put the caravan's horses into the bath as well. All of them!" The Assassin gazed at her moodily. "There would seem to be scarcely anyone here. I see none of his gardeners, I see no secretaries. . . . The Master is badly understaffed. Scutwork of this kind is unworthy of the two of us. I don't understand this."

Hildegart was shocked. "It was well worth doing to rid ourselves of those evil foreign Turks, but we can't possibly stable horses in that beautiful marble bath."

"Stable them? My dear, we are to kill the horses and throw them down into the mine. That's what the Master has written for us here. See if there's not some mistake, eh? You were always so good at interpreting."

Hildegart closely examined the spattered parchment. The Blemmye's queer handwriting was unmistakable, and his Arabic had improved with the years. "These orders are just as you say, but they make no sense. Without pack-horses, how am I to return to Tyre, and you to Alamut?"

Sinan looked at her in fear. "What are you telling me? Do you dare to question the Silent Master's orders?"

"No, you're the man," she told him quickly. "*You* should question his orders."

Hildegart had not had an audience with the Blemmye in some eight years. Their only communication was through couriers, or much more commonly, through the messenger birds.

In earlier days, when his writings had been harder to inter-pret, Hildegart had almost been a body servant to the Blemmye. She had fetched his ink, brought him his grapes, bread, and honey, and even seen him off to his strange, shrouded bed. Then she had left him to dwell in his Paradise, and she had lived for many years many leagues away from him. As long as they were still writing to each other, however, he never complained about missing her.

The Blemmye gave her his old, knowing look. His eyes, round, black, and wise, spread in his chest a hand's span apart. The Blemmye wore baggy trousers of flowered blue silk, beautiful leather boots, and of course no headgear. He sat cross-legged on a velvet cushion on the floor of his office, with his Indian inks, his wax seals, his accounting books, and his elaborate plans and parchments. The Blemmye's enormous arms had gone thinner with the years, and his speckled hide looked pale. His hands, once so deft and tireless, seemed to tremble uncontrollably.

"The Master must be ill," hissed Hildegart to Sinan. The two of them whispered together, for they were almost certain that the Blemmye could not hear or understand a whispered voice. The Blemmye did have ears, or fleshy excrescences anyway, but their Silent Master never responded to speech, even in the languages that he could read and write.

"I will formally declaim the splendid rhetoric that befits our lordly Master, while you will write to him at my dictation," Sinan ordered.

Hildegart obediently seated herself on a small tasseled carpet.

Sinan bowed low, placing his hand on his heart. He touched his fingertips to lips and forehead. "A most respectful greeting, dread Lord! May Allah keep you in your customary wisdom, health, and strength! The hearts of your servants overflow with joy over too long an absence from your august presence!"

"How are you doing, dear old Blemmye?" Hildegart wrote briskly. She shoved the parchment forward.

The Blemmye plucked up the parchment and eyed it. Then he bent over and his wrist slung ink in a fury.

"My heart has been shattered / the eternal darkness between the worlds closes in / my nights burn unbroken by sleep I bleed slowly / from within / I have no strength to greet the dawn / for my endless days are spent in sighing grief and vain regrets / the Light of All My Life has perished / I will never hear from her again / never never never again / will I read her sweet words of knowledge understanding and consolation / henceforth I walk in darkness / for my days of alien exile wind to their fatal climax."

Hildegart held up the message and a smear of ink ran down it like a black tear.

The two of them had never had the least idea that the Blemmye's wife had come to harm. The Blemmye guarded her so jealously that such a thing scarcely seemed possible.

But the mistress of their Silent Master, though very female, was not a Blemmye at all. She was not even a woman.

The Blemmye led them to the harem where he had hidden her.

This excavation had been the Blemmye's first great project. He had bought many slaves to bore and dig deep shafts into the soft Dead Sea limestone. The slaves often died in despair from the senseless work, perishing from the heat, the lack of fresh water, and the heavy, miasmic salt air.

But then, at Hildegart's counseling, the hapless slaves were freed and dismissed. Instead of using harsh whips and chains, the Blemmye simply tossed a few small diamonds into the rubble at the bottom of the pit.

Word soon spread of a secret diamond mine. Strong men

from far and wide arrived secretly in many eager gangs. Without orders, pay, or any words of persuasion, they imported their own tools into the wasteland.

Then the miners fought recklessly and even stabbed each other for the privilege of expanding the Blemmye's diggings. Miraculous tons of limestone were quarried, enough rock to provide firm foundations for every structure in the Blemmye's Paradise. The miners wept with delight at the discovery of every precious stone.

When no more diamonds appeared, the miners soon wearied of their sport. The secret mine was abandoned and swiftly forgotten.

Within this cavernous dugout, then, was where the Blemmye had hidden his darling.

The Silent Master removed a counterweighted sheet of glass and iron. From the black gulf, an eye-watering, hellish stink of lime and sulfur wafted forth.

Strapping two panes of glass to his enormous face, the Blemmye inhaled sharply through his great trumpet of a nose. Then he rushed headlong into the stinking gloom.

Hildegart urged Sinan to retreat from the gush of foul miasma, but the Assassin resisted her urgings. "I always wondered what our Master did with all that brimstone. This is astonishing."

"The Blemmye loves a creature from Hell," said Hildegart, crossing herself.

"Well, if this is Hell, then we ourselves built it, my dear." Sinan shrouded his eyes and peered within the acid murk. "I see so many bones in there. I must go in there, you know, I must bear witness and write of all this. . . . Why don't you come along with me?"

"Are you joking? A mine is no place for a woman!"

"Of course it is, my dear! You simply must come down into Hell with me. You're the only aide memoire available, and besides, you know that I rely on your judgment."

When Hildegart stiffly refused him, Sinan shrugged at her womanly fears and rushed forward into the gassy murk. Hildegart wept for him and began to pray—praying for her own sake, because Sinan's salvation was entirely beyond retrieval.

At the fifth bead of her rosary, the brave Assassin reappeared, half-leading his stricken Master. They were tugging and heaving together at a great, white, armored plate, a bone-colored thing like a gigantic shard of pottery.

This broken armor, with a few tangled limbs and bits of dry gut, that was all that was left of the Blemmye's Lady. She had been something like a great, boiled, stinking crab. Something like a barb-tailed desert scorpion, living under a rock.

In her silent life, cloistered deep within the smoking, stony earth, the Blemmye's Lady had fed well, and grown into a size so vast and bony and monstrous that she could no longer fit through the narrow cave mouth. Sinan and the Blemmye were barely able to tug her skeletal remnants into daylight.

The Blemmye pawed at a hidden trigger, and the great iron door swung shut behind him with a hollow boom. He wheezed and coughed and snorted loudly through his dripping nose.

Sinan, who had breathed less deeply of the hellish fumes, was the first to recover. He spat and wiped his streaming eyes, then gestured to Hildegart for pen and ink.

Then Sinan sat atop a limestone boulder. He ignored her questions with a shake of his turbaned head and fervently scribbled his notes.

Hildegart followed the laboring Blemmye as he tugged at

his bony, rattling burden. The Silent Master trembled like a dying ox as he hauled the big skidding carcass. His sturdy leather boots had been lacerated, as if chopped by picks and hatchets.

Ignoring his wounds, the Blemmye dragged the riddled corpse of his beloved, yard by painful yard, down the slope toward the Dead Sea. The empty carapace was full of broken holes. The she-demon had been pecked to pieces from within.

Hildegart had never seen the Blemmye hurt. But she had seen enough wounded men to know the look of mortal despair, even on a face as strange as his.

The Blemmye collapsed in anguish at the rim of the sullen salt lake.

Hildegart smoothed the empty sand before him with her sandaled foot. Then she wrote to him with a long brass pin from the clasp of her cloak. "Master, let us return to your Paradise. There I will tend to your wounds."

The Blemmye plucked a small table knife from his belt and scratched rapidly in the sand. "My fate is of no more conse-quence / I care only for my darling's children / though born in this unhappy place / they are scions of a great and noble people."

"Master, let us write of this together in some much better place."

The Blemmye brushed away her words with the palm of his hand. "I have touched my poor beloved for the last time in my life / How pitifully rare were our meetings / We sent each other many words through the black gulfs and seas amid the stars / to understand one sentence was the patient work of years / her people and mine were mortal enemies amid the stars / And yet she trusted me / She chose to become mine / She fled with me to live in exile to this distant unknown realm / Now she has left me to face our dark fate alone / It was always her dear way to give her life for others / Alas my sweet correspondent has finally perished of her generosity."

The Blemmye tugged in fitful despair at his lacerated boots.

Resignedly, Hildegart knelt and pulled the torn boots from her Master's feet. His wounds were talon slashes, fearsome animal bites. She pulled the cotton wimple from her head and tore it into strips.

"I promised her that I would guard her children / sheltering them as I always sheltered her / That foolish vow has broken my spirit / I will fail her in my promise, for I cannot live without her / Her goodness and her greatness of spirit / She was so wise, and knew so many things / Great marvels I could never have guessed, known, or dreamed of / What a strange soul she had, and how she loved me / What wondrous things we shared together from our different worlds / Oh, how she could write!"

Sinan arrived. The Assassin's eyes were reddened with the fumes, but he had composed himself.

"What have you been doing?" Hildegart demanded, as she worked to bind the Blemmye's bleeding, toeless feet.

"Listen to this feat of verse!" Sinan declared. He lifted his parchment, cleared his throat, and began to recite. " 'With my own eyes, I witnessed the corpses of the massacred! Lacerated and disjointed, with heads cracked open and throats split; spines broken, necks shattered; noses mutilated, hair colored with blood! Their tender lips were shriveled, their skulls cracked and pierced; their feet were slashed and fingers sliced away and scattered; their ribs staved in and smashed.

With their life's last breath exhaled, their very ghosts were crushed, and they lay like dead stones among stones!' "

Hildegart's bloodied fingers faltered on the knot of her rough bandage. The sun beat against her bared head. Her ears roared. Her vision faded.

When she came to, Sinan was tenderly sponging her face with water from his canteen.

"You swooned," he told her.

"Yes," she said faintly, "yes, that overcame me."

"Of course it would," he agreed, eyes shining, "for those wondrous verses possessed me in one divine rush! As if my very pen had learned to speak the truth!"

"Is that what you saw in Hell?" she said.

"Oh no," he told her, "that was what I witnessed in the siege of Jerusalem. I was never able to describe that experience before, but just now, I was very inspired." Sinan shrugged. "Inside that ugly mine, there is not much to see. There is dark, acrid smoke there, many chewed bones. The imps within, they screeched and rustled everywhere, like bats and lizards. And that infernal stench!" Sinan looked sidelong at the Blemmye's wounded shins. "See how the little devils attacked him, as he walked through the thick of them, to fetch out their dam."

Though the Blemmye did not understand Sinan's words, the tone of the Assassin's voice seemed to stir him. He sat up, his black eyes filmy and grievous. He took up his knife again, and carved fresh letters into the sand. "Now we will take the precious corpse of my beloved / and sink her to her last rest in this strange sea she loved so much. / This quiet lake was the kindest place to her of any in your world."

Sinan put his verses away, and pulled at one whitened limb

of the Blemmye's ruined lover. The bony armor rocked and tilted like a pecked and broken Roc's egg. The wounded Blemmye stood on his bleeding feet, lifting and shoving at the wall of bone with all his failing strength. The two of them splashed waist-deep into the evil water.

As the skeleton sank into the shallows, there was a sudden stirring and skittering. From a bent corner of the shell, shaking itself like a wet bird, came a small and quite horrible young demon. It had claws, and a stinging tail, and a circlet of eyes like a spider. It hopped and chirped and screeched.

Sinan wisely froze in place, like a man confronting a leopard. But the Blemmye could not keep his composure. He snorted aloud and fled splashing toward the shore.

The small demon rushed after the Blemmye as if born to the chase. It quickly felled him to the salty shore. At once, it began to feed on him.

Sinan armed himself with the closest weapon at hand: he tore a bony flipper from the mother's corpse. He waded ashore in a rush, and swung this bone like a mace across the heaving back of the imp. Its armor was as tough as any crab's, though, and the heavy blow only enraged it.

The little demon turned on the Assassin with awful speed, and likely would have killed a fighter less experienced. Sinan, though, was wise enough to outfox the young devil. He dodged its feral lunges, striking down and cracking the vulnerable joints in its twitching, bony limbs. When the monster faltered, foaming and hissing, he closed on it with a short, curved dagger from within his robe.

Sinan rose at last from the young beast's corpse, his robes ripped and his arm bloodied. He hid his blade away again, then dragged the dead monster to the salt shore. There he heaved it with a shudder of loathing into the still water beside its mother.

Hildegart knelt beside the panting Blemmye. His wounds had multiplied.

The Blemmye blinked, faint with anguish. His strength was fading visibly, yet he still had something left to write. He scraped at the sand with a trembling fingertip. "Take me to my Paradise and bind my wounds / See to it that I live / I shall reveal to you great wonders and secrets / beyond the comprehension of your prophets."

Sinan took Hildegart by the arm.

"I'm no longer much concerned about our horses, my dear," he told her. He knelt and smoothed out their Master's writing. A spatter of his own blood fell on the sand beside the Blemmye's oozings.

"That ugly monster has hurt you, my brave hero!"

"Do you know how many times this poor old body of mine has known a wound?" Sinan's left arm had been badly scored by the creature's lashing tail. He gritted his teeth as she tied off his arm with a scarf. "What a joy that battle was, my darling. I have never killed anything that I wanted to kill so much."

The Blemmye propped his headless body on one elbow. He beckoned at them feebly.

Hildegart felt a moment of sheer hatred for him, for his weakness, for his foolish yieldings to the temptations of darkness. "What it is that the Blemmye wants to write of now, these *great secrets* that he promises us?"

"It will be much the same as it was before," Sinan said with disgust. "That mystical raving about the Sun being only a star. He'll tell us that other stars are suns, with other worlds and other peoples."

Hildegart shivered. "I always hated that!"

"The world is very, very old, he'll insist on that nonsense, as well. Come, let us help him, my dear. We shall have to patch the Master up, for there is no one else fit to do it."

"Thousands of years," Hildegart quoted, unmoving where she stood. "Then, thousands of thousands of years. And thousands, of thousands, of thousands. Then thirteen and a half of those units. Those are the years since the birth of the universe."

"How is it you can remember all that? Your skills at numeration are beyond compare!" Sinan trembled suddenly, in an after-combat mix of rage, fear, and weariness. "My dear, please give me counsel, in your wisdom: did his huge numbers ever make any sense to you? Any kind of sense at all?"

"No," she told him.

The Assassin looked wearily at the fainting Blemmye. He lowered his voice. "Well, I can fully trust your counsel in this matter, can't I? Tell me that you are quite sure about all that."

Hildegart felt a rush of affection for him. She recognized that look of sincere, weighty puzzlement on his face; he'd often looked like that in the days when they had played chess together, whiling away pleasant evenings as lord and concubine. It was Sinan who had taught her chess; Sinan had taught Hildegart the very existence of chess. Chess was a wonderful game, with the crippled Shah, and the swift Vizier, and all their valiant knights, stern fortresses and crushing elephants. When she began to defeat him at chess, he only laughed and praised her cleverness; he seemed to enjoy their game all the more.

"My dear, brave Sinan, I can promise you: God Himself

doesn't need such infinities, not even for His angels to dance on the heads of pins." Hildegart felt light-headed without her wimple, and she ran her hands self-consciously across her braids. "Why does he think that big numbers are some kind of reward for us? What's wrong with gold and diamonds?"

Sinan shrugged again, favoring his wounded arm. "I think his grief has turned his mind. We must haul him away from his darling now. We must put him to bed, if we can. No man can be trusted at the brink of his lover's grave."

Hildegart gazed with loathing at the demonic skeleton. The dense salt water still bore the she-monster up, but her porous wreck was drowning, like a boat hull riddled with holes. A dark suspicion rose within Hildegart's heart. Then a cold fear came. "Sinan, wait one moment longer. Listen to me now. What number of evil imps were bred inside that great incubus of his?"

Sinan's eyes narrowed. "I would guess at least a hundred. I knew that by the horrid noise."

"Do you remember the story of the Sultan's chessboard, Sinan? That story about the great sums."

This was one of Sinan's Arabic tales: the story of a foolish sultan's promise to a cheating courtier. Just one grain of wheat on the first square of the chessboard, but two grains of wheat on the second, and then four on the third, and then eight, sixteen, thirty-two. A granary-leveling inferno of numbers.

Sinan's face hardened. "Oh yes. I do remember that story of algebra. And now I begin to understand."

"I learned that number story from you," she said.

"My clever darling, I well remember how we shared that tale—and I also know the size of that mine within the earth!

Ha-ha! So that's why he needs to feed those devils with the flesh of my precious pack horses! When those vile creatures breed in there, then how many will there be, eh? There will be hundreds, upon hundreds, multiplied upon hundreds!"

"What will they do to us?" she said.

"What else can they do? They will spill out into our sacred homeland! Breeding in their endless numbers, uncountable as the stars, they will spread as far as any bird can fly!"

She threw her arms around him. He was a man of such quick understanding.

Sinan spoke in a hoarse whisper. "So, darling, thanks to your woman's intuition, we have found out his wicked scheme! Our course is very clear now, is it not? Are we both agreed on what we must do?"

"What do you mean?"

"Well, I must assassinate him."

"What, now?"

Sinan released her, his face resolutely murderous. "Yes, of course now! To successfully kill a great lord, one must fall on him like a thunderbolt from a clear sky. The coup de grace always works best when least expected. So you will feign to help him to his feet. Then, without a word of warning, I will bury my steel blade between his ribs."

Hildegart blinked and wiped grains of salty sand from her cloak. "Does the Blemmye have ribs, Sinan?"

Sinan stroked his beard. "You're right, my dear; I hadn't quite thought that through."

But as they conspired together, the Blemmye himself rose from the bloodstained sand. He tottered and staggered into the stinging salts of the dead lake. His darling had failed to sink entirely from sight.

Half-swimming, their master shoved and heaved at the bony ridges and spars that broke the surface. The waters of the Dead Sea were very buoyant by nature, but the Blemmye had no head to keep above the water. He ignored their shouts and cries of warning.

There he sank, tangled in the bones of his beloved. Minutes later, his drowned corpse bobbed to the surface like a cork.

After the death of the Silent Master, life in the Holy Land took a swift turn for the worse. First, exotic goods vanished from the markets. Then trade faltered. Ordered records went unkept. Currencies gyrated in price. Crops were ravaged and villages sacked, caravans raided and ships sunk. Men no longer traded goods, or learned from one another; they were resolved upon massacre.

Defeat after wave of defeat scourged the dwindling Christian forces. Relentlessly harassed, the Crusaders lurked and starved within their stone forts, or else clung fitfully to off-shore ships and islands, begging reinforcements that were loath to come.

Sinan's Muslim raiders were the first to occupy the Blemmye's Paradise. Sinan had vaguely meant to do something useful with the place. The Assassin was a fiendish wizard whose very touch meant death, and his troops feared him greatly. But armies were low on discipline when loot was near. Soon they were breaking the plumbing, burning the libraries, and scraping at semiprecious stones with the blades of their knives.

Hildegart's own Crusader forces had arrived late at the orgy, but they were making up for lost time. The Christians had flung themselves on the Blemmye's oasis like wolves. They were looting everything portable and burning all the rest.

Six guards dragged Hildegart into Sinan's great black battle tent. They threw her to the tasseled carpet.

The pains of battlefield command had told on the alchemist. Sinan's face was lined, and he was thinner. But with Hildegart as his captive, he brightened at once. He lifted her to her feet, drew his scimitar, and gallantly sawed the hemp ropes from her wrists. "How astonishing life can be!" he said. "How did you reach me amid all this turmoil?"

"My lord, I am entirely yours; I am your hostage. Sir Roger of Edessa offers me to you as the guarantee of the good behavior of his forces." Hildegart sighed after this little set speech.

Sinan seemed skeptical. "How unseemly are these times at the end of history! Your paladin Roger offers me a Christian holy woman for a hostage? A woman is supposed to be a pleasant gift between commanders! Who is this 'Roger of Edessa'? He requires some lessons in knightly courtesy."

Hildegart rubbed her chafed wrists. Her weary heart overflowed toward the Assassin in gushing confidence. "Sinan, I had to choose Roger of Edessa to command this expedition. Roger is young, he is bold, he despises death, and he had nothing better to do with himself but to venture forth and kill demonic monsters."

Sinan nodded. "Yes, I understand such men perfectly."

"I myself forced Sir Roger to appoint me as your hostage."

"I still must wonder at his lack of gallantry."

"Oh, it's all a very difficult story, very. The truth is, Roger of Edessa gave me to you as a hostage because he hates me. You see, Sir Roger dearly loves my granddaughter. This granddaughter of mine is a very foolish, empty-headed girl who despite her fine education also despises me bitterly. When I saw the grip that their unchaste passion had on the two of them, I parted them at once. I kept her safe in a tower in Tyre with my message birds. . . . Roger is a wandering adventurer, a freelance whose family fief was lost years ago. I had a much more prosperous match in mind for this young girl. However, even bread and water could not break her of her stupid habit of loving him. . . . It is her hand in marriage that Roger seeks above all, and for her silly kisses he is willing to face hell itself. . . . Do I tire you with all this prattling, Sinan?"

"Oh no, no, your words never tire me," Sinan said loyally. He sat with a weary groan and absently patted a plump velvet cushion on the carpet. "Please do go on with your exotic Christian romance! Your personal troubles are always fascinating!"

"Sinan, I know I am just a foolish woman and also a cloistered nun, but do grant me some credit. I, a mere nun, have raised an army for you. I armed all these wicked men, I fed them, I clothed them, I brought them here for you to kill those demons with. . . . I did the very best I could."

"That was a very fine achievement, sweet little Hudegar."

"I am just so tired and desperate these days. Since the dark word spread of our Silent Master's death, all my agents have fallen to quarreling. The birds no longer fly, Sinan, the birds go neglected and they perish. And when the poor birds do arrive, they bear me the most awful news: theft, embezzlement, bankruptcies, every kind of corruption. . . . All the crops are burned around Tyre and Acre, Saladin's fearsome raiders are everywhere in the Holy Land. . . . There is famine, there is pestilence. . . . The clouds take the shapes of serpents, and cows bring forth monsters. . . . I am at my wits' end."

Sinan clapped his hands and demanded the customary hostage cloak and hostage hat. Hildegart donned the official garments gratefully. Then Hildegart accepted a cool lime sherbet. Her morale was improving, since her Assassin was so kindly and dependable.

"Dearest Sinan, I must further inform you about this ugly band I have recruited for your daring siege of Hell. They are all Christians fresh off the boat, and therefore very gullible. They are Englishmen . . . well, not English. . . . They are Normans, for the English are their slaves. These are lion-hearted soldiers, and lion-gutted, and lion-toothed, with a lion's appetites. I promised them much loot, or rather, I made Sir Roger promise them all that."

"Good. These savages of yours sound rather promising. Do you trust them?"

"Oh no, certainly not. But the English had to leave Tyre for the holy war anyway, for the Tyrians would not suffer them to stay inside the port. These English are a strange, extremely violent people. They are drunken, foul, rampaging. Their French is like no French I ever heard. . . ." Hildegart put down her glass sherbet bowl and began to sniffle. "Sinan, you don't know what it's been like for me, dealing with these dirty brutes. The decay of courtesy today, the many gross, impious insults I have suffered lately. . . . They are nothing at all like yourself, a gentleman and true scholar."

Despite all difficulty, Hildegart arranged a formal parley between Sinan and Sir Roger of Edessa. Like most of the fighters dying in the Holy Land, Roger of Edessa was a native. Roger's grandfather had been French, his grandmother

Turkish, his father German, and his mother a Greek Orthodox native of Antioch. His home country, Edessa, had long since fallen in flames.

Sir Roger of Edessa was a Turcopole, the child of Muslim-Christian unions. Roger wore a checkered surcoat from Italy, and French plate armor, and a Persian peaked cavalry helmet with an Arabian peacock plume. Sir Roger's blue eyes were full of lucid poetic despair, for he had no land to call his own. Wherever he went in the Holy Land, some blood relation was dying. The Turcopoles, the Holy Land's only true natives, were never considered a people to be trusted by anyone; they fought for any creed with indifference, and were killed by all with similar glee. Roger, though only twenty, had been fighting and killing since the age of twelve.

With Hildegart to interpret for him, Sir Roger and his boldest Englishmen inspected their new Muslim allies. Sinan's best efforts had raised a bare two hundred warriors to combat the fiends. Somewhere over the smoldering horizon, the mighty Saladin was rousing the Muslim faithful to fight yet another final, conclusive, epic battle with the latest wave of Western invaders. Therefore, heroic Muslim warriors willing to fight and kill demons were rather thin on the ground.

Word had also spread widely of the uniformly lethal fate of Sinan's suicide-martyr assassins. Nevertheless, Sinan's occult reputation had garnered together a troop of dedicated fanatics. He had a bodyguard of Ismailis from a heretical madrassa. He had a sprinkling of Fatimid Egyptian infantry and their Nubians, and some cynical Damascenes to man his siege machines. These large destructive weapons, Sinan hoped, were his keys to a quick victory.

Roger examined the uncanny siege weapons with pro-
found respect. The copper kettle-bellies of the Greek Fire
machines spoke eloquently of their sticky, flaming mayhem.
Much fine cedar of Lebanon had been sacrificed for the
massive beams of the catapults.

Roger had been educated by Templars. He had traveled as
far as Paris in their constant efforts to raise money for the wars.
He was incurably proud of his elegant French. "Your Excellency, my pious troops are naturally eager to attack and kill
these wicked cave monsters. But we do wonder at the expense."

Hildegart translated for Sinan. Although the wily Assassin
could read French, he had never excelled at speaking it.

"My son, you are dealing with the Old Man of the Mountain here." Sinan passed Roger a potent handful of diamonds.
"You and your fine boys may keep these few baubles. Inspire
your troops thus. When the very last of these foul creatures is
exterminated within that diamond mine, then we shall make
a full inventory of their legendary horde of jewels."

Roger displayed this booty to his two top lieutenants.
The first was a sunburned English sea captain with vast
mustaches, who looked rather uneasy stuck on horseback.
The second was a large crop-headed Norman rascal, shorn
of both his ears. The two freebooters skeptically crunched
the jewels between their teeth. When the diamonds failed to
burst like glass, they spat them out into their flat-topped
kettle-helmets. Then they shared a grin.

Sinan's Assassin spies had been keeping close watch over
the cave. The small war council rode there together to rec-
onnoiter the battle terrain. Hildegart was alarmed by the
sinister changes that had taken place on the site. The mighty
door of glass and iron had been riddled with pecked holes.

Fresh bones strewed the ground, along with the corpse-pale, shed outer husks of dozens of crabs. All the vegetation was gnawed and stripped, and the dusty earth itself was chewed up, as if by the hooves of stampeding cattle.

Using their pennoned lances, Roger's two lieutenants prodded at a cast-off husk of pinkish armor. Roger thoughtfully rolled a diamond through his mailed fingertips. "O Lord High Emir Commander, this place is indeed just as you told us: a very mouth of Hell! What is our battle plan?"

"We will force the evil creatures into the open with gouts of Greek fire. Then I place great confidence in your Christian knights who charge in heavy armor." Sinan was suave. "I have seen their shock tactics crush resistance in a twinkling. Especially from peasants on foot."

"My English knights will likely be sober enough to charge by tomorrow," Roger agreed. "Is our help required in moving all those heavy arbalests? I had some small acquaintance with those in Jerusalem."

"My Damascene engineers will acquit themselves to our general satisfaction," said Sinan. He turned his fine Arabian stallion. The party cantered from the cave.

"There is also the matter of our battle signals, Your Excellency," Roger persisted gamely. "Your minions prefer kettledrums, while my men use flags and trumpets. . . ."

"Young commander, such a problem is easily resolved. Would you care to join me for this battle on the back of my elephant? With those flags, horns, drums . . . and our translator, of course."

Hildegart was so startled that she almost fell from her mare. "You have an elephant, Sinan?"

The Assassin caught the reins of her restive horse in his

skilled hand. "My tender hostage, I brought you an elephant for the sake of your own safety. I hope you are not afraid to witness battle from atop my great beast?"

She met his eyes steadily. "Trusting in your wise care, I fear nothing, dread Prince!"

"How good you are."

Sinan's war elephant was the strangest creature to answer the call of his pigeons. The gray and wrinkled pachyderm had tramped some impossible distance, from the very shores of Hindustan, arriving thirsty and lean at the Dead Sea, with his great padded feet wrapped in shabby, salt-worn leather. The elephant had many battle scars on the vast bulging walls of his hide, and a man-killing glare in his tiny red eyes. His ivory tusks were carefully grooved for the insertion of sharp sword blades. He wore thick quilted cotton armor, enough for a dozen tents. His towering san-dalwood howdah had a brass-inlaid crossbow, pulled back by two stout whirring cranks, and with forty huge barbed bolts of Delhi steel, each one fit to pierce three men clean through. His Master was a very terror of the Earth.

Hildegart gazed up at the vast beast and back to Sinan with heartfelt admiration. How had the Assassin managed such a magnificent gesture?

On the next day, Sinan made her some formal gifts: an ivory-handled dagger, a helmet with a visor and veil to hide her beardless face, padded underarmor, and a horseman's long tunic of mail. It would simply not do for the common troops to see a woman taking to the battlefield. However, Sinan required her counsel, her language skills, and a written witness to events. Clad in the armor and helmet, she would pass as his boyish esquire.

The dense links of greased mail crunched and rustled on Hildegart's arms. The armor was so heavy that she could scarcely climb the folding ladder to the elephant's gleaming howdah. Once up, she settled heavily into place amid dense red horsehair cushions, towering over the battlefield giddily, feeling less like a woman than an airborne block of oak.

The battle opened with glorious bursts of colored flames. Sinan's sweating engineers kept up a steady pace, pumping gout after gout of alchemical fire down the black throat of Hell.

A half-dozen imps appeared at once at the cave mouth. As creatures inured to sulfur, they seemed less than impressed by the spurts of Greek Fire. The beasts had grown larger now and were at least the size of goats.

At the sight of their uncanny capering, the cavalry horses snorted and stamped below their mailed and armored masters. A few cowards fled in shock at the first sight of such unnatural monsters, but their manhood was loudly taunted by their fellows. They soon returned shamefaced to their ranks.

A drum pounded, a horn blasted, and a withering fire of crossbow bolts sleeted across the dancing crabs. In moments every one had been skewered, hopping, gushing pale ichor, and querulously plucking bolts from their pierced limbs. The men all cheered in delight. Watching through the slits in her visor, Hildegart realized that the imps had no idea that weapons could strike from a distance. They had never seen such a thing done.

Sinan's stores of Greek Fire were soon exhausted. He then ordered his catapults into action. Skilled Damascenes with great iron levers twisted the horsehide skeins until the cedar uprights groaned. Then, with concussive thuds, the machines flung great pottery jars of jellied Naphth deep into the hole. Sullen booms echoed within.

Suddenly there was a foul, crawling clot of the demons, an antlike swarm of them, vomiting forth in pain, with carapaces wreathed in dancing flames.

The creatures milled forth in an unruly burning mob. The fearless Ismaili Assassins, seeking sure reward in the afterlife, screamed the name of God and flung themselves into the midst of the enemy, blades flailing. The bold martyrs swiftly died, cruelly torn by lashing tails and pincers. At the sight of this sacrifice and its fell response, every man in the army roared with the rage for vengeance.

A queer stench wafted from the monsters' burning flesh, a reek that even the horses seemed to hate.

Trumpets blew. The English knights couched their lances, stood in their stirrups, and rode in, shield to shield. The crabs billowed from the shock, with a bursting of their gore and a splintering of lances. The knights, slashing and chopping with their sabers, fell back and regrouped. Their infantry rushed forth to support them, finishing off the wounded monsters with great overhand chops of their long-handled axes.

A column of black smoke began to block the sky. Then a great, choking, roiling tide of the demons burst from their filthy hole. They had been poisoned somehow and were spewing thin phlegm from the gills on their undersides. There were hundreds of them. They leapt over everything in their path, filled with such frantic energy that they almost seemed to fly.

In moments the little army was overrun, surrounded. The Damascenes died screaming at their siege machinery. Horses panicked and fell as lunging, stinging monsters bit through their knees. Stout lines of spear-carrying infantry buckled and collapsed.

But there was no retreat. Not one man left the battlefield. Even those who died fell on the loathsome enemy with their last breath.

Men died in clumps, lashed, torn, shredded. At the howdah's rear deck, Sir Roger pounded a drumskin and shouted his unheard orders. The elephant, ripped and slashed by things no taller than his knees, was stung into madness. With a shattering screech from his curling sinuous nose, he charged with great stiff-legged earthshaking strides into the thickest of the enemy. As the towering beast lurched in his fury, Sinan kept up a cool fire from the howdah's crossbow. His fatal yard-long bolts pierced demons through, pinning them to the earth.

A knot of angry demons swarmed up the elephant as if it were a moving mountain. The evil creatures seethed right up the elephant's armored sides.

Hildegart, quailing within her heavy helmet and mail, heard them crawling and scrabbling on the roof of the howdah as Roger and Sinan, hand to hand, lashed out around them with long blades.

Claws caught within the steel links of her chainmail and yanked her from the howdah.

Along with the demons seizing her, she tumbled in a kicking, scrambling mass from the plunging elephant. They crashed and tumbled through a beleaguered cluster of Egyptians on horseback.

Hildegart lay stunned and winded as more and more of the foul creatures swarmed toward the great beast, their pick-like legs scrabbling over her. Chopped almost in half by the elephant's steel-bearing tusks, a demon came flying and crashed across her. It lay on her dying, and among its many twitching legs, its broken gills wheezed forth a pale pink froth.

Hildegart lay still as death, knowing that many survived battles that way. She was utterly terrified, flat on her back amid a flowing tide of jittering, chattering monsters, men's dying screams, curses, the clash of their steel. Yet there was almost a tender peace in such stillness, for she wanted for nothing. She only wished that she were somehow still in the howdah, together with dear Sinan, to wrap her arms around him one last time, to shield his body from his fate, even at the cost of her own life.

Suddenly, as often happened in battles, there was a weird lull. She saw the blue sky and a rising billow of poisoned smoke. Then the elephant came screaming and trampling over her, blinded, bleeding, staggering to its death. Its great foot fell and rose swiftly. It stamped her flat and broke her body.

Coldness crept around her heart. She prayed in silence.

After some vague time she opened her eyes to see Sinan's torn and bloodied face inside his dented helmet.

"The day is ours," he told her. "We have killed all of them, save a very few that fled into the mine. Few of us survive . . . but none of them can be suffered to live. I have sworn a holy oath that they shall not trouble the next generation. My last two Assassins and I are walking into hell to settle them forever. We shall march into the very midst of them, our bodies laden with our very best bombs. That is a strategy that cannot fail."

"I must take notes for our glorious history," she murmured. "You must write the verses for me. I long to read them so!"

The Assassin eased the helmet from her braided hair and

carefully arranged her limbs. Hildegart could not feel her own numbed legs, but she felt him lift her mailcoat to probe her crushed flesh. "Your back is broken, precious." With no more word than that—for the coup de grace always worked best without warning—she felt a sharp, exciting pang through her ribs. Her Assassin had stabbed her.

He kissed her brow. "No gentleman would write one word about our history! All that sweetness was our secret; it was just for you and me."

The tattered pigeon carried an urgent message:

"MY DARLING: At the evil shores of a dead sea, I have survived a siege of such blood and hellish fire that I pray that no survivor ever writes of it. My command was ravaged. All who came to this land to serve God have died for Him, and even the imps of Satan have perished, leaving nothing but cold ashes and bones. My heart now tells me: you and I will never know a moment's happiness as man and woman unless we flee this dreadful Holy Land. We must seek some shelter far beyond the Gates of Hercules, or far beyond the Spice Islands, if there is any difference. We must find a place so distant no one will ever guess our origins. There I swear that I will cleave to you, and you only, until the day I die.

"Trust me and prepare yourself at once, my beloved, for I am coming to take you from your tower and finally make you mine. I am riding to you as fast as a horse will carry me. Together we will vanish from all ken, so that no man or woman will ever know what became of us."

The laden pigeon left the stone sill of the window. She

fluttered to the floor, and pecked at the useless husks of a few strewn seeds. The pigeon found no water. Every door hung broken from every empty cage. The tower was abandoned, a prey to the sighing wind.

[Though I like writing fantasies, this last story is the only ghost story I've ever written. The dead do not walk the earth—but there is no ghost like a nonperson.]

The Denial

Yusuf climbed the town's ramshackle bridge. There he joined an excited crowd: gypsies, unmarried apprentices, the village idiot, and three ne'er-do-wells with a big jug of plum brandy. The revellers had brought along a blind man with a fiddle.

The river was the soul of the town, but the heavy spring rains had been hard on her. She was rising from her bed in a rage. Tumbling branches clawed through her foam like the mutilated hands of thieves.

The crowd tore splinters from the bridge, tossed them in the roiling water, and made bets. The blind musician scraped his bow on his instrument's single string. He wailed out a noble old lament about crops washed away, drowned herds, hunger, sickness, poverty, and grief.

Yusuf listened with pleasure and studied the rising water with care. Suddenly a half-submerged log struck a piling. The bridge quivered like a sobbing violin. All at once, without a word, the crowd took to their heels.

Yusuf turned and gripped the singer's ragged shoulder. "You'd better come with me."

"I much prefer it here with my jolly audience, thank you, sir!"

"They all ran off. The river's turning ugly, this is dangerous."

"No, no, such kind folk would not neglect me!"

Yusuf pressed a coin into the fiddler's palm.

The fiddler carefully rubbed the coin with his callused fingertips. "A copper penny! What magnificence! I kiss your hand!"

Yusuf was the village cooper. When his barrel trade turned lean, he sometimes patched pots. "See here, fellow, I'm no rich man to keep concubines and fiddlers!"

The fiddler stiffened. "I sing the old songs of your heritage, as the living voice of the dead! The devil's crows will peck the eyeballs of the stingy!"

"Stop trying to curse me and get off this stupid bridge! I'm buying your life with that penny!"

The fiddler spat. At last he tottered toward the far riverbank.

Yusuf abandoned the bridge for the solid cobbles of the marketplace. Here he found more reasonable men: the town's kadi, the wealthy beys, and the seasoned hadjis. These local notables wore handsome woolen cloaks and embroidered jackets. The town's Orthodox priest had somehow been allowed to join their circle.

THE DENIAL

Yusuf smoothed his vest and cummerbund. Public speech was not his place, but he was at least allowed to listen to his betters. He heard the patriarchs trade the old proverbs. Then they launched light-hearted quips at one another, as jolly as if their town had nothing to lose. They were terrified.

Yusuf hurried home to his wife.

"Wake and dress the boy and girl," he commanded. "I'm off to rouse my uncle. We're leaving the house tonight."

"Oh, no, we can't stay with your uncle," his wife protested.

"Uncle Mehmet lives on high ground."

"Can't this wait till morning? You know how grumpy he gets!"

"Yes, my uncle Mehmet has a temper," said Yusuf, rolling his eyes. "It's also late, and it's dark. It will rain on us. It's hard work to move our possessions. This may all be for nothing. Then I'll be a fool, and I'm sure you'll let me know that."

Yusuf roused his apprentice from his sleeping nook in the workshop. He ordered the boy to assemble the tools and wrap them with care against damp. Yusuf gathered all the shop's dinars and put them inside his wife's jewelrybox, which he wrapped in their best rug. He tucked that bundle into both his arms.

Yusuf carried his bundle uphill, pattered on by rain. He pounded the old man's door, and, as usual, his uncle Mehmet made a loud fuss over nothing. This delayed Yusuf's return. When he finally reached his home again, back down the crooked, muddy lanes, the night sky was split to pieces by lightning. The river was rioting out of her banks.

His wife was keening, wringing her hands, and cursing her unhappy fate. Nevertheless, she had briskly dressed the children and packed a stout cloth sack with the household's precious things. The stupid apprentice had disobeyed Yusuf's orders and run to the river to gawk; naturally, there was no sign of him.

Yusuf could carry two burdens uphill to his uncle's, but to carry his son, his daughter, and his cooper's tools was beyond his strength.

He'd inherited those precious tools from his late master. The means of his livelihood would be bitterly hard to replace.

He scooped the little girl into his arms. "Girl, be still! My son, cling to my back for dear life! Wife, bring your baggage!"

Black water burst over their sill as he opened the door. Their alley had become a long, ugly brook.

They staggered uphill as best they could, squelching through dark, crooked streets. His wife bent almost double with the heavy sack on her shoulders. They sloshed their way to higher ground. She screeched at him as thunder split the air.

"What now?" Yusuf shouted, unable to wipe his dripping eyes.

"My trousseau!" she mourned. "My grandmother's best things!"

"Well, I left my precious tools there!" he shouted. "So what? We have to live!"

She threw her heavy bag down. "I must go back or it will be too late!"

Yusuf's wife came from a good family. Her grandmother had been a landowner's fine lady, with nothing more to do than knit and embroider all day. The grandam had left fancy garments that Yusuf's wife never bothered to wear, but she dearly treasured them anyway.

"All right, we'll go back together!" he lied to her. "But first, save our children!"

Yusuf led the way uphill. The skies and waters roared. The children wept and wriggled hard in their terror, making his burden much worse. Exhausted, he set them on their feet and dragged them by the hands to his uncle's door.

Yusuf's wife had vanished. When he hastened back downhill, he found her heavy bag around a street corner. She had disobeyed him and run back downhill in the darkness.

The river had risen and swallowed the streets. Yusuf ventured two steps into the black, racing flood and was tumbled off his feet and smashed into the wall of a bakery. Stunned and drenched, he retreated, found his wife's abandoned bag, and threw that over his aching shoulders.

At his uncle's house, Mehmet was doubling the woes of his motherless children by giving them a good scolding.

As soon as it grew light enough to see again, Yusuf returned to the wreck of his home. Half the straw roof was gone, along with one wall of his shop. Black mud squished ankle deep across his floor. All the seasoned wood for his barrels had floated away. By some minor quirk of the river's fury, his precious tools were still there, in mud-stained wrappings.

Yusuf went downstream. The riverbanks were thick with driftwood and bits of smashed homes. Corpses floated, tangled in debris. Some were children.

He found his wife past the bridge, around the riverbend. She was lodged in a muddy sandbar, along with many drowned goats and many dead chickens.

Her skirt, her apron, her pretty belt, and her needleworked

vest had all been torn from her body by the raging waters. Only her headdress, her pride and joy, was still left to her. Her long hair was tangled in that sodden cloth like river weed.

He had never seen her body nude in daylight. He pried her from the defiling mud, as gently as if she were still living and in need of a husband's help. Shivering with tenderness, he tore the shirt from his wet torso and wrapped her in it, then made her a makeshift skirt from his sash. He lifted her wet, sagging body in his arms. Grief and shame gave him strength. He staggered with her halfway to town.

Excited townsfolk were gathering the dead in carts. When they saw him, they ran to gawk.

Once this happened, his wife suddenly sneezed, lifted her head and, quick as a serpent, hopped down from his grip.

"Look, the cooper is alive!" the neighbors exulted. "God is great!"

"Stop staring like fools," his wife told them. "My man lost his shirt in the flood. You there, lend him your cloak."

They wrapped him up, chafed his cheeks, and embraced him.

The damage was grave in Yusuf's neighborhood, and worse yet on the opposite bank of the river, where the Catholics lived. The stricken people searched the filthy streets for their lost possessions and missing kin. There was much mourning, tumult, and despair.

The townsfolk caught two looters, pilfering in the wreckage. The kadi had them beheaded. Their severed heads were publicly exposed on the bridge. Yusuf knew the headless thieves by sight; unlike the other dead, those rascals wouldn't be missed much.

It took two days for the suffering people to gather their wits about them, but common sense prevailed at last and they pitched in to rebuild. Wounds were bound up and families reunited. Neighborhood women made soup for everyone in big cooking pots.

Alms were gathered and distributed by the dignitaries. Shelter was found for the homeless in the mosques, the temple, and the churches. The dead were retrieved from the sullen river and buried properly by their respective faiths.

The Vizier sent troops from Travnik to keep order. The useless troopers thundered through town on horseback, fired their guns, stole and roasted sheep, and caroused all night with the gypsies. Muslims, Orthodox, and Catholics alike waited anxiously for the marauders to ride home and leave them in peace.

Yusuf's wife and the children stayed at his uncle's while Yusuf put another roof on his house. The apprentice had stupidly broken his leg in the flood—so he had to stay snug with his own family, where he ate well and did no work, much as usual.

Once the damaged bridge was safe for carts again, fresh-cut lumber became available. In the gathering work of reconstruction, Yusuf found his own trade picking up. With a makeshift tent up in lieu of his straw roof, Yusuf had to meet frantic demands for new buckets, casks, and water barrels. Price was no object and no one was picky about quality.

Sensing opportunity, the Jews lent money to all the craftsmen of standing, whether their homes were damaged or not. Gold coins appeared in circulation, precious Ottoman sultani from the royal mint in distant Istanbul. Yusuf schemed hard to gain and keep a few.

When he went to fetch his family back home, Yusuf found his wife with a changed spirit. She had put old Mehmet's place fully into order: she'd aired the old man's stuffy cottage, beaten his moldy carpet, scrubbed his floors, banished the mice, and chased the spiders into hiding. His uncle's dingy vest and sash were clean and darned. Old Mehmet had never looked so jolly. When Yusuf's lively children left his home, Mehmet even wept a little.

His wife flung her arms around Yusuf's neck. When the family returned to her wrecked, muddy home, she was as proud as a new bride. She made cleaning up the mud into an exciting game for the children. She cast the spoilt food from her drowned larder. She borrowed flour, bought eggs, conjured up salt, found milk from heaven, and made fresh bread.

Neighbors came to her door with soup and cabbage rolls. Enchanted by her charming gratitude, they helped her to clean. As she worked, his wife sang like a lark. Everyone's spirits rose, despite all the trials, or maybe even because of the trials, because they gave people so much to gripe about. Yusuf said little and watched his wife with raw disbelief. With all her cheerful talk and singing, she ate almost nothing. That which she chewed, she did not swallow.

When he climbed reluctantly into their narrow bed, she was bright-eyed and willing. He told her that he was tired. She obediently put her cool, damp head into the hollow of his shoulder and passed the night as quiet as carved ivory: never a twitch, kick, or snore.

Yusuf knew for a fact that his wife had been swept away and murderously tumbled down a stony riverbank for a distance of some twenty arshin. Yet her pale skin showed no bruising anywhere. He finally found hidden wounds on the soles of her feet. She had struggled hard for her footing as the angry waters dragged her to her death.

In the morning she spoke sweet words of encouragement to him. His hard work would bring them sure reward. Adversity was refining his character. The neighbors admired his cheerful fortitude. His son was learning valuable lessons by his manly example. All this wifely praise seemed plausible enough to Yusuf, and no more than he deserved, but he knew with a black flood of occult certainty that this was not the woman given him in marriage. Where were her dry, acidic remarks? Her balky backtalk? Her black, sour jokes? Her customary heartbreaking sighs, which mutely suggested that every chance of happiness was lost forever?

Yusuf fled to the market, bought a flask of fiery rakija, and sat down to drink hard in midday.

Somehow, in the cunning pretext of "repairing" their flood-damaged church, the Orthodox had installed a bronze bell in their church tower. Its clangor now brazenly competed with the muezzin's holy cries. It was entirely indecent that this wicked contraption of the Serfish Slaves (the Orthodox were also called "Slavish Serfs," for dialects varied) should be casting an ungodly racket over the stricken town. Yusuf felt as if that great bronze barrel and its banging tongue had been hung inside his own chest.

The infidels were ringing bells, but he was living with a corpse.

Yusuf drank, thought slowly and heavily, then drank some

more. He might go to the kadi for help in his crisis, but the pious judge would recommend what he always suggested to any man troubled by scandal—the long pilgrimage to Mecca. For a man of Yusuf's slender means, a trip to Arabia was out of the question. Besides, word would likely spread that he had sought public counsel about his own wife. His own wife, and from such a good family, too. That wasn't the sort of thing that a man of standing would do.

The Orthodox priest was an impressive figure, with a big carved staff and a great black towering hat. Yusuf had a grudging respect for the Orthodox. Look how they'd gotten their way with that bell tower of theirs, against all sense and despite every obstacle. They were rebellious and sly, and they clung to their pernicious way of life despite being taxed, fined, scourged, beheaded, and impaled. Their priest—he might well have some dark, occult knowledge that could help in Yusuf's situation.

But what if, in their low cunning, the peasants laughed at him and took advantage somehow? Unthinkable!

The Catholics were fewer than the Orthodox, a simple people, somewhat more peaceable. But the Catholics had Franciscan monks. Franciscan monks were sorcerers who had come from Austria with picture books. The monks recited spells in Latin from their gold-crowned Pope in Rome. They boasted that their Austrian troops could beat the Sultan's janissaries. Yusuf had seen a lot of Austrians. Austrians were rich, crafty, and insolent. They knew bizarre and incredible things. Bookkeeping, for instance.

Could he trust Franciscan monks to deal with a wife who refused to be dead? Those celibate monks didn't even know what a woman was for! The scheme was absurd.

Yusuf was not a drinking man, so the rakija lifted his imagination to great heights. When the local rabbi passed by chance, Yusuf found himself on his feet, stumbling after the Jew. The rabbi noticed this and confronted him. Yusuf, suddenly thick of tongue, blurted out something of his woes.

The rabbi wanted no part of Yusuf's troubles. However, he was a courteous man, and he had a wise suggestion.

There were people of the Bogomil faith within two days' journey. These Bogomils had once been the Christian masters of the land, generations ago, before the Ottoman Turks brought order to the valleys and mountains. Both Catholics and Orthodox considered the Bogomils to be sinister heretics. They thought this for good reason, for the Bogomils (who were also known as "Cathars" and "Patarines") were particularly skilled in the conjuration and banishment of spirits.

So said the rabbi. The local Christians believed that the last Bogomils had been killed or assimilated long ago, but a Jew, naturally, knew better than this. The rabbi alleged that a small clan of the Old Believers still lurked in the trackless hills. Jewish peddlers sometimes met the Bogomils, to do a little business: the Bogomils were bewhiskered clansmen with goiters the size of fists, who ambushed the Sultan's tax men, ripped up roads, ate meat raw on Fridays, and married their own nieces.

Next day, when Yusuf recovered from his hangover, he told his wife that he needed to go on pilgrimage into the hills for a few days. She should have pointed out that their house was still half wrecked and his business was very pressing. Instead she smiled sweetly, packed him four days of home-cooked provisions, darned his leggings, and borrowed him a stout donkey.

No one could find the eerie Bogomil village without many anxious moments, but Yusuf did find it. This was a dour place where an ancient people of faith were finally perishing from the earth. The meager village clustered in the battered ruin of a hillside fort. The poorly thatched hovels were patched up from tumbledown bits of rock. Thick nettles infested the rye fields. The goats were scabby, and the donkeys knock-kneed. The plum orchard buzzed with swarms of vicious yellow wasps. There was not a child to be seen.

The locals spoke a Slavish dialect so thick and archaic that it sounded as if they were chewing stale bread. They did have a tiny church of sorts, and in there, slowly dipping holy candles in a stinking yellow mix of lard and beeswax, was their elderly, half-starved pastor, the man they called their "Djed."

The Bogomil Djed wore the patched rags of black ecclesiastical robes. He had a wall-eye and a river of beard tumbling past his waist.

With difficulty, Yusuf confessed.

"I like you, Muslim boy," said the Bogomil priest, with a wink or a tic of his bloodshot wall-eye. "It takes an honest man to tell such a dark story. I can help you."

"Thank you! Thank you! How?"

"By baptizing you in the gnostic faith, as revealed in the Palcyaf Bible. A dreadful thing has happened to you, but I can clarify your suffering, so hearken to me. God, the Good God, did not create this wicked world. This evil place, this sinful world we must endure, was created by God's elder archangel, Satanail the Demiurge. The Demiurge created all the Earth, and also some bits of the lower heavens. Then

Satanail tried to create Man in the image of God, but he succeeded only in creating the flesh of Man. That is why it was easy for Satanail to confound and mislead Adam, and all of Adam's heritage, through the fleshly weakness of our clay."

"I never heard that word, 'Demiurge.' There's only one God."

"No, my boy, there are two Gods: the bad God, who is always with us, and the good God, who is unknowable. Now I will tell you all about the dual human and divine nature of Jesus Christ. This is the most wonderful of gnostic gospels; it involves the Holy Dove, the Archangel Michael, Satanail the Creator, and the Clay Hierographon."

"But my wife is not a Christian at all! I told you, she comes from a nice family."

"Your wife is dead."

A chill gripped Yusuf. He struggled for something to say.

"My boy, is your woman nosferatu? You can tell me."

"I don't know that word either."

"Does she hate and fear the light of the sun?"

"My wife loves sunlight! She loves flowers, birds, pretty clothes. She likes everything nice."

"Does she suck the blood of your children?"

Yusuf shook his head and wiped at his tears.

The priest shrugged reluctantly. "Well, no matter—you can still behead her and impale her through the heart! Those measures always settle things!"

Yusuf was scandalized. "What would I tell the neighbors?"

The old man sighed. "She's dead and yet she walks the Earth, my boy. You do need to do something."

"How could a woman be dead and not know she's dead?"

"In her woman's heart she suspects it. But she's too

stubborn to admit it. She died rashly and foolishly, dis-
obeying her lord and master, and she left her woman's body
lying naked in some mud. Imagine the shame to her spirit!
This young wife with a house and small children, she left
her life's duties undone! Her failure was more than her
spirit could admit. So, she does not live, but she stubbornly
persists." The priest slowly dipped a bare white string into
his pot of wax. " 'A man may work from sun to sun, but a
woman's work is never done.' "

Yusuf put his head in his hands and wept. The Djed had
convinced him. Yusuf was sure that he had found the best
source of advice on his troubles, short of a long trip to
Mecca. "What's to become of me now? What's to become
of my poor children?"

"Do you know what a succubus is?" said the priest.

"No, I never heard that word."

"If your dead wife had become a succubus, you wouldn't
need any words. Never mind that. I will prophesy to you of
what comes next. Her dead flesh and immortal spirit must
part sometimes, for that is their dual nature. So sometimes
you will find that her spirit is there, while her flesh is not
there. You will hear her voice and turn to speak; but there
will be no one. The pillow will have the dent of her head,
but no head lying there. The pot might move from the stove
to the table, with no woman's hands to move it."

"Oh," said Yusuf. There were no possible words for such
calamities.

"There will also be moments when the spirit retreats and
her body remains. I mean the rotten body of a woman who
drowned in the mud. If you are lucky you might not see that
rotten body. You will smell it."

"I'm accursed! How long can such torments go on?"

"Some exorcist must persuade her that she met with death and her time on Earth is over. She has to be confronted with the deceit that her spirit calls 'truth.' She has to admit that her life is a lie."

"Well, that will never happen," said Yusuf. "I never knew her to admit to a mistake, since the day her father gave her to me."

"Impale her heart while she sleeps!" demanded the Djed. "I can sell you the proper wood for the sharpened stake—it is the wood of life, *lignum vitae,* I found it growing in the dead shrine of the dead God Mithras, for that is the ruin of a failed resurrection. . . . The wood of life has a great herbal virtue in all matters of spirit and flesh."

Yusuf's heart rebelled. "I can't stab the mother of my children between her breasts with a stick of wood!"

"You are a cooper," said the Djed, "so you do have a hammer."

"I mean that I'll cast myself into the river before I do any such thing!"

The Djed hung his candle from a small iron rod. "To drown one's self is a great calamity."

"Is there nothing better to do?"

"There is another way. The black way of sorcery." The Djed picked at his long beard. "A magic talisman can trap her spirit inside her dead body. Then her spirit cannot slip free from the flesh. She will be trapped in her transition from life to death, a dark and ghostly existence."

"What kind of talisman does that?"

"It's a fetter. The handcuff of a slave. You can tell her it's a bracelet, a woman's bangle. Fix that fetter, carved from the wood of life, firmly around her dead wrist. Within that wooden bracelet, a great curse is written: the curse that bound the children of Adam to till the soil, as the serfs of Satanail, ruler and creator of the Earth. So her soul will not be able to escape her clay, any more than Adam, Cain, and Abel, with their bodies made of clay by Satanail, could escape the clay of the fields and pastures. She will have to abide by that untruth she tells herself, for as long as that cuff clings to her flesh."

"Forever, then? Forever and ever?"

"No, boy, listen. I told you 'as long as that cuff clings to her flesh.' You will have to see to it that she wears it always. This is necromancy."

Yusuf pondered the matter, weeping. Peaceably, the Bogomil dipped his candles.

"But that's all?" Yusuf said at last. "I don't have to stab her with a stick? I don't have to bury her or behead her? My wife just wears a bracelet on her arm, with some painted words! Then I go home."

"She's dead, my boy. You are trapping a human soul within the outward show of rotten form. She will have no hope of salvation. She will be the hopeless slave of earthly clay and the chattel of her circumstances. For you to do that to another human soul is a mortal sin. You will have to answer for that on the Day of Judgment."

The Djed adjusted his sleeves. "But, you are Muslim, so you are damned already. All the more so for your woman, so . . ." The Djed spread his waxy hands.

The rabbi had warned Yusuf about the need for ready cash.

• • •

When Yusuf and his borrowed donkey returned home, foot-sore and hungry after five days of risky travel, he found his place hung with the neighbors' laundry. It was as festive as a set of flags. All the rugs and garments soiled by the flood needed boiling and bleaching. So his wife had made herself the bustling center of this lively activity.

Yusuf's smashed straw roof was being replaced with sturdy tiles. The village tiler and his wife had both died in the flood. The tiler's boy, a sullen, skinny teen, had lived, but his loss left him blank-eyed and silent.

Yusuf's wife had found this boy, haunted, shivering, and starving. She had fed him, clothed him, and sent him to collect loose tiles. There were many tiles scattered in the wrecked streets, and the boy knew how to lay a roof, so, somehow, without anything being said, the boy had become Yusuf's new apprentice. The new apprentice didn't eat much. He never said much. As an orphan, he was in no position to demand any wages or to talk back. So, although he knew nothing about making barrels, he was the ideal addition to the shop.

Yusuf's home, once rather well known for ruckus, had become a model of sociable charm. Neighbors were in and out of the place all the time, bringing sweets, borrowing flour and salt, swapping recipes, leaving children to be baby-sat. Seeing the empty barrels around, his wife had started brewing beer as a profitable sideline. She also stored red paprikas in wooden kegs of olive oil. People started leaving things at her house to sell. She was planning on building a shed to retail groceries.

There was never a private moment safe from friendly interruption, so Yusuf took his wife across the river, to the Turkish graveyard, for a talk. She wasn't reluctant to go, since she was of good birth and her long-established family occupied a fine, exclusive quarter of the cemetery.

"We never come here enough, husband," she chirped. "With all the rain, there's so much moss and mildew on great-grandfather's stone! Let's fetch a big bucket and give him a good wash!"

There were fresh graves, due to the flood, and one ugly wooden coffin, still abandoned above ground. Muslims didn't favor wooden boxes for their dead—this was a Christian fetish—but they'd overlooked that minor matter when they'd had to inter the swollen, oozing bodies of the flood victims. Luckily, rumor had outpaced the need for such boxes. So a spare coffin was still on the site, half full of rainwater and humming with spring mosquitos.

Yusuf took his wife's hand. Despite all her housework— she was busy as an ant—her damp hands were soft and smooth.

"I don't know how to tell you this," he said.

She blinked her limpid eyes and bit her lip. "What is it you have to complain about, husband? Have I failed to please you in some way?"

"There is one matter. . . . a difficult matter. . . . Well, you see, there's more to the marriage of a man and woman than just keeping house and making money."

"Yes, yes," she nodded, "being respectable!"

"No, I don't mean that part."

"The children, then?" she said.

"Well, not the boy and girl, but . . ." he said. "Well, yes, children! Children, of course! It's God's will that man and woman should bring children into the world! And, well, that's not something you and I can do anymore."

"Why not?"

Yusuf shuddered. "Do I have to say that? I don't want to."

"What is it you want from me, Yusuf? Spit it out!"

"Well, the house is as neat as a pin. We're making a profit. The neighbors love you. I can't complain about that. You know I never complain. But if you stubbornly refuse to die, well, I can't go on living. Wife, I need a milosnica."

"You want to take a concubine?"

"Yes. Just a maidservant. Nobody fancy. Maybe a teenager. She could help around the house."

"You want me to shelter your stupid concubine inside my own house?"

"Where else could I put a milosnica? I'm a cooper, I'm not a bey or an aga."

Demonic light lit his wife's eyes. "You think of nothing but money and your shop! You never give me a second glance! You work all day like a gelded ox! Then you go on a pilgrimage in the middle of everything, and now you tell me you want a concubine? Oh, you eunuch, you pig, you big talker! I work, I slave, I suffer, I do everything to please you, and now your favor turns to another!" She raised her voice and screeched across the graveyard. "Do you see this, Grandmother? Do you see what's becoming of me?"

"Don't make me angry," said Yusuf. "I've thought this through and it's reasonable. I'm not a cold fish. I'm living with a dead woman. Can't I have one live woman, just to warm my bones?"

"I'd warm your bones. Why can't I warm your bones?"

"Because you drowned in the river, girl. Your flesh is cold."

She said nothing.

"You don't believe me? Take off those shoes," he said wearily. "Look at those wounds on the bottoms of your feet. Your wounds never heal. They can't heal." Yusuf tried to put some warmth and color into his voice. "You have pretty feet, you have the prettiest feet in town. I always loved your feet, but, well, you never show them to me, since you drowned in that river."

She shook her head. "It was *you* who drowned in the river."

"What?"

"What about that huge wound in your back? Do you think I never noticed that great black ugly wound under your shoulder? That's why you never take your vest off anymore!"

Yusuf no longer dared to remove his clothes while his wife was around, so, although he tried a sudden, frightened glance back over his own shoulder, he saw nothing there but embroidered cloth. "Do I really have a scar on my back? I'm not dead, though."

"Yes, husband, you are dead," his wife said bluntly. "You ran back for your stupid tools, even though I begged you to stay with me and comfort me. I saw you fall. You drowned in the street. I found your body washed down the river."

This mad assertion of hers was completely senseless. "No, that can't be true," he told her. "You abandoned me and the children, against my direct word to you, and you went back for your grandmother's useless trousseau, and you drowned, and I found you sprawling naked in the mud."

" 'Naked in the mud,' " she scoffed. "In your dreams!" She

pointed. "You see that coffin? Go lie down in that coffin, stupid. That coffin's for you."

"That's your coffin, my dear. That's certainly not my coffin."

"Go lie down in there, you big hot stallion for concubines. You won't rise up again, I can promise you."

Yusuf gazed at the splintery wooden hulk. That coffin was a sorry piece of woodworking; he could have built a far better coffin himself. Out of nowhere, black disbelief washed over him. Could he possibly be in this much trouble? Was this what his life had come to? Him, a man of circumspection, a devout man, honest, a hard worker, devoted to his children? It simply could not be! It wasn't true! It was impossible.

He should have been in an almighty rage at his wife's stinging taunts, but somehow his skin remained cool; he couldn't get a flush to his cheeks. He knew only troubled despair.

"You really want to put me down in the earth, in such a cheap coffin, so badly built? The way you carry on at me, I'm tempted to lie down in there, I really am."

"Admit it, you don't need any concubine. You just want me out of your way. And after all I did for you, and gave to you! How could you pretend to live without me at your side, you big fool? I deserved much better than you, but I never left you, I was always there for you."

Part of that lament at least was true. Even when their temperaments had clashed, she'd always been somehow willing to jam herself into their narrow bed. She might be angry, yes, sullen, yes, impossible, yes, but she remained with him. "This is a pretty good fight we're having today," he said, "this is kind of like our old times."

"I always knew you'd murder me and bury me someday."

"Would you get over that, please? It's just vulgar." Yusuf reached inside the wrappings of his cummerbund. "If I wanted to kill you, would I be putting this on your hand?"

She brightened at once. "Oh! What's that you brought me? Pretty!"

"I got it on pilgrimage. It's a magic charm."

"Oh how sweet! Do let me have it, you haven't bought me jewelry in ages."

On a sudden impulse, Yusuf jammed his own hand through the wooden cuff. In an instant, memory pierced him. The truth ran through his flesh like a rusty sword. He remembered losing his temper, cursing like a madman, rushing back to his collapsing shop, in his lust and pride for some meaningless clutter of tools. . . . He could taste that deadly rush of water, see a blackness befouling his eyes, the chill of death filling his lungs—

He yanked his arm from the cuff, trembling from head to foot. "That never happened!" he shouted. "I never did any such thing! I won't stand for such insults! If they tell me the truth, I'll kill them."

"What are you babbling on about? Give me my pretty jewelry."

He handed it over.

She slid her hand through with an eager smile, then pried the deadly thing off her wrist as if it were red-hot iron. "You made me do that!" she screeched. "You made me run into the ugly flood! I was your victim! Nothing I did was ever my fault."

Yusuf bent at the waist and picked up the dropped bangle between his thumb and forefinger. "Thank God this dreadful thing comes off our flesh so easily!"

His wife rubbed the skin of her wrist. There was a new black bruise there. "Look, your gift hurt me. It's terrible!"

"Yes, it's very magical."

"Did you pay a lot of money for that?"

"Oh yes. I paid a lot of money. To a wizard."

"You're hopeless."

"Wife of mine, we're both hopeless. Because the truth is, our lives are over. We've failed. Why did we stumble off to our own destruction? We completely lost our heads!"

His wife squared her shoulders. "All right, fine! So you make mistakes! So you're not perfect!"

"Me? Why is it me all the time? What about you?"

"Yes, I know, I could be a lot better, but well, I'm stuck with you. That's why I'm no good. So, I don't forgive you, and I never will! But anyway, I don't think we ought to talk about this any more."

"Would you reel that snake's tongue of yours back into your head? Listen to me for once! We're all over, woman! We drowned, we both died together in a big disaster!"

"Yusuf, if we're dead, how can you be scolding me? See, you're talking nonsense! I want us to put this behind us once and for all. We just won't talk about this matter any more. Not one more word. We have to protect the children. Children can't understand such grown-up things. So we'll never breathe a word to anyone. All right?"

Black temptation seized him. "Look, honey, let's just get in that coffin together. We'll never make a go of a situation like this. It can't be done. That coffin's not so bad. It's got as much room as our bed does."

"I won't go in there," she said. "I won't vanish from the Earth. I just won't, because I can't believe what you believe, and you can't make me." She suddenly snatched the bangle from his hand and threw it into the coffin. "There, get inside there with that nasty thing, if you're so eager."

"Now you've gone and spoiled it," he said sadly. "Why do you always have to do that, just to be spiteful? One of these days I'm really going to have to smack you around."

"When our children are ready to bury us, then they will bury us."

That was the wisest thing she had ever said. Yusuf rubbed the words over his dead tongue. It was almost a proverb. "Let the children bury us." There was a bliss to that, like a verse in a very old song. It meant that there were no decisions to be made. The time was still unripe. Nothing useful could be done. Justice, faith, hope, and charity, life and death, they were all smashed and in a muddle, far beyond his repair and his retrieval.

So just let it all be secret, let that go unspoken. Let the next generation look after all of that.

Or the generation after that. Or after that. Or after that. That was their heritage.